DEATH *in*
SHAMBLES

Also by Stephen Alter

NON-FICTION

Wild Himalaya: A Natural History of the Greatest Mountain Range on Earth
Becoming a Mountain: Himalayan Journeys in Search of the Sacred and the Sublime
All the Way to Heaven: An American Boyhood in the Himalayas
Amritsar to Lahore: Crossing the Border Between India and Pakistan
Sacred Waters: A Pilgrimage to the Many Sources of the Ganga
Elephas Maximus: A Portrait of the Indian Elephant
Going for Take: The Making of Omkara and Other Encounters in Bollywood

FICTION

Birdwatching: A Novel
Feral Dreams: Mowgli and His Mothers
In the Jungles of the Night: A Novel About Jim Corbett
The Cloudfarers
The Secret Sanctuary
Neglected Lives
Silk and Steel
The Godchild
Renuka
Aripan and Other Stories
Aranyani
The Phantom Isles
Ghost Letters
The Rataban Betrayal
Guldaar

DEATH *in* SHAMBLES

A HILL STATION MYSTERY

STEPHEN ALTER

ALEPH BOOK COMPANY
An independent publishing firm
promoted by *Rupa Publications India*

First published in India in 2023
by Aleph Book Company
7/16 Ansari Road, Daryaganj
New Delhi 110 002

Copyright © Stephen Alter 2023

The author has asserted his moral rights.

All rights reserved.

This is a work of fiction. Names, characters, places, and incidents are either the product of the author's imagination or are used fictitiously and any resemblance to any actual persons, living or dead, events or locales is entirely coincidental.

No part of this publication may be reproduced, transmitted, or stored in a retrieval system, in any form or by any means, without permission in writing from Aleph Book Company.

For sale in the Indian subcontinent only.

ISBN: 978-93-95853-06-4

1 3 5 7 9 10 8 6 4 2

Printed in India.

This book is sold subject to the condition that it shall not, by way of trade or otherwise, be lent, resold, hired out, or otherwise circulated without the publisher's prior consent in any form of binding or cover other than that in which it is published.

For Sunil Arora
Cambridge Book Depot

Author's Note

In 1978, I published my first novel, *Neglected Lives*, which was set in a fictional hill station called Debrakot. Forty-five years have passed since that book came out and I've written a variety of stories since then, but Debrakot has always remained in my mind, partly as an imagined place but also as a literary refraction of my home town, Mussoorie. In this new novel, we return to Debrakot, though much has changed since my young protagonist, Lionel, escaped to the mountains after a forbidden love affair in Lucknow. This time, he has come back to settle in Debrakot, four and a half decades later, following his retirement from the Indian Police Service. *Neglected Lives* was a youthful romance, containing elements of the grotesque but full of hope and expectations while *Death in Shambles* is a darker book in which Lionel investigates a murder involving mysterious and disturbing events.

One

Mornings in Debrakot always begin with a residual sense of discontentment, especially during the monsoon when the mist outside my windows is as thick as felt. A sodden, grey shroud hides the oak and rhododendron trees at the edge of the garden. Even the flowerpots on the veranda, full of pink geraniums and dangling fuchsia, are drained of colour and almost disappear. Sometimes it feels as if the world beyond the house has been erased and I am adrift in a sea of clouds.

My home is called Thornfield Lodge, named after the grand manor house in Charlotte Bronte's novel, *Jane Eyre*, which was published in 1847, five years before this bungalow was built. An element of irony must have influenced the choice of the name because it is a modest building, not nearly as palatial as Lord Rochester's gothic residence, where he kept his mad, Creole wife locked away in an upstairs room. Many of the oldest houses in Debrakot have literary appellations from poems and novels that were popular when they were built. In a hill station like this, first settled by the English, Scots, and Irish, stories are embedded in the foundations. I like to think that every house on this hillside is a mystery waiting to be solved.

My name is Lionel Carmichael and I am a retired police officer. My final posting was as deputy inspector general, DIG (Kumaon). It didn't end well. I was suspended during my last year of service for breaking the nose of a prominent politician. It's a long, uninteresting story and I've tried my best to forget the details, though I can still feel my knuckles crunch against the bastard's nasal cartilage, shoving it up into his sinuses, a satisfying feeling of justice delivered, even if it brought my career to an ignominious end.

I suppose there's no point in brooding over the incident, though I can't quite rid myself of the anger and humiliation. The inspector general (IG) above me, a bloody Thakur swine, took special pleasure in launching an inquiry and making sure that I was found guilty of indiscipline and insubordination. He had an instinctual prejudice against Anglo-Indians, even if my grandfather served in the police long before his ancestors uncrossed their legs and got off their charpais.

At the end of it, I handed in my resignation six months before I was scheduled to retire, a compromise that allowed me to avoid going before a judge and left me with a pension that was a few rupees short of the full amount I was due. It's been exactly a year and seven months since I stepped down. I don't know why I keep track of the days, now that I'm unemployed. Perhaps calendars and wristwatches will lose their importance after a while, but for the moment, I'm still a punctual man.

8 a.m. Time for a shit, shower, and shave.

⁂

During the monsoon the bathroom mirror fogs up immediately because there's so much humidity in the air. As the last of the hot water trickled out of the tap, I knew it would go cold before I finished. Wiping away a circle of condensation, I caught sight of myself staring out of the glass, like a face peering through the porthole of a submarine. The grey stubble on my chin makes me look older than I think I am, though I've never had youthful features. Not good-looking, either. Too long in the jaw, though a trim moustache helps break up my profile and hides the fullness of my upper lip. My late mother, God rest her soul, claimed that my eyes were English—blue and bloodshot. The rest of my face could be Indian, though that's not quite accurate, neither the complexion nor the bone structure. Sometimes I think I look a bit like one of those composite drawings of police suspects, vaguely recognizable but not a true likeness.

In Nainital, where I was posted in 1980, soon after I joined the UP Police, we hired a sketch artist from time to time. He was a teacher at Sherwood College and worked for the police on the side. I never had much faith in him, though he did help us solve one or two crimes. His portraits seemed more romantic than realistic. The process was crude and inexact, as the witness tried to recall the details of a criminal's face and the art teacher's timid pencil traced out lines that were soon erased and redrawn according to retracted or adjusted memories. It's remarkable how quickly we forget what someone looks like.

Every morning, when I squint into the mirror, it takes me a moment to recognize myself and there's always an impulse to add a little more hair on top and a few less wrinkles around the chin. Only a mother would have loved a face like this. She often told me I looked like the actor, Richard Harris, which isn't true at all. I've never been much of a ladies' man and after my wife, Sylvia, left me twenty-six years ago, I've maintained a modicum of celibacy. Nevertheless, my mother had other ideas on the subject and she kept her eye out for women that I might marry, even if I wasn't interested.

Meanwhile, Sylvia ran off to Melbourne with her shippy and never once replied to my aerogrammes. Mother died three years ago of a brain haemorrhage, while she was in church, probably praying that I would find another wife.

As I finished shaving and changed into a fresh shirt, I could hear old Badlu the cook arguing with the milkman outside the kitchen door, a regular routine.

'Look at this!' he cried, as I entered. Holding up the degchi into which the dairywalla had poured two measures of viscous fluid from his milk can, he added, 'Half of it is water!'

'No, bhaiji,' Raipal Singh replied. 'I swear it's straight from the udders of my buffalo but these days, with all the rain, the grass it eats is soaking wet and the milk gets diluted.'

'Rubbish!' Badlu cried.

Though the two men are roughly the same age and about the same height, that's where the similarities end. Badlu is balding and well-fed, with a pair of thick-rimmed glasses that give him an owlish appearance. Raipal is gaunt and lean-featured, his greying hair tucked beneath a wool cap. You can tell he's a hillman, used to working outdoors and climbing steep trails, while Badlu is heavier around the waist, with the lethargic manner of a plains dweller, despite his sharp tongue.

Raipal crouched on the kitchen steps, sealing a milk can with wadded leaves and a wooden stopper. He carries the cans in a rope mesh satchel, all the way from his village on the far side of the hill, walking twenty kilometres round trip.

'Sahib!' he greeted me, as the cook disappeared back into the kitchen to boil the milk. 'I need your help.'

Raipal knows I'm a soft touch and I will always slip him a hundred, if he asks for an advance.

'What is it now?' I answered, trying to sound intimidating. 'Not a loan?'

'No, sahibji, something else,' he said. 'My son, Suraj, has disappeared.'

'Again?' I said. 'He's probably run off with another girl.'

'Not this time, sahib. He vanished on Thursday. Yesterday, we tried to file a missing person report with the police but nobody will listen,' he said. 'Maybe you could have a word with the SHO.'

'I'm retired,' I told him. 'I have no authority any more.'

The mist was turning to rain. Raipal's clothes were already wet. His umbrella was in tatters and he wore a pair of plastic shoes that were cracked at the toes and looked as if they were about to fall apart.

'But they will listen to you.'

He knows that the station house officer (SHO) in Debrakot still treats me with respect. Inspector Thapliyal started his career under me when I was posted in Kashipur, ten years ago.

'Maybe your son has gone off to get a job in Delhi,' I suggested. 'He's tired of looking after buffaloes and digging up potatoes.'

'No, sahibji. Something has happened to him, I know,' Raipal replied, tears forming in his eyes. 'Suraj must be in trouble.'

'All right,' I agreed, retreating behind the screen door, which was beaded with moisture. 'I'll have a word with Thapliyal.'

Raipal gave me a grateful salute and opened his umbrella before heading off to deliver the rest of his milk.

Inside the kitchen, Badlu was hovering over the gas range to make sure the milk didn't boil over.

'You see, no cream at all!' he complained before asking, 'Have you had your breakfast?'

'I had a toast.'

'No eggs? Cornflakes?'

I shook my head and set off for my study, when the telephone began to ring. Its shrill cackle startled me because the damn thing seldom works and I can go weeks without a call or a dial tone. Either monkeys snap the connection by swinging on the cables, or a branch happens to fall in a storm. The linesman takes several days to come and inspect the damage. Not long ago, someone stole two hundred metres of copper cable, the most serious crime we've had on this hillside since I returned to Debrakot. They caught the bugger, trying to sell it off to a scrap dealer in town.

When I picked up the phone, I could hear a faint voice drowning in static. It took me a moment to recognize who it was.

'Thapliyal!' I shouted. 'Long life! I was going to give you a call.'

'Sir! Hello?' I could barely hear him.

'What's that?' I yelled into the receiver. 'What did you say?'

He now raised his voice over the interference on the line. 'Shambala Villa,' he cried. 'Sir, there's been a murder!'

'What? Where?' I replied.

'Two bodies!'

'When?'

'Last night. Sir, can you come, please? I need your advice.' Thapliyal uttered a few more words but his voice was breaking up.

'Are you still there?' I asked.

'Yes, sir. Sorry to trouble you, sir.'

'Not at all,' I said. 'I'll be over in twenty minutes.'

When I put down the receiver, Badlu stood in the doorway looking at me.

'What is it?' he asked, always protective.

'Nothing,' was my reply. 'I just need to go out for a bit.'

'It's raining,' he said. A heavy downpour was drumming on the sheet metal roof, a percussive crescendo.

'Yes, I know,' I answered, impatiently. 'Don't worry. I'll take an umbrella, and my raincoat.'

Badlu worked as a cook for my mother for thirty-two years. He comes from Lucknow, originally, though he has lived in Debrakot for the past two decades. Following my mother's death, I kept him on and he has assumed her role, fussing over me, as if I am still a forgetful schoolboy.

Two

More than one path leads from Thornfield to Shambala Villa. The shortest is a narrow, winding trail that cuts across the southern face of the ridge. An easier route follows the old bridle trail to the top of the hill and then descends gradually past several other homes. Because of the rain, I chose the longer path but, on the way down, it had turned into a river of mud and I wished I'd worn my gumboots. Of course, I could have waited until the downpour eased, but there had been a note of urgency in Thapliyal's voice.

Shambala Villa is a sprawling, rundown building with a rusty, corrugated metal roof. Most residents in Debrakot call it Shambles, for obvious reasons. The house looks abandoned, especially during the monsoon when the gardens are a jungle of weeds. As I entered through the gate, the windows were dark, though I could make out a single low-wattage bulb burning in the hall. A constable was standing just inside the main door and saluted as I left my umbrella and raincoat on a hook in the screened porch. Though I considered removing my wet shoes, the frayed jute carpeting was sure to be full of scorpions and spiders. Besides, the police had already tracked mud into the house.

Thapliyal was in the hallway, smoking a cigarette, which he hid behind his back as soon as I appeared. We shook hands and I gave him a moment to get rid of the cigarette while I examined a portrait in the hall, a dingy photograph of a sour-faced European woman with piercing eyes and a hat that looked like a dead pheasant perched on her head. This was the first time I'd been beyond the front gate of Shambala Villa and the derelict conditions extended indoors. Ancient coats of whitewash on the inner walls were blistered and peeling. The discoloured marble tiles on the floor of the hall were cracked and several were missing. Cobwebs clung to every corner and the musty pungency of mildew and mould filled the air.

'Two bodies, you said?'

Thapliyal nodded. He is one of the most competent police officers I've known, slightly built but physically strong and mentally as sharp as they come.

'Where are they?'

'In the kitchen, sir,' he replied, gesturing towards a door that stood ajar at the end of the hall. The dim yellow light from the single bulb overhead barely extended that far into the shadows. Passing through the door, I entered a drawing room, full of bookcases, two mismatched chairs, and an overstuffed sofa coming apart at the seams. A standard lamp with a crooked shade had been switched on and a faint, spectral aura filtered through a skylight that also admitted a trickle of rain, which had left a damp patch on the carpet. Another door opened from the drawing room into a storeroom lined with steel cupboards and shelves stacked with household relics, old kerosene heaters, and dented tin trunks. Beyond this lay the kitchen, which had two windows that ushered in a watery grey light from outdoors. The only other illumination came from a flickering tube light on one wall, which cast a fluorescent glow on the scene.

The first body I examined was hanging from the ceiling by a length of rope tied to a hook screwed into one of the wooden beams. It was a woman, dressed in a faded green cotton sari. The pallu had fallen off her shoulder and cascaded to the floor, though her bare feet were about half a metre off the ground. Her dark, lank hair was open over her shoulders and the woman's neck was twisted to one side. Her face seemed remarkably calm. She was heavily made-up, with kajal around her eyes, powdered cheeks, and lipstick on her mouth. Her arms hung by her sides, surrendering to the complacency of death. A small abrasion was visible on the inside of her wrist, though I couldn't see it clearly because her hand was partly hidden by the sari's folds. Her blouse was loose fitting, as if she had no breasts.

A two-burner cooker sat on a marble countertop, attached to a gas cylinder. The kitchen was also equipped with an ancient coal stove that looked as if it hadn't been used for years, a black, wrought iron beast with a gaping maw and a crooked chimney that disappeared through a sooty hole in the ceiling. The slate flagstones of the kitchen were awash in blood, which came from the second victim, slouched against the stove. He had several wounds on his chest and stomach, as well as a slashed throat. I recognized Reuben Sabharwal immediately, though I'd met him only two or three times. Even in death, his bearded face bore the solemn expression of a man consumed by dark, metaphysical broodings. The only time we'd spoken was a brief conversation about the transmigration of souls, which he had initiated at the funeral of another neighbour, eight months ago. I couldn't help wondering if his spirit had escaped from his body at the moment of death or whether it still lay imprisoned within his corpse, waiting to be released.

Over the years, I have seen my share of murders, from meagre, impoverished deaths in village huts and city slums to lavish displays of bloodshed in extravagant mansions, but the scene of the crime at Shambles was one of the gloomiest I've ever witnessed. Part of it may have been the grim weather outside but the interior of the house added to the horror of this macabre tableau. A kitchen knife, presumably the murder weapon, lay on the floor beneath the woman's left foot. On the counter was a wooden cutting board, where the knife had been used to peel and chop onions before it was employed in the deadlier act. One of the constables was dusting the knife for fingerprints while another was doing the same on the doorknob, though I didn't have a lot of confidence that they would find anything.

'Why haven't you cut her down?' I asked, turning to Thapliyal.

'We're waiting for the photographer to show up,' he said. 'She was obviously dead when we got here an hour ago.'

'How did you find out?'

'The maid discovered them this morning. She's the daughter of the chowkidar, Charan Das. He called us....' Thapliyal explained.

'No shortage of footprints,' I remarked, surveying the bloodstained floor.

'Yes, but anything outdoors has been washed away, and most of the prints are ours. The constables are careless about these things.'

'I can see that,' I said. 'What do you make of it?'

'My first impression?' he asked. Thapliyal has a reserved but thoughtful manner and he doesn't jump to conclusions. Cleanshaven and with a pensive, boyish expression, he appears younger than he is, in his mid-thirties.

I nodded, looking up into the face of the dead woman, her eyes open in a morbid stare.

'It looks as if she killed him with the knife, then hanged herself,' said Thapliyal. 'A murder–suicide. They must have fought over something. She lost her temper and stabbed him to death, then took her own life.'

'Who is she?' I asked.

'I don't have a full name,' he replied. 'The chowkidar said she was known as Meena. She's been living here for a couple of months but never went out.'

'And her relationship to Sabharwal?'

'No idea,' said the SHO, 'But we can assume....'

'Have there been any others staying here?' I asked.

'The house is run like an ashram,' Thapliyal explained, 'for religious retreats. They offered yoga courses and spiritual workshops. The chowkidar says that sometimes as many as ten or fifteen people stayed here, but mostly it was just Sabharwal. He's a guru of some sort. Or was. He called himself Reuben Bhagwan.'

I had heard that Reuben styled himself as a god-man and his followers looked upon him as a personification of divinity, even if the house he lived in was a dilapidated slum.

At this point, Thapliyal let out an apologetic cough. 'Sir?'

'What is it?' I asked.

'I need your help, if it's not too much trouble,' he said. 'The state finance minister is arriving today and his visit will take up all of my time for the next three days. I wonder if you'd be willing, sir, to assist with the investigation.'

'I'm not sure that's a good idea,' I said. 'Retired officers aren't usually....'

Just then, we heard a commotion near the entrance to the house and moments later two figures blundered into the kitchen. One of them was another constable and the other was Vipin Verma, a photographer from Rajhans Studio in town. Most of his work involved following honeymooning couples around and taking pictures at scenic spots. Whenever the police needed photographs of road accidents or property encroachments, Vipin was called in. From the look in his eyes, I could tell he wasn't prepared for what he saw. His hair was wet from the rain and he had his camera wrapped in a plastic bag, which he had difficulty opening, because his hands were trembling.

'Why don't I let you do your work in here,' I suggested, 'while I take a look around the rest of the house?'

Thapliyal nodded, as I retreated back into the hall where the woman in the photograph gave me the evil eye. Two of the four doors off the hall were closed. When I turned the brass knob of one, it came off in my hand. A nudge from my shoulder pushed it open. Inside, it was as dark as Plato's cave. Searching about for a light switch, I finally found one, which turned on a bare bulb on the wall. The room was relatively large, about six metres by eight, with a high ceiling, though it seemed cramped because of the five beds that occupied the space. All of them had lumpy cotton mattresses, without sheets or any other bedding. It looked like a school dormitory or a prison cell. A curtained archway led into another, smaller room that contained three more beds, beyond which lay a bathroom and a toilet.

There wasn't much more to investigate in the bedrooms, so I retraced my steps to the hall and tried the other door, which seemed to be locked. Out of the corner of my eye, as I turned away, I spotted a drop of red on the floor, next to my foot. In the dim light, I had to take a second look, leaning down and confirming that it was blood. About two feet away was another drop leading back into the bedroom. Unlike the stains in the kitchen, these were tiny spots, an uneven string of fresh punctuation marks on the floor. For a moment, I stopped cold, wondering why I hadn't seen them before. The blood trail seemed to end at the locked door but then, with a sudden sense of irritation and relief, I realized what it was.

Rolling up my right pant leg, I checked my ankle and found the tell-tale ooze of blood on my lower calf, just above the sock, which was also stained. A leech had climbed up my shoe and fastened on to my leg, as I was walking over from Thornfield. Now that it had gorged itself and fallen off, my blood was dripping on to the floor. Pulling up my sock to cover the bite and staunch the bleeding, I searched around for the leech and finally found it, bloated and squirming, just inside the bedroom door. I left it there. My calf itched slightly though I hadn't felt anything until then. Every monsoon, I get two or three leech bites, though I'm usually careful and keep checking my shoes whenever I'm outdoors.

After this brief distraction, I turned back to searching the rest of the house. Shambles was like a labyrinth, and I retraced my steps into the drawing room. It was strewn with books and papers, which I decided to leave for later. At this point, I was looking for obvious clues or, perhaps, another body.

Aside from the passageway leading into the kitchen, the drawing room opened on to a long veranda, glazed with chequered windows. Many of the panes of glass were broken or cracked. This narrow corridor extended for about thirty metres, along the north side of the building, with several entrances leading back into the house. The first of these provided access to a dingy warren of rooms, crammed full of old furniture and boxes that didn't look as if they had been opened for years.

The next door allowed me to enter what I assumed was the locked room off the hall. It was the same size as the bedroom but furnished in a completely different manner. Finding a switch by the door, I turned on an overhead lamp, dangling from the ceiling. The floor was covered in Afghan carpets, some of which looked as if they might be valuable, though they were badly frayed and threadbare. A full-length mirror with a dark wooden frame hung from one of the walls, like a doorway leading into an identical room. In the centre of the floor was a round table that stood about two feet off the ground, with cushions all around, so that eight or ten people could gather in a circle. Covering the table was a cheap block-printed cloth. On the walls were several thangka scrolls, depicting elaborate Tibetan mandalas. Devil masks had also been hung at eye level and there was a wooden altar on one side, with a collection of brass and copper votive lamps. A moth-eaten fly whisk made from a yak's tail lay next to a strange looking bell, with a handle shaped like the hood of a cobra. In the centre of the altar was a statue of a winged goddess, with two serpents entwined atop her head, like a crown. Above this was the Egyptian symbol ankh that I initially mistook for a crucifix. More than a dozen candles of different sizes surrounded the altar. All of these had burned down to tumescent stubs of coagulated wax. A stale fug of incense filled the room and the remains of joss sticks had left a sprinkling of ash on the altar. The room was obviously the inner sanctum of Shambala Villa, some sort of prayer room or shrine.

Before I was able to investigate further, someone shouted from the other side of the door. I tried the knob but it was still locked, so I quickly made my way back through the glazed veranda to the drawing room, just as Vipin the photographer appeared with a look of alarm on his face.

'What is it?' I demanded. 'What's wrong?'

'Come quickly, sir,' he said, ducking back into the cluttered passageway leading to the kitchen.

I followed on his heels and when I arrived at the scene of the crime, I could see that they had cut the rope from which the woman's corpse had been suspended and the body lay crumpled on the floor. Her sari was now completely unwound and without a petticoat, so the body was naked from the waist down.

As I stepped forward to get a better look, Thapliyal stated the obvious.

'Sir, it's a man!'

Three

By the time I got home, the rain had stopped, though waves of mist kept rolling in over the ridge, swirling through the trees like a rising tide. My thoughts were equally opaque, as if the weather had fogged my mind. On one level the crime seemed obvious. Thapliyal was probably correct to assume that Sabharwal had been stabbed first. His attacker, the young man dressed as a woman, presumably hanged himself out of desperation or remorse. The only question remaining was for us to determine what motives might have driven someone to commit such a violent and fatal act. Somehow, instinctively, I felt the answer lay inside the house itself. If only buildings could be interrogated! We weren't likely to find a note of confession or any other obvious clue like a letter that may have aroused jealousy or a stolen object that possessed greater value than life itself.

After my initial shock, the fact that the dead woman in the sari had turned out to be a man didn't surprise me much. Over the years, having observed all kinds of sexual disguises and permutations, I've grown to understand that gender can be as elastic as our imaginations allow.

Yet, the first assumption all of us made—Thapliyal, the constables, the photographer, and myself—when we caught sight of the dead man's genitals, was that somehow the answer lay in this fact alone. His true identity had been kept hidden and he'd used a feminine alias 'Meena', which seemed to suggest some sort of prurient guilt beyond the stabbing itself. Nevertheless, on my way home from Shambles, I discarded these thoughts, knowing that we were simply jumping to unwarranted conclusions. More important was the relationship between the two dead men. Were they friends? Lovers? Fellow seekers of sacred truths? I felt that Meena must have participated in Sabharwal's cult, though I couldn't be sure. The two of them had been together in the house and if there was no physical intimacy between them, then surely there was a spiritual bond.

I was an hour late for lunch, and Badlu was waiting impatiently in the kitchen. When I told him that I had no appetite and he could leave the food on the stove, he looked at me with a disapproving scowl.

'Why aren't you eating?' he said. 'It's almost two o'clock.'

'There's been a murder,' I explained. It was pointless hiding the news from him for it would soon be out, travelling around the hillside like Chinese whispers.

'Murder?' Badlu's eyes opened wide behind the thick lenses of his glasses.

'At Shambala Villa. Sabharwal is dead and one of his guests,' I said.

The old man shook his head. 'A lot of strange things happen there,' he said. 'That house is cursed.'

'Why do you say that?' I demanded.

'To even talk about it brings bad luck,' he muttered.

'What do you mean?' I demanded.

'That place is haunted,' he replied.

'I don't think it was a ghost that committed the murders,' I said.

'Who can say?' Badlu shrugged. 'Bad things happen there.'

'How do you know?'

'Charan Das has worked there as long as I've been here in Debrakot. Before Sabharwal took over, an Englishwoman stayed at Shambala Villa for years, until she died.' Badlu stared at the ground.

'Did the Englishwoman own the house?' I asked. 'What was her name?'

'Miss Muckanjee. I don't know if the property belonged to her but she lived there for as long as anyone can remember. Reuben moved in much later. People say he took advantage of her. By then she was losing her mind.'

'But if it's such a terrible place, how can Charan Das have worked there for so long?' I asked.

'Finding a job isn't easy. Most of the time he works outdoors and has nothing to do with what happens inside,' the cook replied.

'But his daughter helps with the housework. She's the one that found the two bodies this morning,' I said.

Badlu nodded. 'Poor girl. She has no choice.'

'Why?'

'Her husband left her, the year after their marriage. She was forced to come back to her father's house....' Badlu stopped himself and shook his head.

'Go on,' I said.

'The girl suffers from fits and gets possessed.'

∽

Nobody is really sure how Debrakot got its name. The most popular theory suggests that it is an Anglicized corruption of Devtakot, because of a rustic temple to a local deity that lies two kilometres east of Thornfield, beyond the edge of town. Others have argued that the first Englishman who built a house here, Thomas Chisholm, had a wife named Deborah and he christened the hill station in her honour, though documentary evidence of this is scarce and Chisholm's house was demolished long ago.

I was born here, though most of my childhood was spent in Lucknow, where my parents lived. My first memory of this town dates back to the age of twenty, when I escaped to Debrakot after falling in love with a Hindu girl. Sujeeta's family had me beaten up and threatened my life after she got pregnant. The whole experience was traumatic and my parents sent me up to the hills to stay with close family friends, Brigadier Teddy Augden and his wife, Natalie. They had no children of their own and looked upon me as a surrogate son. After they died, I inherited Thornfield Lodge from them. It's a relatively large property, about ten acres, and there used to be a fruit orchard the Brigadier had planted—plums, peaches, and apples—which is now overgrown. Most of the trees have been destroyed by monkeys.

The original plan had been for me to live up here for the rest of my life. Initially, it looked as if that might happen. Sylvia and I met through a mutual friend in Delhi where she was in college. On a reckless impulse, we got married soon afterwards, believing that we would live happily ever after in this idyllic setting. Debrakot is situated amidst forested hills with a line of Himalayan snow peaks visible to the north. The climate is pleasant, at 2,000 metres above sea level, but the isolation can be stifling. The town is a poor cousin to larger, better-known hill stations like Nainital and Mussoorie. Most people don't even know it exists. When I came here from Lucknow, Debrakot was mostly deserted and many of the properties had been abandoned. In those days there was no motor road connecting the town to the plains. People rode horses up the hill, or were carried in dandies, unless they chose to walk. That changed the year Sylvia and I got married, when a new road was completed, winding its way up from Kanjiwalla at the foot of the hill.

Suddenly, Debrakot had a future, but not for us. Sylvia quickly got bored with hill station life and it became obvious that we couldn't support ourselves from the orchard. The year Brigadier Augden died, a hailstorm destroyed the entire crop and the next year I waged a constant war against monkeys and birds, who defeated me in the end. Sylvia decided that we should move back to Delhi. I sat for the State Public Services Commission exam and became a policeman. It wasn't exactly the career I'd dreamed of but there was security in the job and a sense of authority that I enjoyed. Besides, my grandfather and two uncles had been police officers.

At the same time, my marriage was falling apart. Sylvia had got pregnant and then lost the child. She was unhappy being posted in lonely mofussil towns like Mainpuri and Etawah, which were even more provincial than Debrakot. Eventually, she left me and went back to her parents for a while before meeting a merchant navy captain who was emigrating to Australia. I didn't contest the divorce and that was the end of that. To get over the unhappiness, I threw myself into my work with renewed determination. What I enjoyed most about being a policeman was the unpredictable nature of the job, as well as the day-to-day routines of solving crimes and enforcing the law. By the time I was promoted to superintendent of police (SP), I had a reputation for being an honest officer who wouldn't accept a bribe. Before long, I was taken on deputation by the Central Bureau of Investigation (CBI), which was the most fulfilling period of my career, working on difficult, high-profile cases often involving corrupt civil servants and politicians.

The year after I joined CBI, my father died and my mother decided that she would leave Lucknow and move up to Debrakot. Though I had been employing a caretaker to look after Thornfield Lodge there was the constant worry about leaving the house unoccupied. My mother had always loved gardening and the flower beds came back to life under her supervision. Soon enough, she made a few friends and her time in Debrakot was probably the happiest years of her life. My younger brother Tony had moved to Bombay. He and his wife produced two grandchildren and they would come up to see her twice a year. I also made regular visits, whenever my work permitted. Altogether, it was a good arrangement and I was content to remain single, despite a few casual affairs over the years, none of which amounted to much.

Now that I'm retired, I wonder sometimes how different my life might have been if I hadn't joined the police. Perhaps I would have found a job in the corporate sector, like Tony, and made a good deal more money. But I'm not sure it would have given me the same satisfaction as being a policeman. As my rank increased, I missed the rough and tumble of an investigation and I didn't particularly enjoy the ceremonial duties that came with my promotions. In 1999, after I had transferred back from CBI to the Uttar Pradesh Police, the new hill state of Uttaranchal was being formed. Senior officers were given the choice of staying with the UP cadre or opting for Uttaranchal, which I did, because Debrakot was now part of the new state, later renamed Uttarakhand. By then I was an SSP, and I was promoted to DIG soon afterwards. It seemed likely that I would retire as an IG, if I kept out of trouble and curried favour with my superiors.

Of course, that didn't happen in the end. I had made a number of enemies along the way, mostly because I didn't tolerate corruption. My years with the CBI had reinforced these convictions and eventually I ran afoul of a timber contractor in Rudrapur, who had all sorts of political connections. The whole thing blew up in my face and I retreated to Debrakot to lick my wounds.

I have to admit that I miss being a policeman, not the uniform or the saluting, or sitting on a stage at public functions and making speeches. More than anything, I wish I could go back to being an investigating officer, getting my hands dirty in society's ugly secrets, and putting two and two together to make six. Police work is largely a rational pursuit, an opportunity to employ logic and common sense, as well as a critical eye. That's all I've ever wanted to do and the murder at Shambles now gave me an opportunity to see if I was still up to the task.

Four

At half past four in the afternoon, I went across to call on Gladys Ahluwalia. Her cottage, Glenwood, lies about a hundred metres above Shambala Villa, on a parallel ridge to the west. My mother was a close friend of Gladys, who is in her early nineties now. Most of her life has been spent in Debrakot and I knew that if anyone could tell me the history of Shambles, Gladys was the person to ask. The only problem is that she's stone deaf.

Despite this fact, Gladys had already heard about the murder. After greeting me at her front door, she led me inside to her drawing room. Though she uses a cane, her back is remarkably straight and her hair still has some colour in it, carefully plaited and pinned up in a grey bun. Her face reveals her age, wrinkles under the powder, but her eyes are those of a sixteen-year-old.

'What's your theory, Lionel?' she demanded. 'Do you think Reuben was a homosexual? It wouldn't surprise me. But why would that young man have killed him? Jealousy? Greed? Revenge?'

She dropped into an upholstered chair and waved her cane for me to take a seat on the sofa to her right.

'News travels quickly, doesn't it?' I said.

'What's that?' she replied. 'I don't think so! Reuben never had much money.'

'How did you learn what happened, Gladys?' I asked, raising my voice.

'The chowkidar couldn't possibly have done it,' she insisted. 'Charan Das is a bit of a rogue but a good man underneath.'

'I wasn't suggesting....' I started to say before she interrupted.

'You'll have some tea, won't you?' Gladys asked and then without waiting for an answer, she called out. 'Shanti! Chai lao!'

Through the brocade curtains in the doorway behind us, I saw a movement in the shadows and knew that the maid had been waiting for her orders.

'Gladys, I wanted to ask you about the house?' I said.

She shook her head. 'No, Lionel. I'm not surprised. Sabharwal was a shifty blighter. Never trusted him.'

I raised my voice even louder. 'The house! Who owns it?'

Gladys laughed. 'You don't have to shout, Lionel. Which house?'

'Shambala Villa! Shambles!'

She shook her head impatiently. 'That's the new name that Reuben gave it. It used to be called Cairngorm, back when Rosemary McKenzie first bought it.'

'When was the name changed?' I asked.

'Rosemary was a strange bird. Flighty! Scottish blood but none of that stoic highland spirit. She was into meditation and claimed she could levitate. Believe you me!' Gladys chuckled. 'I'm a sceptic when it comes to these things but she was doing yoga before it became a fad. I used to tease her—"Rosemary you're going to tie yourself in knots." But she never understood a joke, looking at me with her big wide eyes and saying, "It's not what you think, Gladys. Most of it has nothing to do with our bodies. It stretches the mind and exercises the soul!" Dear girl! She was too gullible and trusting... anyone could say anything to her about spiritual auras or astral travel and she would lap it up like a kitten that's been given a saucer of cream. She claimed to be a disciple of Annie Besant, but Rosemary only came to India after the war, just before Independence. I used to say to her, "Annie Besant died long ago, in 1933. How can you be her disciple?" And Rosemary would smile like a child and say, "Annieji speaks to me all the time." She was into all of that mumbo jumbo—séances and clairvoyance.'

As Gladys paused to catch her breath, I asked, 'How did she get the house?'

For a moment, it seemed as if she hadn't understood my question and there was a confused look on her face but she quickly recovered. 'Rosemary bought it from an army officer who was heading back home in '47. Things were going cheaply in those days. I doubt she paid more than five thousand for it. Property values were always depressed in Debrakot. For years, nobody wanted to buy here and people sold their homes for the value of the sheet metal roofs....'

Shanti came in with two cups of tea on a tray and a plate of ginger biscuits.

'Help yourself to sugar!' Gladys instructed me.

'Did Reuben buy the house from her?'

She heard me clearly this time, or perhaps she read my lips.

'Not at all!' she said. 'He was always a scrounger. I know I shouldn't speak ill of the dead, but I could tell he was after the property from the start. Rosemary was growing senile and got herself into debt. Reuben helped empty her bank account with all of his schemes. Can you believe it? He constructed a windmill and said it would generate enough electricity for all of us. Failed miserably! Anyway, Rosemary owed the bania quite a bit of money and he acquired the property in exchange for clearing her debts.'

'Which bania?' I asked.

Gladys laughed. 'Am I being interrogated by the police? Lionel, you must first read me my rights!'

I smiled and took a biscuit.

'Lala Satish Aggarwal, of Hilltop Stores. He's always claimed he owned the house and filed a case against Reuben right after Rosemary died. It's been languishing in the courts for the past eighteen years, but you can be sure Aggarwal will lay claim to it now, with Reuben out of the picture.'

'Do you think Satish Aggarwal could have killed him?' I asked.

'Absolutely,' said Gladys, misunderstanding my question. 'Rosemary was convinced the house was haunted.'

I repeated my question, but Gladys still didn't hear what I said, and rambled on: 'She used to tell me that one of the spirits living in the house with her was an Egyptian princess, the daughter of Tutankhamun.'

Giving up, I asked. 'But how did a pharaoh's daughter end up in Debrakot?'

'It was all some sort of spiritual fantasy,' she said. 'And Reuben encouraged her. I say, can you believe it? He once told me that he was an incarnation of the Egyptian god Osiris. Imagine, he expected me to swallow such rubbish!'

'But a lot of his followers thought he was god,' I said.

She waved a finger at me.

'Blasphemy!' she said.

I stayed another half hour with Gladys, and she told me that she thought Reuben's cult involved satanic rituals. She is a staunch member of the Church of England, as was my mother, though Gladys only attends services at St. John's now on Christmas and Easter because it's hard for her to get out of the house. Her maiden name is Hearsey and she is a direct descendant of the famous Anglo-Indian soldier of fortune and Himalayan explorer, Hyder Jung Hearsey. As a young woman Gladys defied her parents and married a Sikh officer in the armoured corps, who was killed in the 1971 war with Pakistan.

∞

It was beginning to grow dark by the time I left Glenwood but I was keen to visit Shambles once again. When I arrived at the door, a single constable was on duty, dozing in the entry hall. He stood up with a startled expression as soon as I entered and mustered an awkward salute. Thapliyal had left instructions that nobody was allowed into the house, except for me. The finance minister had arrived and most of the police force in Debrakot were preoccupied with his visit.

The constable on duty was a young man and I made a point of asking his name, trying to put him at ease.

'Jagdeep Negi, sir,' he replied, standing stiffly, as if on parade.

'And how long have you been in the police?' I asked.

'Three months, sir,' he answered.

'And are you happy with your work?' I inquired.

He replied in the affirmative and I made some sort of encouraging remark before turning to enter the house, but as I did, the constable said, 'Sir....'

'What is it?' I asked.

'Sir, I have a request....' He stammered.

I nodded for him to continue.

'Sir, would it be possible for the SHO to post another constable here with me?' he asked.

'You'll have to speak to him about that yourself,' I said. 'I have no authority. Why? Are you afraid to be alone in this house?'

'Yes, sir,' he admitted, lowering his head. 'There are sounds from inside, someone walking about, but when I go in, nobody is there.'

'Nonsense,' I scolded him. 'How are you going to be a successful policeman if you're scared of ghosts?'

Though I felt sorry for the young man, being alone on night duty, there was no point in encouraging his fears. The gathering twilight had cast the inner rooms into complete darkness. As soon as I entered the hall, the electricity went off, as it does on a daily basis. If there is a problem with a power connection, anywhere on the hillside, everything is shut down while repairs are carried out.

Fortunately, I'd brought a torch. Its yellow beam tunnelled through the gloomy entrance hall and I wondered whether any of the ghosts would appear. The two bodies had been removed and taken to the mortuary at the municipal hospital, where post-mortems are performed. This morning, one of the constables had discovered an assortment of drugs in the house, mostly hashish and heroin, as well as several bottles of pills, and a collection of used syringes. Thapliyal had taken all of it away for analysis.

The drugs were found in a suite of rooms that appeared to be Sabharwal's private quarters on the east side of the house. There was only one entrance, at the end of the glazed veranda, beyond the door leading into the prayer room. With the help of my torch, I made my way back to these rooms, wanting to examine them on my own. In the morning there had been too much confusion, with half a dozen policemen searching through the house. Like the rest of Shambles, the bedroom suite was in a state of neglect and disrepair, though the rooms showed evidence of recent occupancy, including a half-empty bottle of vodka and a packet of Charminar cigarettes, three of which had been smoked. The entire space was in disarray, with clothes draped over chairs and on a dresser. In the cupboard, I found several un-ironed saris on hangers and half a dozen khadi kurtas, similar to the one that Reuben was wearing at the time of his death.

A quilt on the bed lay rumpled in an untidy heap, while the two pillows were each dented, presumably by two separate heads. All of this made it seem likely that both victims we'd found that morning had slept here in recent days. Over the years, I've learned to read the dishevelled contours of unmade beds as carefully as a palmist examines the creased lines on a person's hand. It's not an exact science but one can gather a good deal of information from the way the sheets have been kicked aside or a blanket lies askew, not to mention the stains and hairs one finds. Most of us spend at least a third of our lives in bed, and often much more, not just to sleep but in convalescence, despair, indolence, and passion. An unmade bed can reveal dreams and fantasies enveloped in its folds and creases, as well as unrequited lusts and aching sorrow. But as I stared at this bed it suggested nothing at all, beyond a hint of loneliness and fear.

The bottom sheet had not been washed in a while and the cheap cotton fabric was torn along one edge, exposing a pink foam mattress underneath. On the bedside table, I found a book. Judging from the reading lamp and the packet of cigarettes, I guessed this was the side where Reuben slept. Picking up the book, I saw it was a heavy tome, *Isis Unveiled*, the pages yellowed with age and the cover coming loose at the binding. On the opposite side of the bed lay a set of blue glass bangles as well as a couple of soiled tissues. The beam from my torch also picked out a single hairpin.

Next to the bedroom was a dressing room with a second cupboard, one of those heavy, old-fashioned almirahs that used to frighten me as a boy. They look like giant coffins standing upright. When I opened it cautiously, the torchlight penetrated the shadows and a faint scent of camphor and mothballs emerged. Several long robes were draped on hangers, similar to academic gowns but made of heavier fabric and embroidered with cryptic designs and symbols in dull, metallic hues. I guessed these were costumes used during rituals performed in the secret sanctuary at the heart of the house.

The constable on duty had offered to accompany me inside but I had told him to remain on guard at the front door, so I was alone. For a brief moment, I felt a passing presence and glanced around. A narrow window was covered with a tattered drape and I was surrounded by shadows. In that fleeting instant, I almost sensed that Reuben had returned as a spirit to keep me from prying into his affairs. Shaking off this premonition, I let my torch explore the contents of the cupboard. At the bottom lay a collection of old shoes. On the lower, right-hand side of the almirah were two drawers. The upper one slid open without resistance. It contained a clutter of objects that seemed to have some ritual purpose, including a conch shell and a pair of tiny brass cymbals. These were jumbled together with a couple of prayer wheels and some other spiritual accoutrements.

The second drawer had jammed because of monsoon humidity. I struggled with it for a few minutes and was about to give up when it finally surrendered with a reluctant groan of swollen wood. It was almost empty, except for a human skull, from which the lower jaw was missing. It was old and yellowed, the kind of anonymous relic one finds in biology labs, used for studying anatomy. The only other object in this drawer was a bullwhip made of braided leather, which was covered with mildew. In the yellow light from my torch, it looked like a snake coiled up beside the skull.

Five

Like most houses on the hillside, Shambala Villa had a set of servants' quarters on the property, where the chowkidar lived. The low, two-room building that Charan Das occupied was in even worse repair than the main house and looked more like a cowshed than a human dwelling. The roof had been patched with tin canisters flattened out and wedged under the rusty metal sheets, which were coming loose at places. One section had been covered by a blue plastic tarpaulin to prevent leaks.

Light rain was falling and the drizzle sifted through my torch beam as I climbed the steps to the quarters. A sour, charred fragrance of burning oak branches emerged from cracks in the door and smoke was spilling out from under the eaves of the roof. When I knocked there was silence. After a pause, I tried again, a little louder this time, calling out Charan Das's name. I couldn't blame him for being cautious after what had happened in the main house. Finally, the hasp inside rattled and the door was pulled inward, creaking on its hinges. A young woman, with the pallu of her sari drawn modestly over her head, stood in silhouette peering out at me.

'Is Charan Das here?' I asked.

She nodded, stepping aside to let me enter.

The old caretaker was seated on the far side of an open clay hearth. With some difficulty he got to his feet and folded his hands. A short, angular man, he was wearing a khaki shirt over loose trousers and his face had a wizened, gnome-like expression.

'Sahib,' he said. 'Why did you bother? I could have come to your house.'

Charan Das is someone I've known for years, a familiar figure on the hillside. He had done a few odd jobs for me to supplement the pittance he received from Reuben Sabharwal. Occasionally, I got him to help me with the gardening and he would sometimes show up for no reason at all, except to complain about his employer, who was always late paying his salary. In winter he would bring gunny sacks of pine cones to sell as kindling. Charan Das was in his seventies and he could no longer chop wood or do heavy tasks, though I paid him daily wages to clear the drains after the monsoon or rake the leaves under the chestnut trees.

He gestured for me to sit on the string cot that stood against one wall and told his daughter to make some tea.

'No, thank you,' I said. 'Please don't. I just wanted to speak to you for a few minutes.'

A cloud of woodsmoke hung from the rafters and I lowered myself to the cot so I could breathe. The only light in the room came from the fire, which cast flickering shadows on the walls. The chowkidar's quarters were like a village hut in some rural settlement far back in the hills, beyond the reach of electricity or running water. In one corner I could see the components of a crude still and I knew that he made his own liquor. Hanging from a nail on the wall, I noticed a large brass and copper drum. Charan Das was a musician too and he was often called to lead wedding processions or to beat a loud tattoo for ceremonies and celebrations at the Devta's temple on the outskirts of Debrakot.

'It's a terrible thing that's happened,' said Charan Das. 'Nobody deserves to die that way, neither by stabbing nor by hanging.'

'I heard your daughter found the bodies this morning?' I said, turning to the woman, who was crouched by the fire, feeding a few twigs into the flames. At my remark, I could see her flinch.

Charan Das replied. 'Yes, it came as a shock to both of us. I've never seen anything so terrible in my life.'

'Who was this Meena?' I asked. 'The man disguised as a woman.'

'We had no idea!' Charan Das claimed. 'She was like so many others who came here—a chela, one of Reuben's devotees.'

'You never suspected Meena was a man?'

Charan Das shook his head. 'I don't pay much attention to what goes on inside the house.'

'What about you?' I asked his daughter.

She simply shook her head in mute denial.

'Sahib, you know I wasn't happy working here,' Charan Das said. 'Reuben never paid my wages on time and he would shout at me if the water ran out or something broke. I did my work, cutting the grass and looking after the property as best I can. Working here for twenty years, I've grown old and poor.'

'You still play your drum,' I said. 'That must earn you something, and you sell your liquor.'

He shook his head and gazed into the fire with a lost expression.

'What do you think happened?' I asked, after a pause.

Charan Das shrugged. 'They must have fought over something and she killed him. I mean, *this man* killed Reuben, then hanged himself.'

'The rope he used,' I asked. 'Is it something you recognize?'

The old man nodded. 'Yes, it was kept in the storeroom. Before the dog died, it was used to tie him up in the yard so he wouldn't run away.'

'How did he fasten it to the hook on the beam?' I asked. 'The kitchen ceiling is at least twice my height.'

'He must have used the stepladder,' said Charan Das.

'I didn't see a ladder,' I said. 'Where is it kept?'

'Also in the storeroom,' said Charan Das, a quizzical look on his face.

'If he put it back before hanging himself, how did he get the noose around his throat? He had to be standing on something,' I said.

'Maybe he climbed on to the kitchen counter and jumped from there,' Charan Das suggested.

'That's possible,' I agreed, though I wasn't convinced. 'It must have happened during the night. Did you hear anything?'

'Nothing,' said the old man. 'The rain was heavy and drowned out any sounds. Often, I could hear Reuben shouting and arguing, but not last night.'

'What sort of rituals did he perform? I saw the room with the round table and candles.'

'Some sort of puja and prayers. I never understood his religion,' Charan Das shook his head. 'His followers called him Bhagwan.'

'Didn't he try to get you involved or explain his teachings?' I asked.

'No,' said Charan Das. 'Most of the time, he wouldn't let me enter that part of the house.'

Though I was seated below the layer of smoke, my eyes were burning and it was difficult to breath, but there was one more question.

'Did Meena come here alone, or was there anyone who accompanied her?'

The old man thought for a bit before he replied.

'I think she came with someone, a young man. I don't know his name. He didn't stay but he visited, once in a while,' the chowkidar explained. 'There were so many people who came and went it was hard to tell them apart.'

'What was his relationship with Meena?'

'I don't know, a friend perhaps,' said Charan Das. 'I never wanted to know what was going on inside that house.'

˜

When I reached home, it wasn't particularly cold, but I lit a fire in the fireplace to drive away a lingering dampness in the air, as well as the pall of death. Unlike the open hearth at Charan Das's quarters, the fire in my drawing room gave off no smoke, though the faint scent of burning oak was the same. The electricity had come back on by now, but I switched off my reading lamp and let the burning logs illuminate the room. My recent memory of the skull and whip in the almirah drawer still disturbed me but the flames in the hearth were comforting. A purifying beauty exists in fire, a primal source of light and warmth that burns away the shadows in our souls.

Rum is also an essential element of life. Pouring myself three fingers in a cut glass tumbler, I added an equal measure of water. Unlike whisky, which I seldom drink, rum has a mildly medicinal flavour, with a hint of raw cane juice and caramel. Some people prefer to add lime or Coke but for purists like me, plain water is the only acceptable form of dilution. I don't add ice.

Badlu had tried to extract more information from me about the murder, but I disappointed him, saying he could go home and I would heat up the leftovers from lunch for my dinner. His quarters are not as humble as Charan Das's dilapidated shed and Badlu has a wife, as well as a son and daughter-in-law, who share three rooms in a pucca building, next to the old stables.

As the alcohol began to unknot the riddles in my brain, I stared into the fire as if trying to interpret the dancing symbols in the flames. I wasn't convinced about the hanging, even if the young man had climbed on to the kitchen counter and jumped. This explanation was too tidy and the idea that a murderer would put away a stepladder, before killing himself, seemed unlikely. But more than this minor inconsistency, there was something else about the two murders that still puzzled me. Violent deaths usually explain themselves, by which I mean there is generally enough evidence in plain view to draw preliminary conclusions. In this case, however, some of my initial observations raised more questions than answers.

Beyond the startling fact that Meena had turned out to be a man, there was a basic contradiction in the crime scene, for I'd noticed that the sari he was wearing was unstained. If, indeed, he had stabbed Reuben, and then hanged himself, the clothes he was wearing would have been covered in blood. Added to this was the fact that his corpse didn't exhibit the usual signs of a hanging. I've seen plenty of suicides in my time, many of them carried out with a rope or a length of cloth tied to a ceiling fan. Those who hang themselves often involuntarily void their bowels. And in every case I've witnessed, the victim died with a contorted grimace on his or her face. Some even had their tongues hanging out. But at Shambles, the corpse's face bore a calm, almost passive expression.

In addition to these nagging questions, I felt sure there was something I had failed to see in the house, a missing piece of evidence I'd overlooked. The inner prayer room with its strange, mystical decor and furnishings seemed perverse in many ways, from the twisted features of the devil masks and occult objects to the bulbous shapes of melted candlewax. It was like an elaborate stage setting for a grotesque, theatrical charade. Yet, I knew better than to make a hasty judgement. Even for someone like myself, who has no religious convictions, it is a mistake to dismiss the beliefs of others. Though I found it difficult to take the cult seriously, with its religious paraphernalia, robes, fly whisk, and other fetish objects, I knew that if I was going to untangle the truth, I had to understand what those symbols meant.

I guessed that the book I'd taken from Sabharwal's bedside table might offer some clues. Allowing myself a few more minutes of soothing firelight, I finished my drink before pouring another and switching on the reading lamp.

Isis Unveiled was an old edition, though more recent than the book's original publication date of 1877. Helena P. Blavatsky—the author's name was intriguing, as was the faux Egyptian motif on the cover. On the flyleaf of the book, I noticed Rosemary McKenzie's name, written in blue ink with a spidery hand. Flipping through the pages, I scanned the table of contents, which was divided into two parts: I. Science, II. Religion.

The chapter titles gave little away—'Old Things With New Names' and further down the list 'India: The Cradle of Race'. Part II included a chapter, 'Christian Crimes and Heathen Virtues' which tweaked my imagination. Turning to that section of the book, I read the opening paragraph:

> For such men as Plotinus, Porphyry, Iamblichus, Apollonius, and even Simon Magus to be accused of having formed a pact with the Devil, whether the latter personage exists or not, is so absurd as to need but little refutation. If Simon Magus—the most problematical of all in a historical sense—ever existed otherwise than in the overheated fancy of Peter and the other apostles, he was evidently no worse than any of his adversaries. A difference in religious views, however great, is insufficient *per se* to send one person to heaven and the other to hell.

Though I had no argument with Madame Blavatsky's conclusion, the references to ancient philosophers passed way over my head. Nevertheless, the rum helped me persevere for a while longer. What I discovered in the book was a strange combination of semi-reasonable, rational arguments about the universality of religious experience muddled up with mystical enigmas and pseudo-science that invoked shamans, sorcery, and black magic. At the end of the book was a passage that began with somewhat abstract conclusions but quickly detoured into phrenology and craniometrical theories.

> Civilized Western nations lack the phenomenal powers of endurance, both mental and physical, of the Easterners; the temperamental idiosyncrasies of the Orientals are utterly wanting in them. In the Hindu, the Arabian, and the Tibetan, an intuitive perception of the possibilities of occult natural forces in subjection to human will comes by inheritance; and in them, the physical senses as well as the spiritual are far more finely developed than in the Western races. Notwithstanding the notable difference of thickness between the skulls of a European and a southern Hindu, this difference, being a purely climatic result due to the intensity of the sun's rays, involves no psychological principles.

Though I've always tried to keep an open mind to the beliefs of others, my own cranium seemed too thick to absorb these ideas and I set the book aside, gazing through the amber lens of my glass of rum at the dying flames in the grate. Policemen aren't mystics or philosophers, as a rule. Our sense of right and wrong lies not in intellectual abstractions or rhetorical arguments but in the harsh reality of spilled blood and broken bones, as well as the crude depravities of human nature.

Six

After a brief spell of unexpected activity, my landline had gone dead again and Thapliyal was forced to dispatch two constables on a motorcycle to deliver a message. The state finance minister, Jagdamba Panwar, was inviting me to lunch at the Sunnyview Manor Hotel on the other side of town. My instincts told me I should decline but I knew that Jagdamba was an influential politician and Thapliyal's career might suffer if I didn't show up. Aside from that, I had known the finance minister when I was posted in Pauri years ago. At that time, he was just starting out in politics and I found him pleasant enough. We'd even played cricket together.

Our part of town has remained largely unaffected by the developments on the other side of Debrakot. When the motor road arrived, forty years ago, it happened to wind its way up from the last hairpin bend and joined the Mall Road at Rana Chowk, five kilometres from Thornfield, on the western end of the ridge. As people began to rebuild the deserted shops and hotels, which had lain dormant for years, they naturally concentrated on that area, where tourists were likely to arrive. Within a decade, more than a dozen cheap hotels had cropped up, along with restaurants, video arcades, and souvenir shops. After years of isolation and neglect, Debrakot suddenly saw a flurry of unplanned construction. Most of it was done in a haphazard, makeshift manner. Old buildings were torn down and new dwellings erected, without any concern for whether the hill station had enough water or electricity to support the expansion. 'Holiday Homes in the Himalayas' were advertised in the newspapers, with pictures of quaint little cottages facing the snow peaks. In fact, most of these new dwellings were dingy, concrete flats that overlooked similar eyesores perched on precipitous slopes.

The eastern side of the town, where I live, has been spared because the Mall Road ends abruptly at the foot of a steep incline, popularly known as Switchback Road—a narrow, winding track that climbs to the top of our ridge. Several corners are so tight that vehicles have to stop and reverse to get around the turn. Every year, at least one car goes off the side of the road, usually with fatal results. Because of this obstacle, properties like mine, as well as Shambles, remain largely unchanged and unspoiled, except through the natural process of decay.

Sunnyview Manor, on the other hand, was once a large, stately home owned by a prominent landowner from Bareilly. He sold it to a hotel chain that turned the estate into Debrakot's only four-star hotel. (The fifth star requires a swimming pool, which isn't possible, given our water shortages.) I do my best to avoid going to that side of town because of chronic traffic jams. The hotel itself is a new structure made mostly of glass and steel. It attracts wealthy tourists and caters to the nouveau riche. The restaurant serves a standard Punjabi–Mughlai buffet that gives me heartburn just looking at the scarlet and saffron sauces, swimming with grease.

Setting aside my reservations, I told the constables that the SHO could kindly send a jeep to pick me up at the foot of Switchback Road, at half past twelve. I preferred to walk across there from Thornfield, rather than risk a police vehicle's brakes failing on the treacherous descent.

When I arrived at Sunnyview Manor, Jagdamba was holding court in the ballroom of the hotel, which is used mostly for weddings. He had put on a good deal of weight since we'd last met. In his crisp, white kurta–pajama, with a striped lavender scarf, he looked like an emperor at his durbar. Thapliyal received me in the lobby and led me forward. I was surprised when Jagdamba greeted me effusively, for it was one of his party colleagues whose nose I'd broken nineteen months earlier. But all of that seemed to have been forgiven and he embraced me like a long-lost friend. The other supplicants, mostly local politicians and merchants who had come to request favours, as well as a few journalists, watched me with suspicion as I was seated on the sofa next to the minister.

'How many years has it been, Lionel bhai,' he asked, 'since I hit those three sixes off you? Are you still a pace bowler?'

'Unfortunately, these days it's nothing faster than leg spin.'

In Pauri I had formed a police eleven to boost community relations and we played against local sporting clubs. Jagdamba had been a wicketkeeper for the Pauri Cricket Association, one of the more competitive teams. Judging by his current girth, the only deliveries that might get past him these days would be declared wide.

Ignoring everyone else, we chatted for a while as Jagdamba kept patting my arm and laughing at my stories. I immediately sensed that he was after something and it soon came out. Before we went in to lunch, the finance minister asked me to accompany him to another room, where we were out of earshot of the others.

'Thapliyalji told me about this terrible murder,' said Jagdamba. 'How could anything like this have happened in such a quiet hill station like Debrakot?'

'Who knows?' I said with a shrug. 'Bad things happen everywhere.'

'Yes,' he nodded with a serious frown. 'But it is unfortunate that a town with a peaceful reputation should be the scene of an ugly murder like this.'

A look of distaste crossed his amiable features and he fell silent.

'What is it, Jaggu bhai?' I asked, knowing that he was waiting for his cue.

'This boy....' he said, then paused. 'The one who died with the rope around his neck, we've learned that he is the son of one of my constituents. They've identified him from his photo. It's a good family, very prominent in Haridwar. I don't want their personal loss to be made worse by too much publicity, you know.'

'When was he identified?' I asked. 'I didn't know.'

'Thapliyal will give you more details,' Jagdamba explained. 'The chief minister was informed and he's asked that you proceed with discretion and avoid speaking to the press.'

I had to laugh. 'But I'm not officially involved in the case,' I said. 'You know I'm retired. I was only helping out because Thapliyal asked me.'

'Yes, yes, of course,' Jagdamba replied, his hand on my shoulder, as large as a wicketkeeper's glove. 'We want you to be involved.

Unofficially, of course, but it would be a huge help if you could solve this case without all of the usual scandal and controversy.'

'I don't understand,' I said. 'Whatever I discover, I will pass on to Thapliyal. It's his case, after all.'

'Absolutely!' said Jagdamba, his eyes shifting away from mine. 'But, in this matter, a little spin bowling would be useful because the pitch is sure to turn.'

'You know I've always kept a straight line and length,' I replied.

Jagdamba nodded. 'Lionel bhai, that's how I've always remembered you. Even when we were on opposing teams, I knew you played with a straight bat.'

A short while later, I cornered Thapliyal after we had served ourselves lunch from the buffet. He gave me a sheepish look.

'Sir, no butter chicken?' he asked, looking at my plate, which contained a small helping of rice with a little dal and vegetables.

'I'm watching my weight,' I said. 'Now, come on, tell me what's happening. It sounds as though this case is more complicated than it seems.'

'Yes.' Thapliyal nodded, with a morose expression.

'Jaggu bhai says you've identified the young man. Who is he?'

'Kunal Vaidya. The eldest son of Dr Pran Vaidya, the herbalist from Haridwar who runs the Ayurvedic Wellness Centre. He's a rich and powerful man. Most of the politicians are in his pocket,' Thapliyal explained after chewing a mouthful of chicken and rice.

'Doesn't he own the Aranya Nivas Ashram, near the ruins of the old Debrakot brewery?' I asked.

Thapliyal nodded.

'Then why was his son living at Shambala Villa?'

'He left home and became a follower of Sabharwal's, one of his devotees,' Thapliyal explained.

'How old was he?'

'Twenty-three.'

'So, what are we supposed to do?' I demanded. 'There isn't much room to manoeuvre here. As you said, yourself, the evidence seems to show that the young man killed Sabharwal, then took his own life.'

'Of course,' Thapliyal agreed, 'but they want us to be discreet.'

'In what sense?' I asked, though I knew the answer already.

'They don't want it to get out that he was wearing a sari...you know how the media will play that up,' said Thapliyal, after taking another bite of butter chicken. He already looked as if he was suffering from indigestion.

'But it's bound to get out,' I said. 'One of your constables is sure to have told his wife and I already know that people are talking. Gladys Ahluwalia knows. So does Charan Das. It's not a secret any more.'

'Sir, I'm sorry to have involved you in this,' Thapliyal apologized.

'It's not your fault,' I said.

The food on my plate remained untouched and I felt a sinking sensation of nausea in the pit of my stomach, knowing that once politics began to play a part in an investigation there was very little chance that we would discover the truth.

∽

As I was leaving the hotel after extracting myself from Jagdamba's presence—he hugged me affectionately before I left—the media cornered me in the lobby. Most of them were young men I know or recognize, though I try to keep a distance from the press, now that I'm retired. They have a way of moving about as a pack and ambushed me before I could escape. Several of the reporters represent local television stations, carrying microphones and cameras. Others work for national and regional newspapers, both in Hindi and in English. Always on the lookout for a story, they tend to follow senior politicians and administrative officials about, hoping for a scandal or a statement that might generate a headline.

'Sir! Sir! One minute please,' a reporter called out in English. 'Can we have a bite, please, sir. One bite?'

'A bite?' I asked, without trying to hide my irritation.

'Sound bite, sir,' another explained, thrusting his microphone in my face.

'What about?' I demanded.

'The two murders, sir. Who were the victims?'

The journalist that asked me this question is named Ratan Chauhan. He is infamous in Debrakot for extorting bribes in exchange for not filing a story. If someone has cut a tree without the forest department's permission or built something illegally, Chauhan shows up with his camera and will only leave after he's been paid off to keep things quiet.

'Was one of the victims a woman?' Chauhan asked.

'You'll have to ask the police. I'm a retired officer....'

A chorus of protest greeted my statement.

'But we know, sir, that you are assisting with the investigation. Why were they murdered?' one of the older journalists, Gyan Chand, asked.

'If I knew the answer to that,' I replied, 'the case would be solved!'

'But, sir,' another television reporter called out. 'How were they killed?'

His microphone was labelled NUZ10.

'Again, you'll have to ask the SHO,' I said. 'I'm sure he will provide details whenever it's appropriate. I'm just a neighbour....'

'But, as a neighbour, how does it make you feel?'

'It doesn't matter what I feel....' I said. 'Now, please excuse me....'

Folding my hands, I tried to push my way out of the circle, but I was surrounded and it was hopeless trying to break free. Finally, I relented and gave them their 'bite', making a few innocuous remarks about the general lack of crime in Debrakot and how these murders were an exception. I also explained that I had full confidence in the SHO, Inspector Thapliyal, who was a 'very diligent and committed officer'. Though they looked disappointed, the journalists reluctantly dispersed, letting me go home.

Seven

Early on in my career, as a young police officer, I developed a habit of taking afternoon naps. It helped me concentrate through the rest of the day and made up for many late nights. As a rule, predators are nocturnal creatures. Most crimes occur after dark and I would often be roused from sleep to investigate burglaries, dacoities, or suspicious deaths. On the other hand, the hours between 2 and 4 p.m. are usually a peaceful period of the day and my naps were seldom interrupted.

When I got home from lunch at Sunnyview Manor it was well past three. Heading straight to bed, I wondered if I would be able to sleep with all of the thoughts circulating through my brain. Eventually, though, I dozed off into the comforting void of slumber 'that knits up the ravelled sleave of care', as Shakespeare put it so eloquently.

Waking out of a dreamless rest is one of the greatest pleasures in life. For a few brief seconds, all of our worries have been erased. I make a habit of lying on my back when I take a nap, so that I don't fall asleep for too long. Opening my eyes, I looked up at the pinewood ceiling, studying the familiar pattern of knots and natural arabesques.

Soon enough, however, I was troubled again by what I'd been told, both by the finance minister and by Thapliyal. It was obvious that efforts were already underway to cover up and distort the facts in this case. As I was lying there, gazing at the designs overhead, I heard Badlu knocking on the door. Checking my watch, I saw that it was half past four.

'Yes, what is it?' I called out.

'Someone is here to see you,' Badlu replied. 'A lady.'

I rose reluctantly from my bed and checked in the bathroom mirror to make sure my hair wasn't out of place, then straightened the seams on my shirt and brushed down the wrinkles to make myself as presentable as possible. It wasn't often that a woman came to call.

Badlu had shown the visitor into the glassed-in porch, having calculated that this was an important guest, not someone who should be kept waiting outside. She rose from her chair as I entered, a tall, graceful figure with long grey hair plaited into a single braid that hung down over her right shoulder as far as her waist. She wore a pale blue sari with a cutwork pattern on the border.

'Please forgive me for disturbing you,' she said in a refined voice that carried traces of a convent education. 'Rita Sabharwal.'

'Hello,' I said, shaking her hand.

'I'm Reuben's sister,' she explained.

'My condolences,' I replied, as she sat down again.

Moments later, Badlu arrived with the tea tray. He knows my habits and the only difference from any other day was that there were two cups instead of one.

I couldn't help noticing that Rita Sabharwal didn't seem particularly upset on account of her brother's death. Her face was calm and composed, with a fair complexion and smooth, well-preserved skin that needed no make-up. The dark eyes that met mine showed little emotion and I could tell immediately that she was trying to evaluate my personality in much the same way as I was gauging hers.

'Did you know Reuben well?' she asked.

'No,' I said, as Badlu withdrew to the kitchen. 'Not really. We met once or twice. I haven't been living here very long...permanently, that is.'

'I was told that you are a retired police officer,' she said.

'Who told you that?' I asked.

'Various people,' she said evasively. 'It's true, isn't it, Mr Carmichael?'

'Lionel...please,' I said. 'Will you have tea?'

'As long as it's not too strong,' she said.

I poured her a cup, which she examined briefly, before nodding.

'Thank you. I don't take milk or sugar,' said Rita, lowering her voice. Then, after accepting the cup she asked, almost as an afterthought, 'Do you have any idea why Reuben was murdered?'

'It's still too early to tell,' I said, 'but it seems he was killed by the young man who hanged himself.'

'I gathered as much,' she said. 'My brother always had bad taste in boys.'

'So, you knew he was gay?' I asked.

'He wasn't exclusive in his sexual preferences,' she said. 'Reuben was promiscuous, and he would sleep with anything that moved.'

I could tell she was eyeing my response, to see if her remark startled me, though I held my teacup steady and returned her gaze with as much equanimity as possible. Very little shocks me any more.

'Did your brother have enemies who might have done this?' I asked.

'Plenty. He had a corrosive personality.'

'I'm guessing you didn't get along with him yourself,' I said.

'Let's just say we were estranged,' she answered abruptly. 'I've only spoken to him two or three times in the past ten years.'

'Where do you live?'

'Delhi,' she said.

'And were you involved in his religious cult?' I asked.

'Our mother was a Theosophist,' Rita replied, taking a sip of tea and then setting it aside. 'Reuben inherited her beliefs, though he took things in a very different direction, a darker side of the truth.'

'What about you?' I asked.

'I'm not involved, though our mother was a strong influence on both of us,' Rita said. 'She was French.'

'And your father was Indian?'

'Yes, Punjabi. Originally from Multan,' she explained.

I hadn't noticed it at first but I could now see a trace of European genes in her features. As if she'd read my thoughts, she asked, 'You're an Anglo-Indian, aren't you?'

I nodded.

'It's strange how our mixed blood gives us a unique perspective. After marrying my father, my mother tried to become an Indian in many ways. She dressed in a sari for as long as I can remember and wore a bindi on her forehead, though her Hindi and Punjabi were atrocious,' Rita said, with a smile.

'But she gave your brother a European name,' I said.

'Jewish, actually. Her family escaped from France just before the Germans invaded. They took the last ship from Marseille to Bombay.'

I was sure that Rita Sabharwal hadn't come to tell me about her ancestry but I didn't interrupt her as she explained how her father had also arrived in Bombay as a refugee during Partition, in 1947. He met her mother by chance, a pair of castaways whose paths crossed in exile.

When she finally paused, looking out the window at the mist that engulfed the trees, I asked. 'Is there anything I can do for you, regarding your brother's death?'

'Actually, two things,' she said, after a moment's pause. 'First of all, I tried to go across and see the house where he lived, but the police won't let me inside. They said I needed your permission.'

'I'm not formally involved in the case,' I said. 'But, perhaps, I could accompany you. Is there anything in particular you're looking for?'

'Not really. I just wanted to see where he lived...take a look around.'

'The house is in a terrible state,' I said. 'We call it Shambles for a reason.'

'I could see that,' she said. 'The whole place is about to collapse.'

'Do you have any interest in claiming the property?'

'Not at all,' she said. 'That isn't my purpose for coming here. Of course, if there is something of sentimental value, perhaps something that belonged to our mother, I might like to take it home with me, but I'm not Reuben's heir and wouldn't want to lay claim to the place. I'm sure it's a legal mess. My brother was careless about these things.' Hesitating for a minute, she added, 'Mind you, at the same time, I won't take any responsibility for his debts.'

'Of course,' I replied. 'But you said there were two things you needed.'

'Oh yes,' she responded. 'I'd like to bury him here.'

'You don't want a cremation?' I asked.

'No,' she said. 'I doubt if there's a Jewish cemetery in this town but I'm sure there must be an old British graveyard.'

'There is, though I'd have to check with the pastor at St. John's,' I said. 'I'm not familiar with church rules and regulations, but of course, I'll try.'

'Thank you,' she answered. 'When would you be free to visit the house?'

'Tomorrow morning?' I said.

'That would be fine. Ten o'clock?' she proposed.

'Yes,' I said. 'By the way, may I ask what you do in Delhi?'

'I have a public relations firm,' she said. 'We represent corporate clients and a few individuals—actors, authors.'

'And where are you staying in Debrakot?'

'At the Sunnyview Hotel,' she said. 'It's the only decent place I could find. Not the most comfortable but clean enough.'

'I was there for lunch today,' I said. 'How did you come across?'

'By car. My driver parked at the top of your path. It's a terrifying road,' she said. 'Everything here is straight up and down!'

'Yes,' I said. 'People who have a fear of heights don't do well in Debrakot.'

❧

I walked Rita Sabharwal up the path to her car, a silver Mercedes that looked as if it had just come out of a showroom. After seeing her off, I decided to take my evening stroll. The weather seemed to be clearing, but I was carrying an umbrella as a precaution. It was almost 6 p.m. Our sunsets during the monsoon can be spectacular and the clouds were already tinted rainbow hues like mother of pearl. The trees were still dripping, branches draped with moss and ferns, but the mist had vanished temporarily and I wondered how much longer the monsoon would continue. Today was the third of September—probably another two weeks of rain to go.

My usual walk circles the top of the hill, a distance of about three kilometres. The furthest point is Hilltop Stores, part of a small bazaar of three shops, from where Switchback Road descends to the main town below. More often than not, I need to pick up a kilo of sugar or a loaf of bread to take home. Lala Satish Aggarwal always greets me with folded hands and an obsequious smile. He is six inches shorter than me and twice my diameter, shaped like a light bulb. Though he presents a timid demeanour and his voice is a high-pitched whisper, he is a shrewd businessman with a ruthless sense of entrepreneurship.

'DIG sahib! Good evening,' he purred, like an asthmatic cat.

'Lalaji,' I said. 'How are things?'

'You know how it is,' he whined. 'Just getting by.'

'What news?' I asked, examining the shelves of tinned goods above his counter, a random assortment of items from condensed milk to cocktail sausages. Nothing ever seemed to be in the same place as it was the day before and the only person who could find what you wanted was the proprietor himself.

'I should be asking you, Carmichael sahib. This murder has terrified everyone. How could such a crime have taken place in Debrakot? My wife and I didn't sleep at all last night.' He paused a moment and eyed me carefully. 'But I'm not surprised someone killed that bastard.'

'Who? Sabharwal?' I said.

'A wicked man,' Aggarwal continued. 'These are the sort of people who should not be allowed up here.'

'I heard you've been fighting in court to get the property from him,' I said.

'He had no right to be living there. I have all the papers in my name but you know how our legal system works. Whoever has occupancy has the upper hand.' His jowls quivered with indignation.

'Well, now that he's dead you can take possession,' I said. 'If your papers are in order.'

'Yes, but....' he whimpered now. 'Everyone will need to be paid off...even the police, I'm sorry to say.'

'Why? If you have a legal claim to the property, it should be yours,' I insisted.

'Sir, you know how this country works.' He cringed a little.

'Did Sabharwal owe you money?' I asked.

'He owed everyone money! But nobody murders someone because

of a debt. It's illogical,' he said. 'Once your creditor is dead, there isn't much chance you'll be repaid.'

'You have a point,' I conceded.

'Reuben fought with many people in town. He had a filthy tongue even though he pretended to be a holy man,' the Lala said. 'I've heard him call people names that I can't repeat.'

'So you think it was revenge?' I asked.

'Who knows?' Aggarwal made a dismissive gesture with one hand. 'I hear that one of his followers died as well. They say he stabbed him and then killed himself.'

'Do you believe that?'

The shopkeeper shook his head.

'No. It's not possible. After killing a dog like Sabharwal, why would you take your own life? There must be someone else involved.'

I said nothing more, scanning the shelves again.

'You're looking for something?' he inquired.

'Mango pickle,' I said. 'Do you have any?'

He nodded and moved sideways behind the counter before leaning down and producing a bottle from the bottom shelf.

Eight

Raipal Singh, the milkman, showed up earlier than usual the next morning, before Badlu had arrived to take charge of the kitchen. I was in my dressing gown, fixing my first pot of tea, when I saw him rapping on the windowpane above the sink. Opening the door, I greeted Raipal, remembering that I hadn't spoken to Thapliyal about his son. With the murder, the boy's disappearance had slipped my mind. Fortunately, however, the problem had solved itself.

'Sahib, Suraj came home yesterday,' Raipal said, a look of relief on his face. 'Without telling us, he had gone to try and join the army in Landsdowne but the Selection Board turned him down.'

'I'm glad he's safe,' I said. 'The police have been busy with other things.'

Raipal nodded. 'Yes, I know. After I spoke with you the other day, I went across to deliver milk to Shambala Villa and I learned that Reuben was dead.'

'Had he been buying milk from you for a long time?' I asked.

'Only the last six months,' he said. 'There was another dairywalla from Kinauli village. But he stopped supplying them after he got bitten by the dog. Reuben sahib also hadn't paid him for several months.'

'I heard the dog died,' I said.

'Yes, someone poisoned it last month,' said Raipal. 'It had bitten several people. They used to tie it up but when it got loose it would attack anyone who passed by the house. I was also afraid of it.'

'Who do you think poisoned the dog?' I asked.

'Probably someone who was bitten,' Raipal replied. 'The only people who could control it were Reuben and Charan Das's daughter, because she fed him.'

'What kind of dog was it?'

'People said it was an Alsatian but it looked more like a street dog,' the milkman replied.

'Did you notice anything at Shambala Villa that might explain why Reuben was killed?' I asked.

Raipal thought for a moment, as if he were trying to decide whether or not to divulge the information. Most people, especially villagers in the hills, are reluctant to point a finger because they believe an accusation might turn against them.

'There was something....' He started to say, then paused again.

'Go on,' I said.

'A month ago, I had delivered milk at Shambala Villa as usual and then I went into town to buy a few things but on my way back to my village, I stopped at the house again because Reuben owed me more than a thousand rupees and I needed the money. When I got to Shambala Villa, I saw Anmol Gupta standing in the kitchen. It was raining and he had left his umbrella outside.'

'Anmol?' I said. 'The chemist who owns Gupta Pharmacy?'

'Yes,' said Raipal. 'He and Reuben were arguing about something. Probably he owed him money as well. I didn't hear most of what they said, but Gupta threatened to report him to the police. Reuben was calling him names and shouting. The dog was tied up under a corner of the veranda and it began to bark. I decided to leave because there was no point in trying to get money out of Reuben, when he was angry like that. By the time I got to the gate, Gupta had come outdoors and picked up his umbrella. It was raining and Reuben followed him outside, abusing the chemist with all sorts of obscenities. Then I saw him go across and untie the dog. Within seconds the animal attacked Gupta, biting him on the legs. He kept hitting the dog with his umbrella and I didn't see what happened after that because I left quickly, afraid the dog might attack me too.'

'Did either of them see you?'

'No, I don't think so,' said Raipal. 'I went straight back home, thinking I should stop delivering milk to Reuben's house...but of course, he still owed me, so I went back the next day...and the dog was dead.'

'You think Gupta poisoned it?' I said.

'I can't say for certain, but....' Raipal left the sentence unfinished while gesturing with one hand to suggest it was obvious.

By this time, Badlu was on his way across from the quarters and Raipal started to take out his milk can, not wanting to make it seem as if he had been gossiping with me. Eyeing us both with suspicion, Badlu greeted me and went indoors to fetch a pan for the milk. I also turned back into the kitchen, realizing that I'd left the tea to steep much longer than usual. It was probably bitter by now.

'Sahib,' Raipal said. 'I need a favour.'

'What is it?' I asked.

'If you could loan me a hundred rupees, I'd be grateful. Now that Reuben is dead, I won't get paid.'

Nodding reluctantly, I went and got my wallet. Badlu gave me a look of disapproval as I handed Raipal the money.

∞

Rita Sabharwal was waiting at Shambles when I arrived. She was sitting outside on a flat rock in the shade of an apricot tree, which the monkeys had dismembered. Today the sky was partly clear and furtive sunbeams slipped through shifting gaps in the clouds.

'Sorry to have kept you waiting,' I said, glancing at my watch, which read exactly 10 o'clock.

'Not at all, I got here early,' she replied with a smile. Instead of a sari, she was wearing jeans and a fleece pullover, though her long grey hair was still plaited in a single braid that reached just below her waist.

The roof of the house looked as if it was about to cave in upon itself, a heap of rusted tin sheets piled on top of cracked masonry walls with cockeyed windows. I felt no desire to go inside again. In the overgrown garden, a few dahlias were blooming, adding a splash of colour to the mass of weeds.

'I'll warn you, it's not pleasant indoors,' I said, 'and if you're at all allergic to mould and mildew....'

'Not to worry,' Rita said. 'I'm prepared for the worst.'

The constable on duty had come out to welcome me with a salute. As we were about to enter the house, I noticed that Charan Das was standing outside his quarters looking down at us. Raising a hand, I called out a greeting and he responded with folded hands. I could tell he was curious about Rita and may have known she was Reuben's sister. In a small town like Debrakot there are no secrets, except for those that really matter, the hidden truths that nobody dares talk about.

We stepped through the inner door off the screened porch and I switched on a light in the entry hall. The feeble glow from a single bulb overhead failed to dispel the gloom inside. Rita immediately noticed the framed photograph of the woman, her eyes fixed on us with sanctimonious intensity.

'This used to hang in my mother's bedroom,' she said with a shudder. 'It always gave me the creeps.'

'Do you know who it is?' I asked.

'Madame Blavatsky,' she said. 'One of the founders of the Theosophical Society. Mama was a great admirer of hers.'

'She must have been a formidable woman,' I said, referring to the photograph.

'Yes,' said Rita, misinterpreting my meaning. 'Our mother had a charisma about her. Reuben was her favourite child. I was an... afterthought.'

'What would you like to see first?' I asked.

'Show me where he died,' she said, without hesitation.

I led the way, switching on another light in the sitting room, which provided enough illumination for us to enter the passage leading to the kitchen. The bodies had been removed but everything else had been left as it was including the dried pool of coagulated gore next to the stove and smeared bloodstains on the walls. Even in the semi-darkness, it was a gruesome scene and when I pressed the switch for the tube light, it blinked several times before casting a bluish-white sheen, like artificial moonlight. Studying Rita's reaction, I could see that she was momentarily disturbed, as anyone would have been, though her face quickly hardened into a look of studied indifference, as she suppressed whatever emotions had arisen.

'What sort of weapon was used?' she asked.

'A kitchen knife. The police have taken it as evidence,' I answered.

A faint odour of death lingered in the room, along with the soapy stench of the kitchen drain and the stale pungency of diced onions, which still lay in a heap on the cutting board. In a basket, by the gas cooker, were a couple of shrivelled potatoes and some sort of leafy green vegetable that had withered since the murder.

'Is that where his friend hanged himself?' said Rita, looking up at the hook in the beam, where one end of the rope was still tied, though it had been cut by the constables about six inches below the knot.

I answered with a nod of my head, wondering what this woman hoped to discover in such a miserable, depressing place. Rita seemed to read my mind, as she turned away from the horrific evidence of her brother's death.

'There was a part of Reuben I never understood. Now that he's gone, I'm trying to comprehend why he was so troubled. Ever since he was a young boy, my brother had an unhappy personality that overshadowed the brilliance of his mind. He was the most intelligent person I've ever known—too smart for his own good...a genius, really. In school the teachers considered him a prodigy, top of his class. Everyone expected great things of Reuben but he dropped out of college after his first year, claiming that education was nonsense.' Rita paused for a moment and looked back at the bloodstains on the floor. 'Though he wasn't a sociable person, people were drawn to him through a kind of reverse magnetism. He combined a cruel cynicism towards others with an unwavering confidence in his own superiority. At times, it seemed to drive him mad. For hours, he could talk with manic eloquence but then he would fall into long, uncomfortable silences, as if his mind were possessed with darkness.'

'I suppose all of us have our own demons to contend with,' I said.

'Did he have a journal or a diary?' she asked.

'Not that I know of,' I said. 'Do you think he kept one?'

'I never saw him writing,' she said, 'though he read a lot. Mostly he expressed himself in a kind of hectoring speech, as if he were giving dictation.'

'You told me he was promiscuous,' I said.

'Yes, it was part of his cynical nature, as if he looked upon sex without any emotions or sentiments, simply a physical need that had to be satisfied by whatever means were immediately possible,' she said, 'pursuing the path of least resistance.'

'Would you say he abused his partners?' I asked. 'Was he sadomasochistic?'

She shook her head but it was almost a shudder. 'I don't think so, at least not through physical violence. It's a strange thing to say but he loved nobody, though others loved him.'

'Do you think he actually believed he was god?' I asked, 'Or was it just an act to dupe his followers?'

Rita seemed surprised by the question.

'I don't know,' she replied. 'Possibly. Reuben had a delusional sense of self-importance. Some of his followers were convinced that he was divine. Perhaps he even convinced himself.'

After a moment of silence, I asked, 'Do you want to see the rest of the house?'

Rita gestured for me to lead the way and we passed through the sitting room again and out on to the enclosed veranda, lined with broken windows. As we entered the prayer room, I heard a rustling sound, probably rats in the rafters, scurrying away. The stale odour of incense still lingered in the air. I had to search for the light switch and finally found it behind one of the thangka scrolls on the wall. When the room was lit up, I heard Rita sigh.

'What is it?' I asked.

'It's the same,' she said in a hushed whisper. 'He recreated our mother's prayer room, almost exactly as it was!'

'Did all of these objects belong to her?' I asked.

'Most of them,' she said. 'I recognize the thangkas and those masks on the walls. She bought them from Tibetan refugees in Delhi back in the sixties, when everything was going cheap.'

Catching sight of the Egyptian statuette on the altar, Rita went across and picked it up. 'This was hers too. Isis. Mama told me she'd bought it in Cairo, when she was a girl. Her father worked for a French cosmetics company, trading mostly in Alexandria. She used to say her fascination for Theosophy began with a visit to the pyramids when she was eight.'

'Is that something you'd want to keep?' I asked, pointing to the statue.

She studied it for a while. 'I don't know. It would seem strange to take it away from here and I'm not sure I'd want it in my house. What's going to happen to all of these things?' she asked looking around the room.

'It's hard to say, but I'm sure the house will be demolished sooner or later and the owner will probably sell off all of the contents and furniture to one of the kabadiwallas in town.'

'That's what mama used for her séances,' she said, pointing to the round table in the centre of the floor. 'I suppose Reuben also communicated with the dead.'

'Well, now that he's among them....' I started to make a joke of it.

She stopped me with her eyes, a look of sudden sadness that revealed for the first time an expression of grief.

'Sorry,' I said. 'I didn't mean to....'

She shook her head and touched my arm, as if to reassure me that I hadn't offended her.

'It's all a bit overwhelming,' she said. 'Standing in this room, I feel as if I've stepped back into my childhood, all the things I'd left behind.'

'Your mother was a medium?' I asked.

'Yes,' Rita replied. 'She called herself a "clairvoyant". People would come to her, wanting to contact someone who had died. As a child, I didn't understand too much of it, and we weren't allowed to enter the room, but I remember peering through a keyhole and watching Mama seated cross-legged on a cushion, stretching out her hands and speaking in a voice that wasn't her own. It frightened me, though Reuben was fascinated by the rituals, anything connected to the occult.'

She went across to the full-length mirror and continued to study the room through the reflection in the looking glass. Turning away, she brushed her hands against a tasselled lampshade. Returning to the altar, Rita touched each of the objects in turn, as if counting them before she stopped and looked at me with a confused expression.

I waited for several moments before prompting her, 'What's wrong?'

'Something is missing,' she finally said. 'Almost everything is here, but one thing I remember...it's gone....'

Nine

Rita stayed at Shambles for a little over an hour but after seeing the prayer room she no longer seemed interested in the rest of the house. I walked her up the path to the motor road at the top of the hill where her Mercedes was parked. It wasn't far, but we took twenty minutes to climb the hill because she walked slowly and stopped several times to catch her breath.

'Yesterday, I spoke to the pastor of St. John's Church,' I said, before she got into her car. 'He says they only permit Christian burials in the main cemetery but there is a plot just below, containing several Parsi graves. He has no objection if you'd like to bury your brother there.'

'Thank you,' she said. 'I'm grateful for all your help. Do you know how long it will take for the police to release his body?'

'I'm afraid it may be three or four more days, at least,' I said.

'I'd like to lay him to rest before I go back to Delhi,' she said, her eyes meeting mine with an earnest, insistent look.

After she drove off, I returned to Shambles. At this point, there was nothing more that I needed to see inside the house, but I knew that Charan Das had gone into town and I had noticed his daughter seated outside. I'd been wanting to question her without her father being present. As I came down the path, I could see that she was still sitting in a patch of sunlight near the entrance to the quarters, cleaning a tray of uncooked rice, picking out bits of husks and stems.

The woman was so focused on what she was doing, she didn't notice me until I was a few steps away, when she looked up with alarm. The first time I'd seen her, I had thought that she might be simple-minded for there was a dazed and troubled look in her eyes. But after I had reassured her that there was nothing to be afraid of, she calmed down and spoke in a subdued, even voice. Her name was Savitri, she told me, and she was twenty-seven years old.

'How long have you been working at the house?' I asked.

'Three years,' she replied.

'And what did Reuben have you do?'

'Mostly cleaning,' she replied. 'Just in the kitchen. Bhagwan didn't let me go into the rest of the house. I washed clothes, as well as dishes and pots.'

'Did he ask you to cook for him?'

'Sometimes,' she said. 'But his devotees usually prepared the meals. I only worked in the mornings for a couple of hours every day.'

'How much did he pay you?'

'I don't know,' she said. 'He gave the money to my father.'

When I asked her if Reuben had ever mistreated her, she shook her head and told me that he was unpleasant with others but generally, he ignored her.

'Sometimes he would speak to me but mostly he acted as if I wasn't there,' she said. 'I went down and did my work, after which I came home.'

'Did you have a key to the house?' I asked.

She shook her head. 'It was never locked.'

'Did you ever see anything that might have suggested that someone would want to kill Reuben or the other victim?' I asked.

She thought for a few moments and then answered.

'Occasionally there were fights and Bhagwan would start shouting but it wasn't anything out of the ordinary. Men argue with each other,' she said, as if it were a fact of life.

'You called him Bhagwan,' I said. 'Is that what he was, a god?'

She smiled for the first time and then looked away.

'That's what he called himself. How should I know?'

'This man, who called himself Meena. Did you think he was a woman?'

'No,' she said, shaking her head. 'I knew he was a man, though he wore a sari sometimes. He had a man's voice and he smoked and drank.'

'Did he speak to you?' I asked.

'Sometimes,' she said. 'He was a nice person.'

'What did he talk about?'

Picking something out of the rice, she tossed it aside.

'He used to tell me that he came from a wealthy family, but he had run away from home because his parents wanted him to get married,' she said.

'Did he ever tell you his real name?'

'Yes, it was Kunal,' she replied.

'What else did he tell you?' I urged her on.

'He told me that he was Bhagwan's slave,' she said. 'But Bhagwan was cruel to him, mistreating him and calling him names. He said he sometimes wanted to leave.'

'Why didn't he?' I asked.

'He had nowhere to go,' she answered. 'He also said that Bhagwan gave him medicines and he needed to take them every day.'

'What kind of medicine?'

'I don't know. He didn't say,' she said.

'Did he have any friends, others who came to the house?'

She nodded. 'There were many people who came and went. Some of them seemed to be friendly with him.'

'Was it only men who came to the house?' I asked.

'No, there were women too. Some stayed for a few hours. Others for weeks. They came and went. I never knew how many people were there. My job was just to keep the kitchen clean, do the laundry, and feed the dog.'

'But I heard that the dog died,' I said.

She was quiet for almost a minute before I prompted her.

'How did the dog die?'

'It just died,' she said softly. 'One morning I came and found it lying outside with white froth around its mouth. It used to bite others but it never bit me. I felt very sad when it died because the dog always greeted me.'

'I heard it was poisoned,' I said. 'Is that true?'

'Who would have done that?' she said, with a sad, lost look on her face.

Just then, I heard a faint, ringing sound coming from somewhere up the hill, like a tinkling of bells. The clouds had rolled in while we had been speaking and visibility was limited. Moments later, a group of ten or twelve people appeared, coming down the path. Emerging from the mist, the figures had a ghostly appearance, walking silently in procession. All of them were wearing simple, khadi clothing made of rough-spun cotton dyed various shades of yellow. The men were in kurta–pajama and the women wore saris or salwar kameez. Most of them had long hair and the woman who was leading the group was carrying something in her hands, while two others had small cymbals that they were ringing together, making a high-pitched sound, like a chorus of cicadas.

Savitri reacted when she saw them, getting to her feet and folding her hands as they passed above us before descending a set of stone steps to a corner of the path that brought them to the front gate at Shambles.

'Who are they?' I asked Savitri, though I'd already guessed the answer.

'Some of Bhagwan's followers,' she said.

As they began to enter the gate, I saw the constable on duty emerge from the house to stop them. Leaving Savitri, I descended the steps from the quarters to Shambles and signalled for the constable to wait a moment. The woman at the front of the group was holding a framed photograph of Rueben, around which she had draped a garland of marigolds. The ringing of cymbals had a piercing intensity.

When the group stopped in front of me, I greeted them and asked who they were and what they wanted.

'We've come to pay our respects to Bhagwan,' the woman said, in a strident voice.

'If you mean Reuben Sabharwal,' I said. 'He's dead.'

'We've come to offer prayers,' the woman insisted.

'You can pray out here, if you wish,' I said. 'But you cannot enter the house because it is a crime scene.'

'Bhagwan has called us here,' said one of the men.

'That's fine,' I replied. 'But, as I said, you can do what you want out here in the yard, but not indoors.'

The constable and I could not have prevented the group from

forcing their way into the house but they seemed peaceful enough, despite the fervour in their eyes. After a few moments, the tension eased and the woman with the photograph went across to the stone where Rita had been sitting earlier in the morning. The group arranged themselves in a circle around the framed portrait and the cymbals finally fell silent. One of the men lit a couple of incense sticks in front of Reuben's picture and they settled into quiet meditation.

Most of the group were in their twenties or thirties and the woman, who seemed to be their leader, may have been ten years older, though it was hard to tell. They had obviously heard about the murders, which had been reported in the newspaper yesterday morning, a short piece that gave no details beyond Reuben's name and a few vague statements that Thapliyal had made to the local press.

Not wanting to leave the constable on his own to deal with the devotees, I waited with him until they finished their prayer vigil. Reuben's disciples might have stayed all day but within an hour it began to rain, lightly at first, and then with increasing intensity. Eventually, the woman stood up and folded her hands in front of the picture, then gestured for the others to depart. They had no umbrellas or raincoats.

'Where have you come from?' I asked her.

'From different places,' she said hurriedly. 'Bhagwan has called us together.'

As I opened my umbrella and watched the motley procession retreat up the hill, I wondered what it was that they had found in this strange man, who seemed to have been anything but a saint, and certainly not a god.

Ten

Bang opposite St. John's Church on the Mall Road is a small shop called Rawat Communications, wedged between a hardware store and a stall selling Tibetan sweaters. Chunky Rawat, the proprietor, sold me my mobile phone a year and a half ago. Every two or three months he tops up my account, though the phone seldom works at home, because there is no signal. I keep thinking I should get rid of the bloody thing but, somehow, these days a mobile phone has become an indispensable device. Aside from marketing messages, I usually get about one or two missed calls a week, which I only discover after it's too late to respond. When I complained to Chunky about the poor service, he offered to sell me a better phone with a SIM card from a more reliable network. After listening to him rattle on about 3G and 4G and various other unintelligible specifications, I simply handed over five hundred rupees and recharged my phone for another two months.

Dark monsoon clouds hovered over Debrakot and a sour stench of mouldering garbage and wet concrete added to the dismal feeling of the morning. Several young rhesus monkeys were doing acrobatics on the wires and cables overhead and I wondered why they didn't electrocute themselves.

Heading back along the Mall Road, I came to an old shop with a new signboard:

A. Hamid & Sons
Antiuqes and Sacondhend Dealers

The misspellings were even more glaring than the fresh green and yellow lettering, but it seemed too late for me to point this out. I had known Abdul Hamid for years and bought a few things from him, including a table lamp to replace one that broke last year in my study at Thornfield.

He greeted me with the courtliness of his generation, while

his son eyed me with the insolence of youth. There was a slight resemblance between father and son, though the boy was clean shaven and sported a Megadeth T-shirt. His hair was bleached blonde while the father was grey-bearded and wore the skullcap of his faith. The shop was full of old things, not all of them valuable, as well as recent reproductions that he passed off as antiques to unsuspecting tourists. Less than fifteen years ago, Abdul Hamid had been a kabadiwalla, or junk dealer, collecting scrap and broken appliances from residents of the town, but he had now elevated himself to being a purveyor of rare antiquities. Whenever anyone of the older residents of Debrakot died or moved away, he would acquire their furniture and other household objects. I often recognized a piece on one of his shelves from the home of a neighbour who had passed on.

'Salaam, sahib,' he said. 'It's been a long time since you paid us a visit.'

I returned his greeting and said, 'My house is full of old things, why would I need to buy any more?'

'Old things still have value,' he replied. 'Perhaps you have something in your house that I could buy.'

'Nothing you'd want,' I said. 'But I've been searching for one thing you might be able to help me find.'

His eyes narrowed as he nodded. An old film poster hung on the wall behind him, *Mera Naam Joker* starring Raj Kapoor. I'd watched the movie as a boy.

'Please tell me,' he said.

'I'm looking for a statue of a dog,' I said.

'A dog?'

'Yes, about this big.' With my hands, I measured out roughly twenty centimetres in the air. 'It's made of pale, yellow stone, like marble.'

The son had turned back into the shop and disappeared, obviously bored with our conversation.

Abdul Hamid shook his head slowly.

'I have no such thing,' he said, then gestured to a pair of bookends on a table nearby, shaped like two Scottish terriers. 'What about these?'

'No, not that,' I replied, 'Are you sure you've never seen a stone dog, with pointed ears?'

His right hand dusted the surface of a wooden side table, half buried under a glacier of old books.

'I don't have it,' he said. 'But I remember seeing what you've described, several months ago. Why do you ask?'

'Someone offered it for sale?'

He nodded.

'Who?' I asked.

'Reuben Sabharwal,' said Abdul Hamid, as if the answer was obvious. 'He called me to his house and said he had old things he wanted to get rid of, so I went, though I wanted nothing to do with him.'

'Did he try to sell you the dog?'

'First, he showed me some worthless paintings as well as a couple of chairs with broken cane seats. I offered him four hundred rupees for the lot but then he brought out the statue of the dog. It was made from a kind of stone I'd never seen before, and the carving was first class.' Abdul Hamid laughed. 'He told me it was from Egypt, thousands of years old. I could tell it was valuable, maybe a hundred years old. When I asked him how much he wanted for it, we went back and forth, and he finally told me that it was worth three lakhs but he would sell it to me for one. I knew it wasn't worth that much and when I offered him five thousand, he lost his temper and started abusing me, calling me names. So, I walked away. What is one to do with people like that?'

'You heard he was murdered?' I asked.

Abdul Hamid nodded. 'One offers prayers for the dead, even if they have cursed you in their lifetime.'

'Do you know if anyone else bought the dog?' I asked.

'No, I never saw it after that. He may have sold it to someone else but not at the price he was asking, I'm sure.'

'Thank you,' I said. 'I'll take my leave.'

'Let me know if you ever have anything for sale,' said Abdul

Hamid, with a hopeful smile.

'I will,' I replied. 'And if you hear of the stone dog, be sure to inform me.'

From there I walked back towards home, and it began to drizzle by the time I got to the subzi mandi, where I bought half a kilo of tomatoes and a cauliflower, the only vegetable that looked fresh. A few steps further on lay Anmol Gupta's chemist shop. Though I don't know him well, we recognize each other, as most everyone does in this town.

'Hello, sirji!' he said, smiling cautiously. A thin, unhealthy man with thick spectacles, lank hair, and restless hands, Gupta looked as if he needed to prescribe himself some vitamins and a tonic.

'Guptaji, good morning,' I responded, scanning the glass cases and shelves, as if trying to recall what I needed.

'Is there something I can get for you?' he asked, with the discretion of a pharmacist who caters to his customer's private ailments and inadequacies.

'Yes,' I said. 'I need some poison.'

From his expression, I could clearly see that I had him on the back foot.

'Poison?' he repeated, as if it was a word he didn't understand.

'Yes, I've got a problem with rats,' I said. 'I need to kill them off.'

The alarmed look on his face subsided. In Debrakot, it is well known that Gupta Pharmacy sells a variety of controlled drugs without prescriptions. Many patients go directly to him, rather than seeing a doctor.

'Sirji, I'm not sure....' he began. 'Haven't you tried to trap them?'

'No, they're too clever and they've been breeding in my house. I need something that will finish them off for good,' I said. 'Don't you carry poison?'

'Well,' he said, glancing about nervously, though we were alone. 'It's not permitted. But I may have something in the storeroom at the back.'

'Please check,' I said.

After he disappeared through a curtained doorway, I let my eyes wander over the assortment of virility supplements and prophylactics in his glass case, including strawberry flavoured condoms that looked as if they might poison a rat.

A few minutes later Gupta returned, shaking his head.

'Sorry, sirji. I thought there might be some from a long time ago, but it's all finished,' he said. I could tell he was lying.

'Any chance you sold some recently?' I asked.

His nervous eyes studied me as he shook his head once more.

'Is there anything else I can get for you?' he inquired.

'Actually, there is,' I said, as if it had just occurred to me. 'I need some painkillers. My back has been giving me a lot of trouble.'

'Crocin?' he asked.

'Something stronger. Would you have any Tramadol?' I said.

He wet his lips. 'Sirji, it requires a prescription.'

'Come on,' I said. 'I don't have time to go to the doctor....'

Gupta's eyes revealed the uneasy calculations he was making in his mind, trying to gauge whether I genuinely needed the pills or was trying to catch him out. Finally, he reached into a drawer behind the counter and took out a leaf of ten tablets, which he slid across the counter.

'And you're sure this will work on my back?' I asked. 'How much?'

He nodded. 'One hundred forty rupees.'

Handing him the money and putting the pills in my pocket, I waited until he raised his eyes and looked at me with a guilty expression.

'Guptaji, I've been told you were at Shambala Villa, Reuben Sabharwal's place, a few weeks ago,' I said, 'And you were bitten by his dog. Is that true?'

He continued to stare at me with a guarded look before responding. 'It was a vicious animal that bit many people....'

'Any chance you might have poisoned his dog?'

This time he didn't try to disguise the alarm on his face.

'No, it wasn't me,' he blurted out.

'Who did it then?'

'How should I know?' Anmol Gupta's voice had gone up an octave.

'What were you doing at Shambala Villa?' I asked.

'Reuben owed me money,' Gupta replied. 'He owed everyone in town.'

'Is that why he was killed?'

His eyes bulged behind the round lenses of his spectacles.

'Sirji....' he folded his hands. 'I had nothing to do with that....'

'Don't worry. I'm not accusing you of murder but the police did find Tramadol and several other drugs in the house,' I said, patting my pocket. 'Perhaps you supplied him with those.'

∞

From Gupta Pharmacy, I took a side gully that led me directly to the police station, which lies next to the courthouse where the sub-divisional magistrate (SDM) presides twice a week. A crowd of loiterers and litigants were hanging around. I greeted those I recognized including Gurpreet Singh, the lawyer who handles my property matters.

Thapliyal was in his office, looking harried as his steno typed up a letter. Though his uniform is always neatly pressed and he is fastidious about his appearance, today he looked dishevelled. Two constables were hovering to one side. Seeing me, the SHO stood up, though I waved him back into his chair.

'Sir, I was going to come over and see you today,' he apologized, brushing a lock of hair away from his forehead. 'The minister finally left last night and I'm catching up on things. You know how it is with VIPs.'

'Very Impossible People,' I said.

'Bring some tea for us,' Thapliyal instructed one of the constables.

'Don't bother....' I started to say but he insisted.

'Sir, you seldom come by to see us. As you know, we policemen survive on tea because we never have time to eat our meals. Or would you prefer coffee?'

'Tea will be fine, thank you,' I said and then, after a pause. 'Any news on the post-mortem?'

Thapliyal nodded and shooed both of the constables out of the room. The steno was still typing with two fingers, the keys on the Hindi typewriter rattling like a hesitant woodpecker. The SHO told him to stop and leave us alone. His order was obeyed with mute indifference.

'Sabharwal was killed with the knife. No doubt about it,' Thapliyal said, once we were alone. 'Eighteen stab wounds, three of which were fatal. The wound on his neck probably killed him and produced most of the blood, though he was also stabbed just below the ribs and once in the stomach. He didn't have a chance.'

'What about Kunal Vaidya?' I asked.

Thapliyal leaned forward, a worried look in his eyes. 'That's the surprise. He didn't die from hanging.'

'Are you sure?' I said.

'There were traces of drugs in his body,' Thapliyal began.

'An overdose?' I asked.

'No,' he said, shaking his head. 'The cause of death was a blow to the back of his head. We couldn't see it because of his long hair but it cracked his skull. Someone hit him with a hammer or the blunt end of an axe,' said Thapliyal, looking through the files on his desk and handing me the post-mortem report.

'The hanging was done to make it look like a suicide,' Thapliyal continued, 'It's likely they were both killed by the same person.'

'A clumsy job, though,' I said. 'You're absolutely sure the injury on the back of the head didn't happen later?'

Thapliyal frowned. 'No. I thought that maybe when we cut him down, his head struck the floor, but the medical examiner feels sure it happened first and then the body was strung up on the rope. There were no bruises on the neck or any other signs of strangulation.'

'Well, this explains why there were no bloodstains on the sari,' I said. 'If he had stabbed Sabharwal eighteen times, he would have been covered with blood.'

Nodding slowly, Thapliyal agreed with me. 'True....'

'But if they were both killed by a third party, who do you think died first?'

'I would assume that Kunal was killed first and then, after

Sabharwal came to see what was going on, the murderer stabbed him with the knife. That would be the logical sequence,' Thapliyal surmised.

'Unless Kunal was killed somewhere else,' I said, 'in another part of the house and then brought to the kitchen to be strung up.'

'Not likely,' Thapliyal shook his head. 'We would have found some evidence. You yourself said that the man who stabbed Sabharwal would have had blood on his clothes as well as his shoes and would have tracked it through the house.'

'Yes, but maybe there were two killers,' I said. 'One person would have a difficult time lifting a dead body and putting a noose around its neck. Even if the corpse was hoisted up with the rope running through the hook, it would have been impossible to tie a knot like that with the full weight of the body hanging off the ground. The rope was definitely tied first and secured to the beam. So, either the victim put the noose around his own neck and hanged himself, or the body was strung up after the victim was dead.'

A few moments later, one of the constables arrived with two cups of tea sloshing on to the saucers while the other brought a plate of biscuits.

Thapliyal gestured for them to serve me first before waving them out of the room. Reaching across his desk, the SHO then poured the spillage from the saucer into my cup and handed it to me with an apologetic gesture. I took a biscuit out of courtesy and dipped a corner in my tea before taking a bite.

Briefly, I told him about my conversation with Anmol Gupta and suggested that they bring the chemist in for questioning.

'Do you think he was involved in the murder?' Thapliyal asked.

'It's possible. I'm sure he supplied Reuben with the drugs he gave his devotees. Whatever it is, Guptaji needs to be given a warning,' I said, taking the leaf of painkillers out of my pocket and sliding them across the desk. 'He sold me these without a prescription.'

Thapliyal examined the pills with a distracted gaze.

'We still don't have a motive,' he murmured, as if talking to himself.

'No. Nothing conclusive,' I answered. 'But maybe it was a robbery.'

'Sir?' Thapliyal gave me a puzzled look. 'There was nothing worth stealing in that house!'

'Not when we arrived,' I said. 'But it seems something is missing.'

Slurping his tea, Thapilyal eyed me over the chipped rim of his cup.

I waited a moment until he'd wiped his moustache with the back of his hand before I told him about Rita and our visit to Shambles. It took several minutes to fill him in on the details, including my conversation with Abdul Hamid.

'Rita came to the house yesterday searching for something but she discovered it wasn't there—an antique sculpture in the prayer room,' I said, 'an Egyptian artifact made of alabaster. It's a statue of Anubis....'

Thapliyal stared at me with a blank expression.

'The sacred jackal,' I explained. 'Guardian of the dead.'

Eleven

Though I've been tempted sometimes to buy a motorcycle, I prefer to move about on my own two legs and Debrakot has always been a town best suited for walking. From the police station to my house is no more than three kilometres if I take shortcuts, and I can usually cover that distance in half an hour. Nevertheless, the steep climbs would be easier on a bike.

When I reached home, I was ready to put my feet up and unravel the snarled threads of the case. But to my surprise, Charan Das was squatting outside the kitchen with Badlu. On seeing me, both men tossed the smouldering butts of their bidis into one of the flowerpots and stood up. I could see that Charan Das had brought a gunny sack full of pine cones.

We exchanged the usual greetings and pleasantries that always serve as a prelude to the main matter at hand. Eventually, Charan Das gestured toward the bag and asked if I needed kindling.

'This is not the season when I usually light a fire,' I said. 'And I think we have some left over in the godown from last winter.'

The old chowkidar gave me a helpless look. 'They will get used some day. And I need the money, since I have no income now.'

'But you said Reuben never paid you,' I replied. 'So what's the difference?'

'Not regularly and never on time,' said Charan Das. 'But occasionally, if he was in a generous mood, he would give me two–three hundred rupees.'

'Where do you think he got his money from?' I asked.

Charan Das shook his head. 'God knows!'

'Did he go to the bank, or ever send you to cash a cheque?' I asked.

'Earlier, sometimes. He used to have an account at the State Bank but for the last two years I never saw him going there,' said the chowkidar.

'He must have had some sort of income,' I said.

'His followers—those who could afford it—gave him donations to pay for their meals and stay,' said Charan Das. Eyeing me with cautious curiosity, he asked, 'Why are you investigating these murders, when it is obvious the boy killed him and then took his own life?'

'In police work, you have to exclude all of the possibilities before you close a case,' I answered.

Badlu looked at him and snorted. 'What would an old fool like you know about investigating a murder? The DIG sahib has solved cases for the CBI that nobody else could figure out. Who are you to give him advice?'

Charan Das lowered his head but I could see the irritation in his eyes.

'There is one thing,' he said with hesitation. 'You asked where he got his money and, truly, I don't know anything about it, but once a week he would go down to Elsworth Cottage, B. K. Ghosh's house. Whenever he came back from there, he seemed to have cash in his pocket. Sometimes he would send me to town to buy vegetables and other supplies, just enough for two or three days. He would also ask me to pick up a bottle of vodka from the wine shop.'

'You think Ghosh was giving him money? For what?' I asked.

Elsworth Cottage lies on a spur of the ridge below Shambles, about three hundred metres down the hill. The main trail descends past several other homes and just below Elsworth is a new bypass road that circles under the town. B. K. bought the place a few years ago. He is some sort of IT entrepreneur, who moved to Debrakot from Delhi and works from home. A few months ago, he invited me over for a drink, though we don't have much in common. I'm sure he thinks I'm an absurd anachronism. When I explained that I don't use a computer, B. K. looked at me with an incredulous expression, then laughed as if I'd told him a joke.

Charan Das responded to my question: 'I don't know what Reuben did at Ghosh's place but he went down every Wednesday afternoon and stayed there for several hours, always alone.'

'And how long had this been going on?'

'More than a year.'
'Did Ghosh come up to Shambala Villa?' I asked.
'Only once or twice, last year,' said Charan Das, 'but not in the past six to eight months, at least.'
'Okay. Thank you,' I said, heading for the kitchen door.
'Sahib....' Charan Das said. '...the pine cones.'
'All right,' I agreed, reaching for my wallet and fishing out two hundred rupees. 'You can put them in the godown.'
'Thank you,' the old man said, 'but there's just one more thing....'
I looked at him with irritation, as if he were trying to wheedle something more out of me.
'This evening we are holding a jagran ceremony. Because of the murders we want to ask the Devi for advice. Who knows if Reuben's spirit is still wandering around the property? We need to protect ourselves,' said Charan Das. 'I know you don't believe in these things, but it is our custom. And I thought, sahib, if you would like to join us, perhaps you might get some answers yourself.'
Once, years ago in Pauri district, I witnessed a spirit possession in which a local deity entered the body of an old man and shook him like a puppet, as he spouted prophecies and pronouncements. Jagran means an 'awakening' and Charan Das was right, it wasn't something I believed in, but the ceremony might reveal other facets of the truth.
'When is this?' I asked.
'Tonight. It will start at about nine o'clock, at my house,' said Charan Das.
'Let's see,' I said. 'I usually go to bed by then. But if I'm awake, I'll drop by to hear what your goddess has to say.'

∽

Immediately following my nap in the afternoon, I set off for Elsworth Cottage, taking the lower path across the steep grass slopes west of my house. During the monsoon the rocks get covered with moss and algae, making them slippery, and I was glad to be carrying my umbrella, which I could use as a walking stick. The weather seemed to be changing, though there had been a brief downpour while I was asleep and the rocks were slick with rain.

Joining the main path, several bends below Shambles, I carried on down until I reached the gate of Ghosh's cottage. He had spent a lot of money fixing it up and the renovations included design elements copied from the pages of *Country Living* combined with incongruous touches of Bengali kitsch. The original cottage had been relatively small and characterless, a bit like a dak bungalow with a sloping tin roof and a veranda at the front. The entire facade had been redone in a cross-timbered Tudor style and the roof had been raised twelve feet to add an upper floor. The windows and woodwork were painted white and an extension had been added at the back, which looked like an ornate conservatory. Its glass roof was decorated with wrought iron finials and filigree.

The gardens had also been relandscaped and a baroque fountain stood in the centre of the yard, spewing a jet of water into the air that splashed on to the ample breasts of two semi-clad nymphs carved out of marble. A small gazebo had been added at one side and two faux Grecian columns, one of which was broken, to make it look like a picturesque ruin. Surrounding this and bordering the lawn were flower beds full of gladioli, dahlias, and other monsoon flowers. In many ways, it was the antithesis of Shambles. Ghosh had also cut a driveway up from the new road and his Audi was parked under a carport that mimicked the lines of the gazebo.

When I pressed the bell on the gatepost, a loud barking greeted me from inside as two Labradors, one white and one black, came running outside. Ghosh appeared moments later, raising a hand in welcome, though I could see the look of uncertainty on his face.

'Lionel! What a surprise! Lovely to see you.'

I opened the gate and patted the dogs, who were circling around my knees with excitement, tails wagging. For a moment, I could see that Ghosh wasn't sure if he should invite me inside.

'Haven't seen you for a while,' I said. 'Just thought I'd drop by.'

'Of course. Of course,' he said, extending his right hand for me to shake and brushing back his long hair with the other. His beard was neatly trimmed, with touches of grey that made him look like an ageing male model. I guessed he was in his late forties though he obviously worked out and kept himself fit.

'Please do come in,' he said at last, deciding that he had no choice.

The dogs followed us back on to the veranda, a section of which had been enclosed, opening into the drawing room. The interior was brightly lit with an ornate glass chandelier that looked like an octopus doing yoga. Seated at the far end of the room, in a wing-backed chair upholstered in chintz, was Rita Sabharwal.

I was genuinely surprised to see her and could sense an awkwardness, mostly in Ghosh's manner, while she kept her cool.

'Small world!' she said with a smile.

'Do you know each other?' B. K. said, with an unconvincing note of surprise.

'We just met a couple of days ago,' I said.

Rita remained seated as I shook her hand, while Ghosh called out to his servant for tea.

'Doesn't B. K. have a charming house?' Rita said.

'Yes, he's done it up beautifully,' I agreed, looking around the room at the various objects d'art, including a porcelain bust of Beethoven next to an expensive-looking music system. Two gilded swans faced each other on the bar, which was shaped to look like an old-fashioned jukebox with an assortment of single malt whiskies on display. The paintings in the drawing room were gaudy abstracts in various shades of orange and red, as if the canvases were aflame.

'So, what have you been up to?' said Ghosh, throwing himself on to a sofa across from the chair I'd chosen. 'Still enjoying your retirement?'

'I suppose,' I said, 'though the monsoon gets depressing.'

'I love it,' said Ghosh. 'As far as I'm concerned, it could be misty and raining all year long. The only thing that worries me are the thunderstorms because they knock out the internet—my lifeline to the world.'

'Have you put in a lightning arrestor?' I asked.

'Yes, everything! The latest technology from Germany as well as half a dozen surge protectors, backup UPS, and inverters that will keep me online twenty-four-seven, even if the lights go off. Of course, there's a generator too,' he said.

'It sounds a bit excessive,' Rita commented.

'I can't afford to be offline, even for half an hour,' he said. 'When I chose to move up here to the hills that was the one decision I made. I needed an uninterrupted high-speed connection. 5 Gigabytes per second.'

Rita laughed. 'I don't know what that means. It's all science fiction to me! Do you understand what he's talking about, Lionel?'

'Not a word of it,' I said, 'As B. K. knows, I don't even own a computer and my mobile phone is a cheap Chinese model that I seldom use because there's no signal at my house.'

'You should get a booster,' B. K. insisted. 'I've been telling you, that's the only solution.'

'Maybe,' I said, 'But I'm quite happy living in the silence and seclusion of the twentieth century. Why do you need all this technology, anyway?'

'A lot of my work requires sending and receiving large files and quantities of data. I have a studio in Delhi and it's essential for me to have access to whatever we're working on.'

'Forgive me, but please remind me, exactly what it is you do?' I asked. 'Last time I was here you explained, but I've forgotten.'

Ghosh leaned forward with an intent look in his eyes.

'We produce content,' he said.

Rita looked at me and smiled, sympathizing with my ignorance.

'Can you be a little bit more specific?' I said. 'What sort of content?'

'The internet has created an insatiable demand for different kinds of programming, from advertisements to emojis and memes, two-minute clips of lions fighting with crocodiles, or a thirty-second time lapse image of a blooming rose. My company, ZenWorks, focuses on nature and spirit. We create content that connects people to things that bring them peace and contentment, tapping into the mystical beauty of the natural world. I have a camera crew stationed up here to capture images of Himalayan birds and animals, clouds and trees, as well as the simple, rural culture of these hills. Not everybody is as fortunate as we are to live in a tranquil, secluded place like Debrakot, so we deliver that experience to their laptop and smartphone screens. For example, I just finished editing a sequence of waterfalls that are so real it almost feels as if the spray is hitting your face. A lot of people use it as a form of meditation.'

The tea arrived in a tiny ceramic pot on a lacquer tray, with three miniature cups without handles.

'I hope you like herbal tea,' said Ghosh. 'I've gone off caffeine. This is an infusion of chamomile and Japanese sea kelp. It cleanses the blood.'

'I'll try anything once,' I said, as he poured the insipid-looking elixir into the cups and handed it around.

'Any more developments?' Rita asked.

'Nothing really,' I said. 'This morning I did have a word with the SHO and he's hoping they can release Reuben's body in a couple of days.'

Rita closed her eyes and nodded.

'Such a ghastly tragedy!' Ghosh exclaimed.

I took a sip of the tea, which had a musty bouquet and tasted as if it had been strained through a dirty sock.

'Did you know Reuben well?' I asked.

Ghosh shook his head. 'Not really. I met him through Rita. She and I have worked together on various projects. It's such a coincidence that her brother and I ended up being neighbours in the hills.'

'The chowkidar at Shambles, Charan Das, told me that Reuben visited you once a week,' I said. 'Is that true?'

My question made him recoil. Rita, however, didn't react.

'He came here from time to time, yes,' said Ghosh.

'What for?'

'He needed money.'

'And you gave it to him?' I persisted.

'At first I loaned him a little and then....' He looked across at Rita, who nodded.

'We might as well tell him,' she said. 'There's nothing to hide.'

'Reuben's grasp of religion and philosophy was remarkable. After I met him, it struck me that he had a compelling message and spoke persuasively, with a lot of charisma. Of course, he already had his cult of devotees, a sad little clique...pathetic, really. But I saw the potential that he could attract a much larger audience online. People are hungry for spiritual truths and Reuben could speak about these things extemporaneously, without a script. I consulted with Rita and came up with a plan. Reuben styled himself as a god-man and we decided to promote him online.'

'As *content*?' I said.

Ghosh hesitated, then nodded.

'Once a week, he came down and recorded half an hour's session, talking about different subjects—duality, astral vibrations, the constitution of the soul. I have a small recording studio at the back but often I had him sit in the garden outdoors to create some atmosphere.'

'And how was it received?' I asked, '...on the internet?'

'Surprisingly well,' said Rita. 'He was a natural.'

'We started by positioning him along the fringes of social media,' said Ghosh, 'places not everyone goes, a niche audience. Fairly quickly, he drew in a large number of followers, so we started a podcast in January. Within the past nine months, he got more than 200k followers. There were people listening to him in Buenos Aires and Belgium. He was trending in Japan and Australia. It was really taking off! People worshipped him.'

'But now, of course, it's over,' said Rita.

I put my cup down on the coffee table.

'What did you pay him?' I asked.

Ghosh shrugged and looked at Rita. 'This was just the beginning,' he said, with a guilty expression.

'A thousand rupees?' I asked. 'Fifteen hundred a week?'

Ghosh studied his cup for a moment.

'Seven hundred fifty for half an hour's recording,' he said. 'But, of course, we were planning to raise it as soon as we monetized the podcast.'

Twelve

The contrast between B. K. Ghosh's home, with its pretentious decor and high-tech gadgetry, and Charan Das's quarters, lit only by firelight, made me wonder if I was still in the same town. The two homes lay ten minutes' walk from each other but they might as well have been centuries apart. Knowing the jagran was sure to start later than I'd been told, I arrived at half past nine, carrying my torch and umbrella. Six men were seated on the floor around the burning hearth. Savitri, the chowkidar's daughter, crouched to one side, her face covered by the pallu of her sari. She did not look in my direction. As before, a haze of woodsmoke hovered under the rafters. Though Charan Das offered me a seat on the charpai, I was happier sitting on the ground with my back to the wall, beneath the choking cloud of smoke. I recognized two or three of the men, who were all from Charan Das's village, Chiryana, twelve kilometres northeast of Debrakot.

Earlier, when I had mentioned to Badlu, as he served me dinner, that I was planning to attend the jagran, he looked at me with disapproval. Being from the plains originally, my cook considers himself a few notches above people from the hills, whom he looks down upon as backward and uncouth.

'They'll make a lot of noise. They'll be drinking too! Why would you want to go and listen to that nonsense?' Badlu said. 'You never know what sort of behaviour you'll witness.'

Despite his warning, I was prepared for whatever might occur during the ceremony, though I felt sure it would be a relatively tame affair.

The sweet, grassy odour of cannabis smoke was in the air and the men were passing around a chillum that must have been laced with bhang. Though the still had been packed away in a corner, I could see two bottles of katchee in the shadows. At first, my presence seemed to put a damper on the gathering but when Charan Das poured a couple inches of the raw liquor into a brass tumbler, I accepted it to signal that I wasn't here as an official representative of the law. After everyone had knocked back several drinks, the drumming began. Though I was offered a second peg of katchee, I declined. The flavour was almost as bad as B. K.'s herbal tea. Besides, I preferred to remain sober this evening.

Instead of the large drum that hung from a nail, Charan Das used a smaller, two-sided hurki, which he braced on one knee and beat with his fingers. Meanwhile, another man had picked up a brass thali, placing the circular tray in front of him on the ground and tapping it with two sticks. The rhythm was erratic at first, and the percussionists were not in sync, though gradually their tempos merged into a steady, hypnotic beat. After a while, Charan Das began to sing and conversations within the room ceased. His voice was rough but carried a tune and had a melancholic timbre. This was the first time I'd heard him sing and I was surprised that someone as old and decrepit as him could draw music from his lungs. The lyrics were in Garhwali, and I could understand only a word or two, though it sounded like an invocation.

Soon after the drumming began, two women and several more men crowded into the room, taking their seats on the floor. They eyed me self-consciously and the women hid their smiles in the sleeves of their sweaters. I had no idea what I might discover, if anything, but through their rituals, Charan Das and his companions were trying to decipher the same puzzles that I was confronting in my investigation.

The thali was now rattling like a cymbal and the pace of the drumbeats had quickened under the chowkidar's fluttering fingers. After fifteen minutes or so, Savitri, who hadn't moved until then, began to shiver and her shoulders started quaking beneath the cotton fabric of her sari. Moments later, she threw back her head and I could see the whites of her eyes in the firelight. Though her lips were now moving, no sound emerged. Her body swayed to the rhythm of the hurki and the clatter of the brass tray, until suddenly she seemed to be pulled from the ground by a force outside her body. For the first time since I'd arrived, I felt uneasy and wondered if I should have taken Badlu's advice and stayed home. As the pallu fell from her head, I could see that Savitri's hair was loose, a dark mass that swung back and forth as she began to dance.

It was not a rehearsed or graceful performance, more of an awkward, whirling stagger. The ring of spectators left little space at the centre of the room while the hearth, which had burned down to coals, also restricted her movements. At several points, she paused and threw a few grains of raw rice at someone in the circle. The goddess had taken possession of the woman and everyone's eyes followed her movements with rapt attention and devotion.

Charan Das had stopped singing now and there was only the beating of the drum and the metallic clamour of the thali, but after a while he sang out a phrase, as if to coax some sort of response from his daughter. Again, I couldn't understand what he was saying but it sounded like a question.

Savitri stumbled backwards, then forwards. Throwing her head from side to side, she uttered a few incoherent sounds before muttering loudly in a voice that sounded more like a man than a woman, coarse and deep-throated. Charan Das called back to her and I heard him say Reuben's name. My seat was about three metres away from the fire, behind two other men. Someone leaned forward and pushed a stick further into the hearth. It flamed up and I could see Savitri's wild expression as she came towards me, her right hand bunched in a fist. Suddenly, she flung a handful of rice at me, which stung as it hit my face. Then she shouted something in my direction, with a hoarse note of anguish.

Most of the gathering was now looking at me with curiosity and alarm, though I had no idea what was being said. The drumming continued and several others began to sway, mesmerized by the beat. The interior of the room, with its windowless walls, felt like the hollow chamber of the drum, as if we had all been sucked inside. I began to feel a sense of claustrophobia and thought of getting up to leave but I was fascinated by the raw energy of the jagran, which had awakened something powerful within this young woman.

Then, all at once, she collapsed, nearly falling into the fire. With a heavy thud, Savitri dropped to the ground, as if she'd fainted, but I could see her body trembling and it was clear she was having an epileptic fit. The drumming subsided and two women crawled forward. They placed their hands on Charan Das's daughter, who was now shaking her head from side to side, teeth clenched and her eyes rolling back into their sockets. Instinctively, I got up to try and help, but the men gestured for me to stay back.

'Don't worry,' one of them said. 'She'll be fine soon enough.'

Stepping through the circle of celebrants, I stooped down and passed out of the door into the darkness. It was a relief to escape the smoke-filled room and the relentless pounding of the drum. Taking a deep breath, I switched on my torch, ready to head home, but before I started down the steps, I heard a voice behind me and knew it was Charan Das.

'Sahib, are you all right?' he called after me. In the torchlight I could see his eyes were glazed, partly from drink but also from the fervour of the drumming.

'I'm fine,' I said. 'It's getting late, so I'll head home.'

'Of course,' said Charan Das. 'I hope you weren't offended by the Devi's words. She spoke to you.'

'I didn't understand,' I said. 'What did she say?'

'She said that if you want to learn the truth, you must offer her a sacrifice.'

⁂

Earlier that morning, we'd conducted a séance of another kind. After B. K. had told me about the recordings Reuben had done, I asked him to show me one or two podcasts. While Rita waited in the drawing room, I was taken to the recording studio where B. K. set me up in front of one of his computers and logged on to a website called, 'The Immortal Portal'. After he'd entered the appropriate passwords and fitted me with a pair of headphones, suddenly there was Reuben, speaking to me from the dead.

The flat screen was large enough to make him appear life-sized and for several seconds I felt as if the computer had allowed me to cross a digital divide into the afterlife. The last time I'd seen Reuben's face it was contorted and drained of colour, a grey, soapy pallor that corpses get within an hour of death. But here he was, looking healthy enough, with intense, unblinking eyes beneath shaggy brows. His beard was a tangle of grey and black, while his thick hair was brushed back from his forehead, falling to within an inch of his shoulders. Like his sister, he had an athletic build but there was something dissolute and debauched about the way he leaned to one side, shoulders slouched. The rough-spun cotton kurta he wore could have been the same one he had on when he was stabbed, though it wasn't stained with blood or shredded by the blade of the kitchen knife.

ZenWorks's technicians had edited and processed the video. The segment began with ethereal music while an animated logo spun out the words:

SPEAKING TRUTH
MESSAGES FROM THE MASTER
REUBEN BHAGWAN

A graphic designer's sleight of hand wove the lettering into cryptic patterns that unwound themselves into words on the screen. As these titles evaporated, the music continued for another ten seconds, while Reuben stared at the camera as if daring his viewers to look away.

When he finally began his discourse, the music faded though it remained in the background like a harmonic drone. He spoke in English and I recognized his accent from the one time we'd had a brief conversation. It was not too different from Rita's, though his voice had a rougher, masculine edge and there was a lilt of condescension to his speech, a note of superiority and entitlement.

The first podcast I listened to was titled 'Am I a god-man?' and he began with a self-effacing disclaimer.

'I am no one,' he said. 'Just a simple ascetic, who lives in the Himalaya, surrounded by the infinite grandeur of these mountains. I am dwarfed by their presence. My existence on earth is little more than the passage of clouds that cast shadows on the trees or allow the sunlight to touch their leaves. All of us are nothing but a constellation of atoms, held together for a finite period of time, a fraction of a second in a moment of eternity. When we die, our life force, like the minerals in our bones and tissues, will disperse and disintegrate into nothingness.'

His voice was carefully modulated, beginning on a soft, almost subdued note. I could tell that an audio engineer had manipulated the volume and resonance of his words, adding a faint echo. Gradually, Reuben began to speak with more passion.

'Each human being contains a kernel of divinity. Some call it the "soul", others the "atman". It is the essence of our spiritual being, contained within corporeal elements of flesh and bone. Some have argued that "brahman", an unknowable manifestation of divinity, and "shuniya", the concept of nothingness, are two separate entities—both the presence and absence of cosmic forces. But, in fact, they are one and the same, illusion and reality, life and death, the false dualities that we have constructed in order to explain the ultimate mysteries of existence....'

Reuben's voice had a hypnotic tone and as he continued with his discourse a smouldering energy infused his speech and drew me in, despite my reservations. The headphones pressed insistently against my temples. Finally, after ten minutes, he came to the question: 'Am I a god-man?'

He asked it almost as a joke and the hint of a smile crossed his face though his demeanour remained sombre as he provided an answer.

'If each of us possesses a germ of divinity, then we are, by definition, manifestations of God. Most individuals are unaware of this but a few, like myself, who are "adepts", recognize and embrace this divine identity. Like "brahman" and "shuniya", I am nothing and everything....'

Before he finished, I gestured for B. K. to show me the next podcast. He had been sitting at the back of the room and came forward to click whatever keys were required. The second discourse began with the same animated logo sequence and mystical music followed by the title 'The Erotic and The Divine'.

This time Reuben was seated in the garden of Elsworth Cottage, next to the fountain with its half-clad nymphs. He was dressed as before in his khadi kurta and cotton churidar, barefoot in the grass. His hair had a windblown look and I wondered if B. K. had asked him to brush it out with his fingers. After glancing at the marble figures, he stroked his beard with a sensuous gesture and began to speak.

'Religion has always employed the metaphor of love to explain our devotion to God. In Judeo–Christian faiths it is a chaste, platonic bond but in other traditions, particularly the hymns of Bhakti poets and Sufi saints, god takes on an erotic quality, the absent lover for whom we feel a passionate longing. Tantric sects advance this concept even further, seeking a carnal union with God.'

His eyes had a penetrating intensity as he spoke.

'God is neither man nor woman but an indefinable, androgynous force that arouses in us a fierce sense of cosmic desire. Yet, even with the opposing anatomies of gender, we are united in the shared experience of sexual climax. It is the secret of maithuna carved into the temples of Khajuraho and Konark, coital truths contained in the pages of the *Kama Sutra*, where the discipline of sexual intercourse brings us to that consummate moment in which we lose all individuality, when it becomes impossible to know where one lover's ecstasy begins and the other's ends, when devotee and master are conjoined in ecstatic bliss....'

By this time, I had listened to more than enough, though I could see how his words might appeal to those who sought some sort of answers beyond the immediate world we live in. He was articulate, possibly even profound, though I couldn't get the disorder and decay of Shambala Villa out of my mind. If Reuben was a god, as he claimed to be, then I wondered why he lived in such squalid conditions rather than surrounding himself with the sublime trappings of paradise. The persona and the cult that he had constructed was no different than the house in which he had lived, a convoluted pyramid of lies that now lay in shambles.

Thirteen

Nine o'clock the next morning, Thapliyal was at my door, accompanied by two constables. The weather had turned nasty again and there was lightning and thunder as well as a deluge of rain. I beckoned them inside and they left their umbrellas in the entryway, dripping pools of water on the floor.

'Why on earth would you come out on a day like this?' I demanded.

'We have a suspect in custody,' Thapliyal announced, with a look of satisfaction. His uniform trousers were wet from the knees down and his hair was beaded with moisture. 'I tried to telephone....'

'It's dead, of course, as usual,' I said. 'Can I get you a towel?'

'No, sir. We will head back now. I just wanted to inform you. Whenever it's convenient, perhaps you could help question the suspect,' said Thapliyal.

'I can come with you straight away,' I said. 'Give me a moment and I'll be ready.'

'Sir, it's raining....' he protested.

'I know,' I answered, impatiently. 'But if you can come all the way here to tell me this, the least I can do is go back to the station with you.'

Once I had put on my raincoat and got my umbrella, we sloshed our way up the path to the turnaround point, where the motor road ends about four hundred metres above my house.

'Sir, you should have this path widened,' Thapliyal suggested tactfully, on our way up the hill, 'so a vehicle can drive to your house.'

'But I don't own a vehicle,' I said. Of course, I knew he meant it would be more convenient for others like himself, but I prefer the sense of separation it gives me from the motorized world. Perhaps I'm selfish, but if someone wants to visit me, they'll need to arrive on foot.

The police jeep had a canvas roof that was leaking like cheesecloth.

As we drove down to the Mall Road, the wipers thrashed back and forth ineffectually and the driver kept brushing the condensation off the windscreen with his sleeve. I was surprised that he didn't drive off the edge of Switchback Road, especially when he had to reverse at three different points to negotiate the hairpin bends. During these manoeuvres it took all my powers of concentration to listen to Thapliyal's explanation of how the suspect had been apprehended.

When we reached the police station, a gushing stream of rainwater was pouring from a broken gutter on the roof and we ducked around it before entering. I shed my raincoat and umbrella, then followed Thapliyal to the lock-up at the back of the station, a dingy set of rooms, no different from a line of cages at a zoo. Two of them were empty but the third housed a young man dressed in T-shirt and jeans, with dishevelled hair that hid most of his face. He was sprawled on the floor as if he was comatose or asleep but when Thapliyal hammered on the bars with his cane, the suspect sat up with alarm.

The constables unlocked the barred door and pushed the young man ahead of them into a room furnished with three plastic chairs and nothing else. Having spent enough time in various interrogation cells over the years, I know that comfort is not a priority. From the way the suspect was seated on his chair, I could tell that he had been given the full treatment already. One of the unwritten rules of police procedure, which I have always tried to discourage, is that suspects are beaten on the buttocks and thighs with bamboo canes, so that no apparent injuries are visible on the face or upper body, though there are plenty of bruises hidden below the waist. It is a crude method of extracting a confession or making sure that all of the facts are provided, without any obvious signs of torture. I could also see that the young man was an addict, suffering from symptoms of withdrawal. His entire body was trembling and his eyes had a dazed and desperate look. His cheeks were sunken and he looked as if he hadn't eaten for several days.

'What is your name?' I asked.

'Deepak Kanojia,' he replied.

'Are you from Debrakot?'

'No,' he said. 'From Moradabad.'

'And what are you doing here?'

All of this information had been provided to me already but I wanted to begin with the basics to try and put him at ease. The suspect explained that he had come to Debrakot three months ago and was living in a rented room below the old Eros cinema. He had recently passed his BSc degree from a college in Meerut and was looking for work.

'Why would you think you might find a job up here in the hills?' I asked.

'Someone told me there was a company that is hiring.'

'There are no companies in this town,' I said. 'It's a tourist resort. The only work here is at hotels and guest houses, nothing for college graduates like you.'

He shrugged with an insolent look on his face.

Thapliyal's cane prodded him just below the ribs and he was warned to show some respect. I could see him wince as he straightened in his seat.

'Where did you find the mobile phone you were trying to sell?' I asked.

He looked me in the eye with a resigned expression.

'It was given to me,' he replied.

'By who?' I asked.

'A friend.'

'What was his name?'

'Kunal Vaidya,' he said. 'I've already told the inspector all this.'

'Why would he give you his phone?' I asked.

'He wanted me to keep it for him.'

My eyes remained fixed on his. 'Why?'

He finally looked away. 'I don't know,' he said. 'Kunal told me to keep it safely. He said he was afraid that someone might steal it.'

'Then why did you try to sell it last night?'

'When I heard that he had died, I decided to get rid of it,' he explained. 'I needed the money.'

'It's an expensive model, an Apple iPhone,' I said. 'Do you know how much it's worth?'

He wet his lips, then shook his head.

'Did you use it at all?'

'No, it is locked. I don't have the code.'

'Do you have a mobile of your own?' I asked.

The young man nodded. 'The police have taken it,' he added.

'When did you first meet Kunal Vaidya?' I asked.

'A few weeks ago. Here in Debrakot,' he said.

'At Shambala Villa?'

Again, he nodded.

'How did you know Reuben Sabharwal?' I asked.

'I met him through another one of my friends. People said he was a saint and if I approached him for help, he would answer my prayers,' he said.

'What kind of prayers?' I asked.

'For finding a job,' he replied. 'For success in life.'

'Did you really think he could help you?' I asked.

'Some called him Bhagwan,' said the suspect. 'When you are desperate like me, with no future, you will pray to anyone who offers help.'

I felt sorry for the young man. He had a pathetic, cornered look in his eyes as he watched me with a combination of fear and distrust.

'Then why did you kill him?' I asked. 'After offering him prayers?'

He looked away into a corner of the room and was silent for several seconds before Thapliyal prodded him again.

'I didn't kill him,' Deepak said.

'Did you kill Kunal Vaidya too?'

'No, I swear. I had nothing to do with it. I only heard what happened yesterday, when someone was speaking about it in the market.'

I studied him for a minute, trying to see if there was any hint of guilt behind the mask of innocence on his face.

'Why was Kunal wearing a sari when he died?' I asked.

'Bhagwan made him put it on,' he said.

'Why?'

'I don't know. He said we needed to understand what a woman feels like. He said we should be devoted to him like wives or daughters.'

'And you did what you were told?' I asked.

Deepak was silent for a minute, then he looked at me with a pained expression.

'We had no choice,' he said. 'Bhagwan forced us to do whatever he asked.'

'Couldn't you have refused?' I said.

'He got angry and hit us sometimes. He would tie us up and leave us like that for hours,' he answered.

'Did he whip you?' I asked.

Deepak nodded. 'Usually, he just threatened but occasionally he gave us a few lashes that left marks on our backs. Once he wrapped the whip around my neck and told me that he would strangle me with it.'

'Was this part of the rituals he performed in that inner room where he had the altar and the low, round table on the floor?'

'Sometimes,' said Deepak. 'On other days, he taught us how to meditate and performed ceremonies to call the dead. He was able to speak with people who were no longer alive.'

The tremor in his hands had grown worse and I could see the veins in his neck as he struggled to stay calm.

'Did Reuben give you drugs?' I asked.

He started to shake his head and bit his lip.

'Don't try to lie to me,' I said. 'I know he gave you pills and other drugs. We found them in the house.'

The young man crossed his arms tightly about his chest, as if he was afraid of falling off the chair.

'Bhagwan said it would help us stay calm,' he said. 'It would give us peace.'

'Did it?' I asked.

'Sometimes,' he said, reluctantly. 'But when the high wore off... it was as if my body was trying to crawl out of my skin.'

'Is that what you're feeling now?' I asked.

He nodded, reluctantly.

'Sometimes Bhagwan wouldn't give us our medicines to punish us.'

'Is that why you killed him?'

The suspect shook his head, staring down at his feet.

'No, I wanted to leave and not go back but he had kept Kunal with him, like a prisoner,' said the suspect.

'How do you mean?' I inquired.

'He controlled us through his words,' he said in a plaintive, troubled voice. 'The way he spoke sometimes, it was as if I couldn't refuse.'

Again, I paused, letting him reflect upon his words.

'Deepak Kanojia,' I said. 'Is that your real name?'

'Yes, sir.' He nodded.

'Do you have any identification? Aadhaar card? Driver's licence?'

He shook his head. 'I lost everything when I came here from Meerut,' he said. 'My wallet was stolen.'

'How do we know that you didn't go back to the house and kill Reuben and your friend, then steal the mobile you were trying to sell?' I asked.

'No,' he insisted. His hands were trembling.

'What kind of idiots do you think we are?' I leaned forward in my chair, with one finger pointed at his face. 'Why would anyone give someone else his phone, just like that?'

There was panic on his face by now.

'Maybe someone paid you to kill them.' I paused for a moment. 'Is that possible? Maybe you are just a hired killer.'

He didn't answer. This time Thapliyal spoke up, raising his cane.

'Go on,' he said. 'Tell us. Are you saying the DIG sahib is lying?'

The suspect shook his head.

'Did they give you money? Or was it drugs?' I asked.

'Who was it?' Thapliyal echoed, the end of his cane punctuating the question.

The young man cried out.

'You're not from Moradabad, are you?' I said.

Trying to get to his feet, the suspect made a futile effort to escape, though there was nowhere he could go and Thapliyal pushed him back into his seat.

'Stealing a mobile phone is a minor crime,' said the SHO. 'We wouldn't even bother filing a case against you. But if you committed murder, we'll hang you, just like you hanged your friend. It's better if you confess now and get it over with because, in the end, we'll make you talk.'

Though the room was cold, Deepak Kanojia was sweating. His shoulders fell and I could see the terror in his eyes.

Fourteen

After the police jeep dropped me above my house, I suddenly remembered that I'd accepted an invitation to lunch that day. It was already noon and I had just enough time to change and set off for Vinita and Gerald Darcy's house. They were celebrating their twenty-fifth wedding anniversary and most of the hillside residents were sure to attend the party. The rain had stopped and the sun was out. Knowing that I would be grilled about the murder by everyone present, I made a mental note of the information I could share in conversation and what details I would keep to myself.

The Darcys's home, Xanadu, is a relatively recent construction, built on the site of a derelict bungalow that I remember with mixed emotions from my first stay in Debrakot, forty-five years ago. The property used to belong to a man named Farleigh, who was an eccentric recluse. He bled himself to death with leeches, which he believed were a cure for everything from hypertension to gout. As a young man, I was fascinated by him but also troubled by the lonely, deranged life he lived. Now that I am about the age that Farleigh was when I met him, there are times when I imagine I could easily become a hermit and end my years in senile solitude, though I doubt very much that I would turn to leeches for solace or healing. The bite on my right calf had dried up but still itched persistently.

By nature, I'm not a sociable person and whenever I arrive at a party there's an immediate instinct to run away. The Darcys's house is a familiar place, however; they are one of the few couples in Debrakot that I can call close friends. Gerry is an Indologist and Sanskrit scholar who translates ancient Buddhist and Hindu texts. He is one of those expatriate Brits who has immersed himself in another culture, though he retains the mannerisms and accent of an Oxford don. With unruly white hair and a carefully trimmed beard, he looks the part of an elderly professor. Approaching eighty, he keeps saying that he will 'Quit India' one day, and return to

England, though I doubt it very much. His wife, Vinita is twenty years younger than him and grew up in London, though her family is originally from Bombay. This is his third marriage and her second. Vinny has an irreverent sense of humour and flirts with me in a harmless sort of way.

They moved to Debrakot ten years ago, and bought the property from a local merchant who had acquired it after Farleigh's death. Demolishing the old bungalow, Gerry and Vinny built a new place, incorporating elements of traditional village homes in the hills, including a slate roof and a pillared balcony on the upper floor. Inside, however, it is a modern home and the Darcys seem to have enough money to keep it up and live a comfortable life.

I was the last to arrive. About thirty guests were seated outdoors beneath a large walnut tree that dominates the yard. With the sun shining it was hard to believe we'd had a downpour that morning.

Vinny kissed me on both cheeks, then led me across to where Gerry was holding forth on little known facts about Chanakya's *Arthashastra*. He interrupted his lecture and greeted me with a wave.

'Ah, Sherlock is here!' he cried.

'Congratulations!' I said. 'Twenty-five years is a great accomplishment.'

I had given Vinny a bouquet of dahlias, picked hastily from my garden. She batted my arm with them. Her large, moist eyes were outlined with kohl and her lipstick was a subtle but seductive red. An attractive woman, Vinny moved with the grace of an Odissi dancer, her gestures playful but precise.

'Why are you congratulating him?' she scolded me with a smile. 'I'm the one who deserves credit for having put up with an old bore like him for so long.'

'I was going to offer you my commiserations,' I said.

'Dear Lionel,' she said, putting her arm through mine. 'Maybe I should run away with you. I've given him the best years of my life.'

Others joined in the teasing including Colonel Kaju Rao, who lives at Middlemarch with his wife, Komal. Geeta Arjunsingh was watching me with a censorious expression. She is one of the women my mother used to say would be a 'good catch', though I've always found her forbidding and humourless. While her features could be described as beautiful there is always a sad, stern look of disapproval in her eyes. Mr and Mrs Gurdeep Singh were part of the circle too, along with his bachelor cousins, Honey and Lucky, who live at Ravenscot. Everyone had drinks in their hands, mostly beer or gin and tonics.

'What will you drink, Lionel?' Gerry called out. 'And don't tell me you're on duty. Vinny, darling, do get him a Bloody Mary. He looks as if he needs one and then we want to hear all about your investigation. Any suspects present?'

Ignoring the question, I let Vinny steer me towards the bar on the veranda. As a rule, I avoid drinking during the day but after having interrogated the young man at the police station, I felt I deserved something stronger than a nimbu pani.

'I'll take Gerry's suggestion,' I said. 'A Bloody Mary, please.'

The bartender, who was actually the Darcy's driver, Pintu, poured out a large peg of vodka over ice, then added tomato juice with a splash of hot sauce.

'Was the murder as gruesome as they say it was?' Vinny asked.

'It wasn't pretty,' I answered, tasting my drink and gesturing for Pintu to add a little more hot sauce.

'Before we join the others,' Vinny whispered, 'I have to tell you something. It's better you hear it from me because I'm sure it will come out sooner or later and I wouldn't want to be accused of withholding evidence.'

Turning away from the bar, we retreated to the far corner of the veranda, shielded by a wisteria trellis.

Vinny gave me a searching look. 'Promise me you won't let on that I'm the one who told you, but Komal Rao was having an affair with Reuben Sabharwal.'

'What?' I said, trying not to look visibly astonished because I knew that Pintu was watching us out of the corner of his eye. 'Are you sure?'

'She told me about eight weeks ago, back in July,' Vinny said.

'Komal confessed that she attended several of Reuben's meditation sessions and after that she met him once or twice for spiritual advice. One thing led to another....'

'Does her husband know?' I asked.

'Of course not,' said Vinny.

'But I can't imagine a more unlikely pair,' I said. 'Komal is such a dutiful army wife. It's hard to imagine her jumping into bed with Reuben.'

'Well, he did have a kind of animal magnetism, that would have been difficult to resist,' said Vinny, with a mischievous smile.

'Maybe. But I don't see it,' I said.

'Lionel, Lionel.' She shook her head. 'For a policeman, you're so naive when it comes to matters of feminine desire.'

'I suppose I'm just old fashioned,' I said. 'Komal doesn't seem the type.'

After a pause, Vinny added, 'Of course, I'm not saying that this had anything to do with the murder.'

'No, of course not,' I replied, taking a sip of the Bloody Mary, the hot sauce singeing my tongue.

'Let's join the others,' said Vinny, 'or else they'll suspect that you and I are starting an affair, on my wedding anniversary.'

She let go of my arm as we stepped off the veranda and I greeted some of the other guests, including the Tandon sisters who live on the other side of town. My mother was a friend of theirs. They used to play bridge with her and Gladys Ahluwalia.

As the two sisters converged on me, I asked, 'Is Gladys here?'

'No, she doesn't go out any more...hearing makes it difficult... housebound...in social gatherings...we dropped in on her this morning... before coming here....' The Tandies have a way of both talking at once, their voices tumbling over each other, so that I find it difficult to understand what they are saying. 'She's very upset about this murder...dreadful tragedy...getting new locks on her doors.'

'I'm sure she'll be fine,' I said.

'Do you think...was he really?...so violent...must have been a crime of p...p...passion!' They blurted out in unison, clutching the stems of their wine glasses.

'Who knows?' I said, my mind still turning over what Vinny had told me. 'Please excuse me. Lovely to see you again.'

Across the lawn, near a hedge of hydrangeas, I caught sight of Komal Rao chatting with the Chopras, who moved to Debrakot this summer. She didn't look particularly distraught for someone whose lover had been stabbed to death. Komal had always struck me as a plain and homely housewife, but I realized that my prejudices were unfair and unfounded.

Vinny had disappeared by now and Gerry was waving to me from his chair. Bracing myself, I noticed that B. K. Ghosh wasn't at the party.

'I bet Lionel already knows who did it?' Colonel Rao said.

From his manner, I could tell that he was unaware that his wife had been sleeping with Sabharwal. In fact, Kaju is oblivious to almost everything except for his own sense of self-importance.

'It's fairly obvious, isn't it?' I replied. 'The young man who hanged himself killed Reuben and then committed suicide.'

'I'm not buying that theory!' said Gerry.

'Makes sense to me.' Kaju Rao responded. 'But tell me, why was this chap wearing a sari?'

'It wouldn't be the first time a man dressed up as a woman,' I said.

'Being a transvestite isn't a crime, is it?' said Gerry.

'Well....' said the colonel. 'From my point of view, it's not normal....'

'Oh, come on, Kaju!' Gerry cried. 'Don't be such a prude. I bet you like to tie on one of Komal's saris once in a while!'

'Never!' The colonel blurted out and I sensed a defensive note of denial in his voice. Though he's retired and a good ten years older than me, Kaju is physically fit and perfectly capable of stabbing someone.

'Seriously, though,' said Gerry. 'Any progress on the investigation?'

A couple of other men had joined us, including the pastor of St. John's Church, Reverend Isaac, and I was conscious that they'd been talking about the murder before I'd arrived.

'The truth is that officially, I'm not involved,' I said. 'The case is being handled by Inspector Thapliyal, the SHO....'

'Yes, but unofficially, we know you're taking charge,' said Kaju.

'Simply helping out,' I said. 'Other than the man who hanged himself we haven't got any suspects.'

'Well,' said Gerry. 'I suppose each of us here had good reason to kill Reuben, since he fought with everyone on the hillside. Two weeks ago, he wrote me a letter saying that I was corrupting Hindu scripture by publishing biased, inaccurate translations. I replied with a short note in which I questioned his knowledge of Sanskrit and called him a pseudo-spiritualist. He took offence and said he would report me for religious intolerance.'

'At least with you it was an intellectual argument,' said Gurdeep Singh, who lives just below Shambles. 'With me it was all about a dead tree that I cut down. He claimed it was on his land. Reuben threatened me with an axe.'

'How did you resolve things?' Gerry asked.

'My axe was bigger than his,' said Gurdeep, laughing. 'He kept threatening to report me to the Forest Department. I did my best to ignore him, but he would send me messages from time to time, saying that I was encroaching on his property, even though he didn't own the house or the land.'

By now a circle of about ten or twelve guests had gathered and everyone had a story to tell about Reuben quarrelling with them or threatening legal action. Reverend Isaac recalled that he had showed up at St. John's on Easter Sunday and began shouting insults, saying that Christians worshipped false prophets. Finally, two men had to usher Reuben out of the church.

At this point I noticed that Komal Rao and the Chopras had joined us. Her eyes were studying me with a pensive expression as we listened to Gerry tell the story about Reuben and the postman. I'd heard this one before and kept watching Komal as Gerry described how Reuben attacked the postman who tried to deliver an overdue electricity bill to his house. He had chased him off the property with a broom.

'Poor fellow, it wasn't his fault but you know how it goes...if all else fails, blame the ruddy postman!' said Gerry, barely able to contain his laughter.

The pained look on Komal's face told me that Vinny's information was probably true though I wondered if things had fallen apart between her and Reuben before the murder. Maybe she'd discovered him with one of the young men, or perhaps he'd tossed her aside and she resented his rejection. Still, I couldn't imagine her wielding a kitchen knife in anger.

Before I could finish my drink, lunch was announced and everyone trooped inside to serve themselves. Staying back with Gerry, who remained in his chair, I wondered if Vinny had told him about Komal's affair. After twenty-five years most couples confide in each other. Either that, or they hoard their secrets.

'So, what's your theory?' I asked. 'You really don't think it was a murder–suicide?'

'Who knows?' he said. 'But it must have been a crime of passion if Reuben was stabbed eighteen times....'

'How did you get that number?' I asked. 'Who told you how many wounds there were?'

'Dr Manchanda, my physician. I went to see him yesterday and he knows the doctor who performed the post-mortem,' Gerry explained.

'So much for police confidentiality,' I said. 'I hope it wasn't anything serious...I mean, your doctor's visit.'

'Nothing really,' said Gerry. 'Just a touch of angina. Twenty-five years of marriage will do that to you.'

'I wouldn't know,' I said. 'Never made it that far.'

'Well, there's something to be said for bachelorhood,' Gerry mumbled, staring into the depths of his empty glass.

'Aren't you going to eat?' I asked.

'Not hungry,' said Gerry shaking his head. 'You go on and help yourself.'

I sat down beside him and swallowed the last of my drink.

'I'll wait a bit,' I said, then glanced at him, 'By the way, what do you know about Theosophy?'

He laughed. 'Do you have all afternoon?'

'No, but honestly, I haven't a clue what it's all about,' I said. 'Someone like you who studies esoteric Eastern wisdom must have some perspective on Reuben's spiritual beliefs.'

'Over the years, Reuben and I had several conversations about religion and he was an intelligent, articulate man but, from what I gathered, he practised a perverted version of Theosophy, turning it into his own personal cult,' Gerry said.

'Tell me more,' I insisted. 'Who was this Madame Blavatsky?'

'A nineteenth century Russian-born mystic, who tried to synthesize all kinds of arcane philosophies from Neo-platonism to Vedanta. Today, I suppose you'd call it "New Age" but it started a century and a half ago. Madame B was fascinated by magic and the occult. Believed in shamans and sorcery, as well as free will and elements of tantric Buddhism thrown in for good measure. She founded the Theosophical Society with an American named Henry Olcott. They moved here to India and set up an ashram down south. They said they were channelling the wisdom of ancient "adepts" and great masters of different faiths. The whole thing would have probably died away and been forgotten except that Annie Besant and Charles Leadbeater revived the society in the 1920s. It got some credibility by aligning itself with India's freedom movement but Leadbeater was a serial pederast and kept getting caught with his hands down one or another young boy's pants. I suppose Reuben was upholding that tradition.'

'Does anyone take it seriously any more?' I asked.

'Plenty of people. Theosophy has an appealing message of universality that many seekers seem to yearn for...along with elements of magic and miracles thrown in to keep it interesting,' Gerry continued.

Just then, I saw Vinny come out and beckon to us impatiently.

'Memsahib calling,' said Gerry, struggling to lift himself out of his chair.

'We'd better do as we're told,' I said.

Fifteen

When one or more of our five senses is lost or diminished, the others step in to compensate. I remember a case I investigated during my time with the CBI, a murder that involved a member of parliament from Goa. Favio Sequeira was a young, up-and-coming politician who'd been a communist for many years but had compromised and joined the ruling party. He was engaged to a fashion model named Stella Pereira but a week before the wedding she was found dead on Vagator Beach, apparently drowned. The local police began by claiming that it was an accident but her family insisted it was murder and the post-mortem revealed high levels of narcotics and alcohol in her blood. Because of the combination of celebrity and politics, the investigation became too hot to handle for the Goa Police and it was turned over to the CBI. At the time, I was working on an extortion case involving two district collectors in Karnataka and I happened to be in Bangalore. Word came down from Delhi that I should hand things over to my subordinates and drive across to Goa, a twelve-hour journey, in those days, over terrible roads.

When I finally got to Panjim, I was put up in a police guest house in Dona Paula. The following morning a DSP named Kenny Braganza briefed me on the case. He seemed to resent my presence but claimed that he was happy to let me take things off his hands because of all the media coverage and pressure from within the local government and party officials. I had to wait a couple of days before two junior officers arrived from Delhi to assist me. In the meantime, I called on Stella Pereira's family. They were, naturally, distraught and kept accusing Favio Sequeira of murdering his fiancé because he was in love with another woman. If you take away all of the tourists and outsiders, Goa is actually a very small town. Almost everyone knows each other, or at least it seemed that way. A week had passed since the girl had died and rumours were flying about like swarms of bats at twilight.

One of the family members was a young girl named Rosie, who was blind. She was Stella's first cousin on her mother's side and the two of them were very close. It turned out that she had been with Stella on the night she died, at a beachfront restaurant in Anjuna. I asked her what she remembered and she told me they had eaten dinner at about ten o'clock and a stranger had offered to drop them home in his car because Stella's driver hadn't shown up. Rosie insisted that neither of them had anything to drink or took any drugs. She was adamant, tears streaming down her cheeks from sightless eyes.

According to her, they drove out on to the main road towards Calangute when suddenly the car turned off on to a rough side track. Stella asked the driver what was going on, but he didn't reply and abruptly pulled over. Another man got into the back seat and Stella started shouting at him angrily. The next thing Rosie knew, she was pushed out of the car and left by the side of the road. She screamed for help but nobody was around and it was only half an hour later that a man came by on a motorcycle and took her home.

I asked if she had heard Stella say anything that might help us identify the attackers. Though Rosie couldn't recall any names, she said the man who got into the car spoke English with a Goan accent. She also remembered one other thing, the smell of a pungent cologne with a strong, musky scent.

As we began to investigate the case, pressure was building to arrest Favio. Stories were circulating that he had an old girlfriend who had persuaded him not to marry Stella. Of course, all of this was speculation but we finally tracked down the man who had been driving the car and he identified a local thug named Elwin Carvalho, claiming he was the one who abducted Stella. Of course, Carvalho denied everything, a cocksure man who kept his shirts unbuttoned to the navel and wore an ivory cross on a gold chain around his neck. I also noticed that he reeked of cologne, so when we called him in for questioning, I arranged for Rosie to be there. She was in the room next door while Carvalho was being interrogated.

Pressing her nose to the gap in the door she took a deep breath. 'It's him,' she said, nodding. Taking her by the hand, I opened the door and led her inside. Carvalho reacted immediately, tensing up when he saw the blind girl, then trying to act as if he didn't know her. But when I asked him a question and he replied, Rosie recognized his voice. We eventually got a confession out of him, using the psychological equivalent of a bamboo cane to the backside. The blind girl's identification may not have held up in court but we didn't need it because Carvalho folded in her presence. He admitted that he'd known Stella when she was starting her modelling career and he didn't like the fact that she was engaged to Favio. He had taken her to a hotel in Vagator and forced her to drink half a bottle of vodka, then shot her up with heroin, and dumped her body in the sea.

My reason for remembering all this?

If a physical disability leads to increased powers of observation, it might be useful to have another conversation with Gladys Ahluwalia. More importantly, at the Darcys's anniversary celebration, near the end of the party, when Gerry and Vinny were cutting a cake, the Tandon sisters (someone, I can't remember who, had renamed them the Tandem sisters) revealed that Gladys had told them she was certain the killer had been a woman.

'How did she know that?' I asked.

'She didn't...someone in the yard...not the young man in a sari... taller...arguing with Reuben....' They explained in stereo.

Skipping my nap, despite the Bloody Mary, I stopped by Glenwood to call on Gladys before going home. It was almost four o'clock and she was sitting by the bay window in her drawing room, when I opened the gate. Recognizing me, she got up and was already unbolting the front door when I got there.

'Lionel!' she said. 'I thought you'd be at the Darcys's do.'

'I was,' I said. 'But I wanted to come and see you before I went home.'

'Well, between you and me, I think Gerry's a snob,' she said, taking my arm as she pulled me into the house. 'Vinny's all right but he's one of those Englishmen who still believes in the class system. How was the party?'

'Dull and exhausting,' I said, knowing she wouldn't hear me.

'They say his first wife was a second cousin of Lord Mountbatten's daughter, Pamela. She left Gerry for a white hunter in Kenya, if you can believe that,' Gladys continued.

'I wanted to ask if you've had any more thoughts on Reuben's murder,' I said, speaking slowly and loudly.

'No. No. I couldn't have made it. They offered to send a dandie with four coolies to pick me up, but I haven't ridden in a dandie for years. My days of socializing are over.'

'The Tandon sisters told me you think it was a woman that killed Reuben.'

Gladys nodded and steepled her fingers.

'The dear Tandies came to call on me this morning. We used to have such fun playing bridge with your mother but now that she's gone, we can't seem to find a fourth. You've never played, have you, Lionel?'

I shook my head.

Fortunately, this time I had brought a notebook and took it out of my pocket.

'What's this?' she said as I wrote out my question in block letters.

Tossing the notebook back at me after reading it, she pursed her lips into a frown and glared at me with accusing eyes.

'If you speak slowly and clearly, I can hear you, my dear. No need to spell it out,' she insisted, then turned her gaze to the window from where she had a bird's eye view of Shambles, on the opposite ridge across the ravine, about a hundred metres lower down.

'It's not as if I make a habit of spying on my neighbours,' she began, 'but this is the chair I like to sit in during the afternoons because the sun slants through the deodar trees. On a clear day I can see all the way to Kanjiwalla and the plains beyond. About a week ago, the day before Reuben was killed, I saw something that I didn't mention to you before. If you look across from here, the front yard of Shambles juts out from the trees like the prow of a ship. It was about this time of day. Shanti hadn't arrived yet to make my tea and I saw two figures in the yard. One of them was Reuben. There was some mist, but I could see him clearly, gesticulating as if he was upset. The second figure wasn't someone I recognized. At first, I thought it was another man, because of the clothes—sweater and trousers—but then she began to wave an arm about and I could see that she had long hair gathered in a single braid that reached below her waist. From here it was like watching a pantomime. They were obviously shouting at each other, though I couldn't hear a thing, of course.'

Gladys stopped for a moment and I could see her fingers trembling as she turned the gold wedding band on her left hand, around and around with her thumb and forefinger, as if she was trying to unscrew it from her hand.

'Why didn't you tell me this before?' I asked. Gladys must have known that the question was coming.

'It's strange,' she said. 'But it was like watching a memory happening right there in plain sight. I may not be able to hear but after I had my cataracts removed, my distance vision is almost as good as it was when I was a girl. I know I should have told you this before but it reminded me of the terrible arguments I used to have with my husband. In fact, I might as well have been watching myself fifty years ago, fighting with Daljeet over some pointless marital dispute. I've been a widow for twice as long as the Darcys have been married, Lionel, but I still regret the awful rows we had. Seeing Reuben and this woman fighting with each other brought back unhappy memories, and it unnerved me.'

'I understand,' I said, noticing that Gladys was weeping. She pulled a hankie from inside the sleeve of her sweater. Removing her glasses, she dabbed her eyes.

'Thank you for telling me,' I said.

'The last time I saw him,' she said, flustered, 'before Daljeet went off to join his regiment on the border, we had an angry quarrel and I said many things I wish I could take back. If my husband had returned home alive, I would have apologized. We always did, but his tank was blown up near Ferozepur and after that....' She shrugged and then bravely pulled herself together, staring out the window.

'I'm sorry to have questioned you like this,' I said. 'But what you've told me is very helpful, Gladys. Are you sure about the woman's hair?'

'Absolutely,' she said. 'I've been thinking about it all this week and I know she's the one that killed him. Of course, I can't prove it but I have a sixth sense.'

I had to smile when she said this. 'I'm sure you do,' I said.

'Oh, Lionel, I'm just a feeble old woman, deaf as a doorknob. You'll have to forgive me.' Her lower lip was quivering again, and she put the hankie to her eyes once more. Then, with a resolute little laugh, she blinked. 'But of course, I've read all of my Agatha Christies and know how clues like this can help solve a case. You probably think her books are nonsense, but I've always loved a good whodunnit and I prefer Miss Marple to that prig, Poirot.'

I reached over and touched her knee gently, a gesture of reassurance. There was a part of me that would have liked to hug her but I knew that Gladys would never have forgiven me. We stared at each other for a moment.

'Thank you, Gladys, but I need to be sure of one thing,' I said, repeating myself and speaking loudly. 'The woman's hair was definitely in a single braid and reached her waist, you're certain of that?'

She nodded. 'No doubt about it! Grey like mine but much longer, plaited all the way down to here.' Her fingertips indicated three inches below her hips.

Sixteen

I arrived at the cemetery about noon, just before the municipal ambulance arrived carrying Reuben's coffin. Rita Sabharwal's Mercedes was parked near the gate, and I saw her standing by herself next to the first line of gravestones that date back to the 1840s. The cemetery is situated in the centre of town, just below St. John's Church. The rows of graves descend from there in shallow steps, like terraced fields. When the cemetery was first established, the slope would have been covered in grass and scrub but now it is overshadowed by giant cypresses and deodars that have grown taller than the bell tower of the church. Several of these trees have been struck by lightning. It was a grey, solemn morning. When I greeted Rita she thanked me for arranging the burial.

Reverend Isaac had been as accommodating as he could, though he'd made it clear that Reuben could not be buried in sanctified ground. Nevertheless, he had arranged for the church watchman to unlock the gate and I had hired four Nepali labourers to dig a grave about two hundred metres down the hill, just beyond the perimeter wall, a section of which had collapsed. Two cows were grazing amongst the headstones. A carpenter that Reverend Isaac recommended had knocked together a pinewood coffin that had been delivered to the mortuary. After it was unloaded from the ambulance, the Nepalis carried it down the winding path between the older graves. Suddenly, I realized that I had forgotten to tell the coffin maker that this wasn't a Christian burial. On top of the box, he had affixed a small wooden cross.

When we finally made it down to the gravesite, climbing over the broken wall, I pointed out the Parsi graves and two or three other headstones that bore simple inscriptions without any symbols of faith. It wasn't a particularly scenic spot, overlooking a clutter of shacks that had come up in the past decade or two, mostly illegal construction perched on a near vertical slope. Charan Das was squatting on the far side of the grave and got up when we arrived. I was surprised to see him but he seemed to have come to the cemetery out of a lingering sense of duty to the man who had exploited him for years.

'I'll remove the cross if you'd like,' I said to Rita. 'The carpenter who makes the coffins assumed your brother was a Christian.'

'How will you take it off?' she asked.

Producing a penknife from my pocket, I unfolded the screwdriver and gently pried it loose. Attached with three thin nails, the cross came off easily and without leaving a noticeable mark.

There was no ceremony, prayers, or eulogy and Rita watched silently as the coffin was lowered into the hole, where a little rain had collected from a shower that morning. The Nepalis knew how to use the ropes since Reverend Isaac had employed them for other funerals. We stood in silence for a minute and then I signalled for them to start replacing the soil, which was a reddish-brown colour streaked with clay. As the men began shovelling the pile of earth back into the ground, it rattled and thudded against the coffin.

The evening before, Thapliyal had sent word that Reuben's body would be released today. Discovering that my landline had miraculously come back to life, I'd called Rita at her hotel. Things had fallen in place as they always seem to do when it comes to funerals, as if the finality of death brushes away any obstacles. I had asked Rita if she wanted to see her brother's body before the box was nailed shut but, fortunately, she declined. Between the knife wounds and the post-mortem incisions, he would have been a hideous sight.

When the grave was finally full, Rita indicated with her eyes that we should leave. Reaching out to help her climb over the stones of the collapsed wall, I was surprised how cold her hand felt and the fact that she held on to me for a little longer than I expected as we started up the path. Near the gnarled roots of a giant cypress, I took a short detour and leaned down to brush the dry needles off a stone.

'My mother's grave,' I explained, looking up at Rita who was watching intently.

'How long ago did she pass away?'

'It's been more than three years.'

We were silent for a moment and then she read the inscription aloud.

'Sleep on now, and take your rest. Matthew 26:45.'

'My mother chose that verse herself, long before she died,' I said with a smile. 'She suffered from insomnia and used to joke that only when she was finally laid to rest, would she get a good night's sleep.'

Rita laughed and looked up into the cypress branches, a lost expression on her face. I wondered if it was guilt or sadness. Maybe both. As we continued up the winding path from one terrace to the next, I explained to her that the oldest graves were near the top and the more recent ones below.

'What happens when the cemetery fills up?' she asked.

'Well, there aren't that many members of the church any more. I think St. John's congregation totals about eighteen and only half of them attend Sunday services. It will take a while to fill up the lower levels.'

'Do you go to church?' she asked.

'No,' I said. 'Not unless I have to attend a funeral or a wedding.'

Again, I stopped and wandered off the path. I'd been carrying the wooden cross from Reuben's coffin, not knowing what to do with it. But now I placed it next to a headstone covered with moss and lichens.

'Whose grave is that?' Rita asked.

'A man named Farleigh,' I said. 'He was an unusual character. Died forty years ago. I knew him briefly.'

'Was he a friend?' she asked.

'No,' I said. 'Just a lonely old man.'

We continued on up to the gate, where her car and driver were waiting.

'Can I drop you home?' she asked.

'No thanks, I'd rather walk,' I said. 'When will you go back to Delhi?'

'Tomorrow, probably,' she said. 'Or perhaps day after. I haven't decided.'

The driver had opened the car door and she was about to step in.

On an impulse, I asked, 'Would you like to have dinner with me this evening? Nothing fancy, I'm afraid, but my cook does a pretty good chicken curry.'

'I'm vegetarian,' she said.

'Ah....' I responded, catching myself and feeling embarrassed now. 'Well, he does a reasonable gobi aloo too, with dal and rice. I also have a good bottle of wine that's been ageing for a while. That is, if you drink....'

'I do, occasionally,' she said with a smile. 'Thank you, Lionel. I'd be happy to join you for dinner. What time?'

'Sevenish,' I said.

∽

On my way home from the cemetery, I stopped at the bazaar to buy a few supplies since I had no idea what vegetables we had at home. In addition to the cauliflower for gobi aloo, a basket of fresh karela at the subziwalla's stall caught my eye. My mother's recipe for bitter gourd as she called it (preferring English to Hindi names), was famous in Lucknow as well as here in Debrakot. All her friends insisted that she make it every time they came over. More like a pickle than a subzi, it is made with mustard oil, vinegar, and tamarind paste as well as a number of other secret ingredients that Badlu has memorized. After buying half a kilo of karela, I also noticed that the subziwalla had some good-looking chausa mangoes, the last of the season. I picked two for dessert. As I seldom entertain, the prospect of Rita's company at dinner brought on a sense of nervous expectancy that surprised me, though I knew there would be at least one awkward moment when I confronted her with Gladys's story.

'Sir, what are you cooking for dinner?' A familiar voice accosted me as I was paying up. When I turned around, there was Inspector Thapliyal out of uniform, with a toddler in his arms.

'Nothing special,' I said. 'And who is this?'

'My younger daughter,' he announced proudly then prompted the little girl to fold her hands in greeting, which she did. Her hair was tied up in ribbons and she was wearing a pink frock.

I brushed a finger against her cheek and she gave me a worried look.

'So beautiful,' I said. 'What's her name?'

'Anoushka. This is her birthday. Three years old. She wants me to buy her some ice cream,' said Thapliyal, then added. 'I'm off duty today.'

'Well, then I won't ask you any questions about the case,' I said.

The girl's eyes watched me with suspicion.

'No, no,' Thapliyal exclaimed. 'I wanted to contact you, sir, but of course your telephone....'

'Dead again,' I said, with frustration.

'Our suspect has escaped,' said the SHO with a frown. 'The constable who was on duty last night took him to use the latrine at about 9 p.m. and he got away somehow. Probably slipped out while the idiot was having a smoke. The constable has been reprimanded, of course, and we're trying to track the suspect down. A lookout notice has been issued.'

'That's unfortunate,' I said, wondering for a moment why Thapliyal would be taking the day off when something as serious as this had happened. Then I saw the look on his face and realized that he had intentionally let Deepak Kanojia escape.

'We hadn't registered a case against him yet,' said Thapliyal, 'because we wanted to find out if he's working for someone else. Regardless, I would have had to release him from custody within twenty-four hours, unless we brought charges against him.'

'You're right,' I said, smiling at his daughter, before patting her cheek again. 'Maybe it's all for the best.'

Thapliyal nodded and I could see that he was pleased with his own ingenuity.

'You're certain you'll be able to find him again, if need be?' I asked.

'We gave him back his mobile yesterday,' Thapliyal explained. 'The battery had died but we noted his number, as well as the prepaid service he uses. As soon as he charges it, we'll be able to trace the signal. Even if he changes the SIM card, we can follow his movements and identify who he's in touch with.'

'And what if he doesn't have an accomplice?' I asked.

'Then we can always arrest him again and charge him with escaping from police custody.'

'Of course. Let's hope for the best,' I said. 'What about the other phone? Kunal Vaidya's mobile?'

'We've kept it as evidence,' he said.

'Were you able to unlock it?' I asked.

'Not yet. But we're working on it,' he replied. 'Are you coming from the cemetery?'

'Yes, Reuben Sabharwal has finally been put in the ground,' I said. 'What about Kunal's body?'

'It was also released this morning. Two family members came to collect it. They've taken him to Haridwar. By now his pyre has probably been lit,' he said.

Thapliyal's daughter was growing impatient, and she whispered something in his ear. He whispered back to her, saying, 'Wait a minute. I'm talking to Uncle.' She looked at me crossly for coming between her and her ice cream.

'I won't keep you any longer,' I insisted and began to move off. 'Anoushka deserves her ice cream, and you should buy one for yourself.'

'Thank you, sir,' said Thapliyal with a grin.

On the way home, I reflected upon the moral ambiguities of police tactics, in which deception is as much a part of the game as trying to determine the truth. Thapliyal's decision to let the suspect escape might be considered a clear-cut case of entrapment but Deepak Kanojia had brought it upon himself, even if he was innocent. And the strategy that Thapliyal had set in motion was not so much directed at our suspect but at those who might have helped him commit the murder. Hopefully, in his eagerness to escape he would lead us to their doorstep.

Seventeen

By the time I reached Hilltop Stores, after climbing Switchback Hill, I realized that I needed to buy something to serve with our drinks in the evening. Living alone, I tend to forget about social rituals and etiquette.

Lala Satish Aggarwal didn't look as if he had moved from his seat behind the counter since my last visit to his shop, a few days ago. He greeted me with folded hands as usual and allowed himself a reluctant smile.

'Greetings, Lalaji,' I said. 'All well?'

'As good as one can expect,' he mumbled, with a fatalistic shrug, 'under the circumstances....'

'Why? What's wrong?' I asked, eyeing the shelves to see what sort of snacks he had in stock.

'You know how it is. Prices keep going up,' he replied.

'But that shouldn't be a problem for you,' I said. 'Inflation is something you can pass on to the customer, at least that's what the economists tell us.'

'Economists!' he said with disdain. 'What do they know about money?'

He seemed more disgruntled than usual and I let the matter rest.

'Do you have roasted cashews?' I asked.

'Yes, these are fresh,' he said, fishing out a small bag from under a pile of other produce on the counter.

'How much?' I asked.

'Two hundred fifty,' he said.

'For a hundred grams?' I blurted out in astonishment. 'That's probably ten rupees a nut.'

'I told you prices are going up,' he said with a miserable look. 'I remember when cashews were a hundred rupees a kilo.'

'What about potato chips?' I asked.

He pointed across to a display in the far corner of the store. Most of the bags were exotic flavours—jalapeno, cheddar, masala—but I finally found one packet of plain salted chips.

'I'll take both of these,' I said, handing him a 500 rupee note.

After adding up the total and passing me the nuts and chips, along with my change, Aggarwal gave me a wary look.

'Have you found the murderer?' he asked.

'Not yet,' I said.

'Any suspects?' he asked.

I shook my head and turned, as if to leave, though I could tell he had something more to say.

'If anyone should have gained from Reuben's death it was me,' he admitted, 'For eighteen years I've been trying to evict him from that property, but I can assure you that I was as surprised as everyone else when I heard that he'd been killed.'

'Of course, Lalaji, I would never suspect you,' I said, trying not to sound disingenuous, for the possibility had crossed my mind.

He didn't look convinced and his eyes fixed me in a belligerent stare.

'Yesterday, I learned something you should know,' he said, with a secretive look, 'though I'm telling you this in confidence.'

'I'll try to be discreet,' I said. 'But if it has any bearing on the case, I would have to share the information with the police and reveal my sources.'

He looked uncomfortable, rearranging several display boxes on the counter in front of him.

'Reuben was trying to sell off part of my property,' Aggarwal said. 'Though he had no title, he made a deal through an agent last month. Shambala Villa has three acres of land, mostly forested slopes. But fifty metres below the house, there's a level patch of ground where someone could build a small cottage. A prospective buyer paid him an advance. I learned all this when I met my lawyer yesterday. The property agent had contacted him and was trying to get the money back. Of course, we had nothing to do with it but Reuben had forged my signature on the documents and tried to make it look as if I had transferred ownership to him. I told you he was a criminal. Now, instead of being able to reclaim the property, I'll have to fight another case in court. The only ones who win at this game are the lawyers,' he said.

'Are you suggesting that the buyer may have killed him, once he discovered that Reuben didn't own the land?' I asked.

'Anything is possible,' said Aggarwal, meeting my eyes with a malevolent gaze.

Just then, a group of tourists entered the shop, talking loudly amongst themselves. Glancing at them, I asked. 'Do you know who the buyer was?'

Ignoring the tourists, he nodded. 'Someone from Haryana.'

I was tempted to wait until the customers had left, to get more details, but the tourists didn't seem to be in any hurry and it was growing late. Badlu still didn't know that he had to prepare dinner for two. Leaving Hilltop Stores, I headed directly home and reached Thornfield at half-past one, still wondering if Lalaji was telling the truth or covering up his own guilt.

⁂

'Do you think you might be capable of murder?'

'I doubt it. I'm not a violent person.'

'But you must own a weapon of some kind.'

'Yes, I have a revolver, though I doubt if I'll ever have any reason to use it.'

'Do you keep it loaded?'

'No, of course not. But I do have ammunition.'

'Have you ever fired at someone? In self-defence, for instance?'

'Only once, a long time ago.'

'Did you hit your target?'

'Yes.'

'And the person died?'

'Unfortunately, yes.'

'You sound as if you regret what you did....'

'Death isn't something I take lightly but in that case I had every justification. If I hadn't fired my revolver, someone else would have died.'

'Who?'

'Another policeman. A fellow officer.'

'When did this happen?'

'Back in 1982, in a town called Etawah. We had gone to arrest a wanted dacoit, with several murders to his name. He was hiding in his sister's home. She denied that he was there but when we forced our way into the house, he was standing in a corner of the room, holding a twelve-bore shotgun. I could tell he was about to fire and, fortunately, the pistol was already in my hand. He hesitated for a fraction of a second, which gave me enough time to put a bullet through his head. The shotgun went off but he was already falling and the pellets hit the floor, near our feet, just missing the officer who was with me.'

'So, you fired instinctively?'

'I suppose, though I'd been trained to use the revolver, and I'm a relatively good shot, so it wasn't just an impulsive or reckless decision. I knew I had to kill him with one bullet.'

'Did you get a medal?'

'No. But there was a commendation noted in my file.'

'Did this experience change you in any way?'

'What do you mean?'

'Did it make you more confident as a policeman to have done something as heroic as that...saving your partner's life?'

'It wasn't particularly heroic, just a quick decision.'

'What was the dacoit's name?'

'Atmaram Gadariya. Better known as Bhurrey Pahalwan.'

'Why do you think you remember his name?'

'It's hard to forget someone you've killed.'

'And you still don't think you're capable of murder?'

'No. Shooting someone in the line of duty isn't the same at all. For one thing, there was no premeditation. I didn't enter the house with any intention of firing my revolver.'

'But you had it in your hand?'

'As a precaution.'

'Did you have nightmares about the encounter, afterwards?'

'I wouldn't call them nightmares. But, yes, sometimes I've had dreams in which I replayed those moments of entering the house and firing my weapon.'

'Would you do it again?'

'Of course. Why are you asking me these questions? You sound like a psychologist or a lawyer.'

Rita sat back in her chair and smiled before taking a sip of her wine.

'I'm sorry. I have a way of demanding answers that can sound quite rude. I didn't mean to interrogate you. Forgive me,' she said.

I laughed. My first glass of rum was empty. We were sitting in the glassed-in porch, the same place where Rita and I had met the first time she came to call on me, right after her brother's death. The sun had gone down in a blaze of saffron vapours behind a rumpled veil of clouds.

Our evening had begun comfortably enough. Rita seemed to be in a relaxed, even ebullient mood when she arrived, as if her brother's burial had released her from any further responsibility. She thanked me again for my help and I sensed that she was genuinely grateful, though there was a part of her that still seemed distant and guarded. Then, after the first fifteen minutes of conversation, she had suddenly asked me if I was capable of murder and proceeded to quiz me with a persistence that was unnerving. I wondered if she had sensed that I was going to question her and was trying to put me off my stride.

Letting it go for a moment, I went to fetch the bottle of wine to top up her glass before refilling my own.

'Are you trying to get me drunk?' she asked with a laugh.

'Not at all,' I said.

'But you're not having any wine yourself. I won't be able to finish the bottle on my own!'

'Don't worry, I'll have a glass with dinner but, for the moment, I prefer my rum and pani.'

'That's what my father used to drink. Old Monk or Hercules XXX,' she said, wrinkling her nose. 'I always thought it smelled like nail varnish remover.'

'Reuben seems to have preferred vodka,' I said.

She winced and shook her head. 'Let's not talk about him.'

'I understand,' I said, 'but I do have a question, since you've grilled me.'

Her eyes expressed caution though the smile was still on her face. 'All right,' Rita conceded. 'Go ahead.'

'When we first met, you mentioned that you came up to Debrakot after hearing about Reuben's death but we have a witness who says you were arguing with him in the front yard of the house the day before he was killed.' I spoke slowly and deliberately, not sure of the reaction this would elicit.

She cocked her head to one side and gave me an irritated look.

'I thought you invited me here for a romantic evening,' she said. 'But now it seems this is part of your investigation.'

I kept my eyes on her. 'I'm not much of one for romance.'

'So, it seems,' she said. 'You're nothing more than a crude policeman who doesn't hesitate to fire his revolver or insult his guests.'

'It wasn't an insult. It was a question,' I said.

'Yes, but then you should have invited my lawyer to dinner as well,' she said, putting her wine glass on the table and starting to rise from her chair.

'Rita,' I said. 'I'm not saying that you are a suspect, just because you had a fight with your brother, but I would like to know why you haven't been completely forthcoming with the truth.... I mean, your relationship with B. K. Ghosh, the fact that you came up here before the murder. It does invite some questions, doesn't it?'

She looked at her wine before picking up the glass and draining it in a single swallow, as if it were medicine. After this Rita turned back to me with a fierce look in her eyes and her cheeks flushed with anger.

'I don't like playing games, Lionel. You should have asked me earlier.'

'I only just found out,' I said. 'And the police confirmed that you've been staying at Sunnyview Manor since the twenty-seventh of August, five days before the murder.'

Rita rose abruptly from her chair.

'I will not put up with this,' she said. 'I thought you were a decent man but now I can see that you were laying a trap for me.'

'Not at all,' I said. 'I simply wanted to give you a chance to explain what's going on.'

'I'm leaving,' she said with an indignant gesture of her head and shoulders, as she picked up her handbag. 'Unless, of course, you're going to arrest me.'

'No,' I said. 'Please don't be angry....'

'Why shouldn't I be angry?' she cried, her voice shaking with emotion. 'I've never been so offended in my life. Goodbye!'

As she began to leave, I followed.

'Rita, it's dark. You don't have a torch. Please stay.'

She did not answer as she stormed out the front door. Her car and driver were waiting at the top of the path. I thought of following her but there was a part of me that didn't care any more. There would be plenty of opportunities for answers to emerge. Until then, I had half a bottle of wine to finish and dinner for two, which I would now have to eat alone.

Eighteen

My mother's marmalade recipe calls for blood oranges, thickly cut with lots of peel and pulp. Last winter, when the fruit was in season, I made a dozen bottles, adding a little ginger to give it some bite. It has a tart sweetness and a slightly bitter aftertaste that lingers on your tongue.

Spreading the marmalade on a slice of toast, I could clearly see the crimson streaks that give the oranges their name. The truth is that I don't eat much breakfast, just enough to cut the acidity from my morning tea, but today Badlu had given me no choice. He had even fried two eggs, without asking if I wanted them. He was in a foul mood because he'd rushed to get dinner ready the night before and then my guest had left without eating, which he took as a personal insult.

'What kind of people do you invite?' he complained. 'They don't have any manners.'

'She was upset,' I said, trying to placate him. 'Her brother was murdered a week ago. It's understandable.'

'Then she should have stayed at home to mourn her brother, not go out drinking wine. You'd saved that bottle for more than a year and then you wasted it on her,' he ranted.

'Forget about it, Badlu!' I said.

'People don't appreciate the time it takes to make good food. They like their hotel-shotel meals. Now the karela and gobi will go to waste.'

'You can take it home with you,' I said. 'Besides, you made enough for six people and I told you only one guest was coming.'

He ignored what I'd said and began muttering about the milkman. 'Raipal Singh still hasn't shown up. It's nine o'clock and no sign of him. If you want more tea it will have to be black.'

Just then, there was a knock at the kitchen door and he turned to answer it. As I suspected, the milk had arrived but instead of Raipal

Singh, his son Suraj had carried it up from the village. After Badlu had showered him with abuse for being late, I called out from the breakfast table asking why his father hadn't come today.

'He's had a fever since yesterday,' he said.

'Is he seriously sick?' I asked.

'No, he'll be fine,' said Suraj with a hesitant look.

'You're not going to run away again, are you?' I said.

'No, sahibji,' he said. 'I didn't run away. I only went to try and join the army.'

As we spoke, he stood in the kitchen pouring milk into the pan that Badlu was holding over the sink.

'Why didn't they let you enlist?' I asked.

'They said I was too short,' he answered.

'How tall are you?'

'Only 161 centimetres,' said Suraj. 'The minimum height is 163.'

By now, I had finished my breakfast. Getting up I went into the kitchen to speak with him. He is a polite but sullen-looking boy and I know he is restless staying at home in the village. His hair is clipped short on the sides, which seems to be the fashion these days, with a forelock that falls over his eyes.

'How old are you?' I asked.

'Twenty-three,' he said.

'Why don't you go to college?' I said.

'Sahibji, I'm only tenth pass. I would have to do my intermediate and my father says there's no point in studying any further.'

'Your father is a fool,' said Badlu.

'Maybe you could get a job as a nightwatchman,' I suggested. 'After this murder, people are worried about security. If you're interested, I'll ask around.'

Suraj nodded without smiling. 'Yes, of course,' he said.

'Do you think you're brave enough to fight off murderers with knives?' said Badlu. 'And you'd have to show up for work on time. Not an hour late....'

'I'm not afraid of anything,' said Suraj, with an aggrieved expression. 'And this morning I would have come on time but with my father sick, I got delayed.'

'Well, I can't promise anything,' I said. 'But I'll try. Meanwhile, maybe you can do something for me.'

Suraj nodded. 'Yes.'

'I need a goat,' I said.

Badlu looked at me with surprise.

'What kind of goat?' Suraj asked, confused.

'Don't you have goats in your village?' I said.

'Yes, of course, there are plenty though my family doesn't own any,' he said. 'We only have three buffaloes.'

'So, can you find out if someone is willing to sell me a goat?' I said.

He nodded again.

'Why do you need a goat?' Badlu asked, as if I'd lost my mind.

'It doesn't need to be full-grown,' I said, ignoring him. 'And not too expensive. Just an ordinary black goat.'

'Black?' said Suraj, still baffled.

'Yes, completely black. No white spots,' I said. 'I need to make a sacrifice at the Devta's temple.'

***

News from Thapliyal was intriguing. I had gone across to meet him at Shambles, where a constable was still on duty guarding the crime scene. Nothing had been moved since the morning of the murder. Curtains of mist enveloped the house and when I arrived at the gate, it looked as if the building had disappeared altogether. But as I approached, the familiar, decrepit silhouette emerged out of a white void, like a photographic image materializing in a developing tray.

After I briefed him on my two conversations from the day before—the first with Lalaji and the second with Rita—Thapliyal told me that they had been able to locate Deepak Kanojia, the suspect who had escaped.

'Just as we had hoped, he charged his mobile yesterday morning, and we traced the signal to Najibabad. He must have gone straight there. The night bus to Delhi from Debrakot leaves here at 10 p.m.

and stops in Najibabad.'

'I thought you issued a lookout notice,' I said.

'That was put out the following morning,' Thapliyal replied with a smile. 'I'm afraid we aren't as efficient as we should be. Anyway, he's made three calls so far and the mobile provider has given us the details. All the calls were to the same number. Though the recipient's SIM is obviously registered under a false name, the location is somewhere in Haridwar.'

'You're sure he isn't the murderer?' I asked.

'It's possible, of course,' said Thapliyal, 'but he denied it and my suspicion is that he's covering for someone else.'

'Did you question Anmol Gupta?'

'Yes, there's already a case against him for selling restricted drugs without a prescription. We threatened to close his shop down. Ultimately, he'll lose his licence, but I don't think he's guilty of murder.'

'He poisoned Reuben's dog,' I said.

'But do you really think he would stab someone with a knife?' Thapliyal argued. 'He doesn't seem capable of physical violence.'

I had to agree. It seemed unlikely.

'And what about Rita Sabharwal?' I asked. 'Has she left for Delhi?'

'No,' said Thapliyal. 'She's still at the hotel and the manager says she's extended her stay by another two days.'

'Not on my account, I'm sure,' I said.

'Maybe she has business with Ghosh,' said Thapliyal. 'Now that her brother is dead, they'll have to find another god-man.'

'That's why I can't believe she had anything to do with his murder, even if she's behaving as if she's guilty,' I said.

'Yesterday, I questioned Ghosh,' said Thapliyal. 'He claims he was at home that night and his servants have vouched for him. He swears he hadn't seen Reuben for three days before the murder.'

'The podcast was recorded every Wednesday,' I said.

'And Reuben was killed on a Saturday night, so it matches Ghosh's story, at least as far as that goes,' said Thapliyal. 'What about Lalaji? Do you believe what he says about Reuben trying to sell off a plot of land?'

'It's perfectly conceivable,' I replied. 'The property dealer or Aggarwal's lawyer should be able to corroborate the facts.'

I could see that Thapliyal was restless and eager to leave.

'If you'll excuse me, sir,' he said. 'I have to attend a function.'

'Another politician in town?'

'No. St. Mary's Convent is having a martial arts display, and I'm the chief guest,' he said, with an embarrassed look.

'Of course, I forgot you're a black belt in karate!' I said. 'Please carry on. I'm going to look around one more time. I still feel we're missing something here.'

Returning to the sitting room, which looked even shabbier than I remembered from my last visit, I picked through the books on the shelf and examined various papers, including several bills that had been crumpled up and tossed in the wastebasket. I had gone over all of this twice before, even the cigarette butts in the ashtray all of which were unfiltered Charminar, the brand Reuben smoked. There was nothing that might have shed light on the crime.

In the kitchen, cockroaches were scuttling about, but they disappeared under the sink and stove as soon as I stepped into the room. By now the bloodstains had dried completely, having turned a dull, dark brown. Standing beneath the severed remains of the rope, I tried to imagine the sequence of events but it was impossible to block out the action in my mind. Without a motive it still had a random, senseless quality, more like an accident than a crime. Obviously, Reuben had been a hateful man in most people's eyes, even if he projected an aura of divinity, but the fact that someone is disagreeable or even vile, doesn't explain a murder. There had to be a compelling reason that led the killer to plunge a knife into his body eighteen times.

Deciding to go back to the inner sanctum, I went outside and entered the enclosed veranda through an external door that was unlocked. This was something I hadn't noted before and I realized that one could access the prayer room without passing through the rest of the house. The light switch was sticky but when I pressed hard, the overhead bulb came on, revealing the same sepulchral scene with the altar and other objects in place. It was like being inside a pharaoh's tomb.

Thangka scrolls displayed the mysterious cartography of Shambala, a paradise encircled with mountains and full of flowing streams and pleasure palaces, deer, and peacocks, an illusion of eternal bliss. Turning away, I caught sight of myself in the full-length mirror on the opposite wall and stopped for a moment, startled by how old I looked. Earlier I had thought of the mirror as an open doorway, its reflection leading into an identical room but now it seemed as if it was nothing more than a dusty looking glass that framed my ageing figure. The grey hair and stooped shoulders were familiar, but it was the eyes staring back at me that were unsettling because any trace of youth was gone. I looked a bit like a ghost in the feeble yellow light, a jaundiced phantom. Had Rita seen me like this the night before? She had accused me of concocting a romantic evening, perhaps to seduce her, and if I was honest with myself the idea had crossed my mind, though I knew it was absurd to even imagine such a thing.

Shaking off these thoughts, I went over to the mirror and noticed something on the glass next to the wooden frame. It could have been a smear of grease or soot, but it was obvious that someone's fingers had touched the mirror and left a mark. Carefully, I examined it and could see multiple prints on the smooth surface, a faint pattern that extended on to the bevelled margins of the glass. Reaching out, I put my fingers behind the frame, about three inches below the marks and gently pulled. After a momentary resistance, the frame came free of the wall and swung towards me with a soft squeak of unoiled hinges.

The mirror was indeed a door, beyond which there was darkness. I could just make out a set of steps ascending a narrow passage. Going across to the altar, I chose a candle that had burned down to three or four inches and pried it loose. A box of matches lay near the incense holder. Lighting the candle, I stepped into the void. The narrow staircase was steep, and the wooden steps creaked as I climbed into the attic, a windowless space about eight metres square and three metres high at its peak. The candle flame illuminated most of the room and I could see a folding cot with bedding and a couple of wooden crates that seemed to serve as tables. At the foot of the bed was a battered suitcase, which was open. It contained a few clothes, nothing more. The corrugated metal roof angled up from all sides, supported by wooden rafters that were cracked and rotting. One had broken, where the roof bulged inwards and there was a puddle of rainwater on the floor. Beneath the bed was a ceramic chamber pot, half-full of urine. This was the source of one of several unpleasant odours, including the sharp scent of kerosene from a hurricane lantern that sat on one of the crates.

I wasn't able to see into the furthest corners of the attic because of the slope of the roof but I spotted a bundle of clothes next to the cot, as if tossed aside in haste. It was a man's trousers, some sort of grey cotton material and a striped blue shirt, full sleeved. Stooping down I was able to reach them with my hand and when I pulled the clothes towards me, I could see that they were badly stained. Blood had soaked through the front of the trousers to below the knees. The shirt was the same, as if someone had spilled a bucket of paint on himself, which had now dried to a rusty brown colour that stiffened the wrinkled fabric like starch.

Nineteen

Justice is a word that is often used with a false sense of surety, as if it were an absolute noun, like life or death. But the truth of it is that fair and just decisions are seldom delivered in a court of law. More often than not, punishments are never commensurate with the crime, especially when it comes to murder. Many people believe in the primitive dictate of 'an eye for an eye and a tooth for a tooth', as well as the need to put murderers to death. For those who follow this line of reasoning, it is a simplistic moral equation: anyone who takes another person's life forfeits his own. Fortunately, as a policeman, my job has always been to investigate the circumstances of a crime and enforce the law, instead of trying to interpret what is equitable and just.

Of course, I'm not saying that Reuben Sabharwal deserved to die but whoever took his life, whether it was the young man hanging from the kitchen ceiling or someone else, the killer clearly had good cause to wield that knife. Reuben was not an innocent victim. He may even have been culpable in his own death. A wise judge would consider the evidence and decide whether the murderer was driven by anger, pain, madness, or a sense of self-preservation. Whatever punishment might be assigned would be weighed in the scales of justice, which are balanced by measures that can never be entirely accurate. Grams or ounces don't tilt the needle but rather the calibrations of a human mind. Our subjective nature is part of our weakness but also the source of our strength.

I have always been opposed to the death penalty because it represents society's emotional response to tragedy, which cannot be reconciled to the vagaries of guilt. In my career, I have arrested half a dozen men who were sent to the gallows. Up until the 1990s, the Uttar Pradesh government and judiciary was still using this form of execution on a regular basis, though it has been discouraged in recent years. Knowing that my actions had led to a person's life being snuffed out in a crude, medieval manner always left me with a sense of remorse and disgust.

When I was posted in Agra in the early eighties, I apprehended a man who had committed three murders. There was no question about his guilt. In fact, he admitted to the killings as soon as we took him into custody. It was a well-publicized case that caught the attention of the national press. The victims were all members of the same family, a jeweller, his wife, and daughter-in-law, who were hacked to death in the house with a savage brutality that shocked the citizenry of Agra. The murderer was a servant, aged twenty-two, employed as a sweeper. He disappeared after the crime was committed and we found him two days later, hiding in an empty wagon, at the railway station. When I questioned him, he broke down without any need for coercion and explained in detail the humiliation and degrading conditions under which the family had forced him to work. All three of the victims had mistreated him from the time he was employed at the age of twelve. For nine years he had submitted to their insults and beatings until finally, something broke inside him and he struck back with a surge of suppressed anger and resentment.

These facts were presented in court but the horror and fear that the case had aroused in middle-class minds could not be counterbalanced by the reality that he had been put to work as a child, cleaning toilets and sweeping the floors for little more than two meagre meals a day. His employers had treated him worse than an animal and abused him constantly. Nevertheless, the judge sentenced the servant to death, after which there was a half-hearted appeal made by an NGO that took up the cause of 'depressed classes'. It was poorly handled by an inept lawyer and the hanging was carried out the following year, just before I was transferred. I have always been haunted by the thought that this troubled and unfortunate young man was put to death with the same unyielding cruelty that our so-called, modern, civilized society had inflicted on him throughout his short, unhappy life.

George Orwell has always been one of my favourite authors, ever since I read *Animal Farm*, when I was a student at La Martiniere College in Lucknow. The book wasn't on our syllabus but one of my masters, Mr Gomes, loaned me a copy and since then I've read all of Orwell's books. Of course, his essay 'A Hanging' was something that reminded me of my own experiences but the book I've enjoyed the most is *Burmese Days*, a novel about Orwell's early career as a colonial policeman.

The day after I discovered the hidden room at Shambles, I took the book off my shelf and began to re-read it. These days I find myself going back to familiar books, instead of reading new novels. Orwell, whose real name was Eric Blair, was born in India and I've always felt a kinship to him, because he started out as a policeman. His prose has the careful concentration of an investigating officer, unwrapping the mysteries of human nature.

I was three chapters into the book, sitting in a cane chair on the veranda, when two Labrador retrievers appeared without warning, sniffing about near the flower beds, as if they'd found a suspicious scent. Moments later, B. K. Ghosh came up the garden path and whistled for the dogs who ignored him. Marking my place in the book and putting it aside, I rose from my chair and waved in his direction. B. K. caught sight of me, lifting both hands in greeting, as if he was going to surrender. When he joined me on the veranda, I offered him tea but apologized that I had no herbal varieties. He declined, claiming he hadn't really meant to drop by.

'Just out for a walk with the dogs,' he said.

The black lab leapt up on to the veranda and sniffed my hand, while the white one began to bark impatiently.

'Shut up, Yang!' Ghosh cried, wagging a finger.

'Is that her name?' I asked.

'Yes, Yin and Yang. As puppies they used to curl up together when they slept, black and white....' B. K. laughed. 'I hope I'm not intruding.'

'Of course not,' I said, knowing that his arrival was no accident. 'I was just sitting here reading.'

'Which book?' said B. K., pretending to be curious.

I showed him the cover.

'Orwell,' he said. 'I haven't read his stuff, but I saw the movie *1984*.'

'The book is better,' I said.

B. K. nodded with a distracted look on his face.

'Any progress on the case?' he asked.

'Not really,' I said, 'though it still seems to have been a murder-suicide. The victim and the perpetrator are both dead.'

'You're sure of that?' he asked.

I shrugged. 'Unless you have another explanation.'

He hesitated, looking away.

'It's really none of my business,' said B. K., 'but I heard what happened with Rita and I wanted to apologize on her behalf. Though she doesn't show it, her brother's death has left her distraught.'

'I thought they were estranged,' I said. 'That's what she told me.'

'Yes and no,' said B. K. 'It was a complicated relationship.'

'She lied to me about her arrival in Debrakot. At first, she said she came here after hearing about Reuben's death but then I learned that she saw him the day before he was killed and they had an argument. What do you know about that?'

B. K. looked down at the polished toes of his shoes and it was a few moments before he replied. 'Reuben thought we were exploiting him and he refused to record any more podcasts until we paid him more.'

'From what I can gather, it's true. You *were* exploiting him,' I said. 'Seven hundred fifty rupees for half an hour of spiritual wisdom seems like slave wages.'

'But you have to understand, we invested heavily in him,' B. K. protested. 'It isn't as if someone can just ramble on about spirituality and people will immediately tune in. There's a lot work that goes into these podcasts, from editing and sound engineering to promotion and publicity. You don't get two hundred thousand followers just because random people are interested in what you have to say. It involves a lot of factors, including expensive algorithms that reach out to potential viewers. Despite what people think, the internet isn't free.'

'Did Reuben even have an internet connection?' I asked.

'No,' said B. K. 'He was a bit like you. Essentially, unplugged.'

'So, he didn't know how much of an online following he had,' I said.

'Not really, but one of his disciples told him. Up until then, he hadn't taken the whole thing seriously. But once he learned how many people were following him, he accused us of cheating him out of the money he thought we had earned.' B. K. explained.

'And wasn't that true?' I asked.

'No. There was certainly potential, and we might have been able to profit off his podcasts but it was all speculation. We'd positioned him effectively and his message had resonance but no money was coming in.'

'So, he was threatening to pull out just as you were about to make a profit?'

'Exactly,' said B. K. 'That's why Rita came up here, to try and persuade him not to quit. But, of course, he thought we were already making a fortune and demanded two lakhs.'

'Had you signed a contract?' I said with a sceptical expression.

'No,' B. K. admitted. 'Reuben wasn't the sort of person who signs contracts. It would have made him suspicious from the start.'

'And this devotee of his, who told him what was going on,' I said. 'Was it the young man who may have killed him and then hanged himself?'

'I have no idea. All I know is that someone showed him one of his podcasts on a mobile phone and pointed out the number of viewers. The truth is, Reuben didn't really understand how it works. You can have thousands of followers but that doesn't mean they're actually watching. The numbers are always inflated.'

'So, was Rita able to persuade him to continue?' I asked, still unconvinced.

'Eventually, yes,' said B. K. 'We offered to help settle some of his debts but he wanted cash.'

'How much did you finally agree to pay him?'

'Fifty thousand,' B. K. answered, 'as a first instalment.'

'That's not a lot of money for you,' I said.

'I didn't have any cash at home, but we promised Reuben that I would go to the bank the next day and deliver the money to him. Of course, the following morning, I got word that he'd been murdered.'

B. K. could see that I was sceptical of his story and he glanced away for a moment, eyeing the two dogs who were still sniffing about like bloodhounds. His overly-earnest, confiding manner suggested that he was trying to put me off the scent, even if part of what he'd said might be correct.

'I'm telling you the truth,' he insisted with an anxious expression. 'Rita can confirm, if you ask her.'

'Somehow, I don't think she wants to speak to me again,' I replied.

B. K. looked flustered in an exaggerated sort of way. 'I certainly hope you don't think she killed her brother!'

'Right now, I can't rule anything out,' I said with a smile. 'For that matter, you might have helped Rita commit the murder.'

He exhaled a forced laugh. 'Come on, Lionel, you're joking, aren't you?'

I shrugged and gave him a questioning look. B. K. is a smooth talker—too clever for his own good. I could tell he was holding something back.

Making a helpless gesture by raising both hands and then folding them together, he implored me, 'How can I convince you that Rita and I are innocent?'

I kept my eyes on him for several seconds before looking away. One of the things I learned, early on in my career, is that when you're trying to get information out of someone, the silences are often as important as the questions.

'Have you heard of the Devta's shrine?' I asked, after a long pause.

He gave me a puzzled look. 'No.'

'It's a small temple, half an hour's walk from here,' I said. 'There's going to be a ceremony this coming Wednesday.'

'What kind of ceremony?' Ghosh asked, confused.

'A sacrifice,' I said, 'to help solve the murders. I've been told the goddess is going to identify the killer. You should come. It might just prove your innocence.'

'Are you serious?' B. K. said.

'Absolutely,' I said. 'You should bring your camera crew along. It might also provide you with some exciting *internet content....*'

Twenty

Thapliyal had his men scour the attic for evidence, including fingerprints, just as they had done in the kitchen. Nevertheless, I wasn't optimistic that anything useful would be found. Forensic science isn't one of the strengths of Debrakot's police force, but there was a clear set of prints on the mirror, which they were able to collect. The other thing they found in the attic was an empty water bottle that also produced some prints and the foil wrapper from a packet of biscuits. Judging by this, we concluded that the person who had occupied the attic was hiding upstairs for at least twenty-four hours after the murder and must have been there when we first arrived at the house.

This was a frustrating discovery and I blamed myself for not having found the hidden doorway earlier. The killer had probably been listening in on our conversations below, waiting for an opportunity to escape. It confirmed my premonition that the house itself was complicit in the crime.

I met Thapliyal again that evening at Shambles, just as the sun was setting over the town, an amber glow tinting the clouds. Lights were coming on in Debrakot, like scattered stars strewn across the dark crest of the ridge. Though it was beautiful, I hardly noticed, angry that the murderer had been lurking so close at hand but now had disappeared.

After briefing Thapliyal about my conversation with B. K., I wondered aloud about the purpose of the secret room in the attic.

'Reuben must have used it as a hideaway and the killer obviously knew about it.'

Thapliyal replied, 'The contents of the suitcase belonged to Kunal Vaidya. There were a couple of notebooks with his name on them, but no recent entries.'

'He was obviously staying up there.'

'But why?' said Thapliyal. 'It has no window, no lights. There were plenty of other beds in the house.'

'Obviously, he was hiding from something,' I said. 'Maybe his family was trying to take him home.'

'Then why would the murderer have gone up there?' Thapliyal asked. 'It doesn't make sense. Why would he stay in the house after committing the crime, instead of just running away?'

'Perhaps it was a ghost,' I said, unable to control my irritation. 'Everybody says this damned house is haunted.'

Thapliyal looked over his shoulder at the tumbledown structure, which seemed to have settled even further into its foundations. With the gathering darkness it looked like a crumbling heap of ruins, lifeless and abandoned. Despite all of the leads we'd followed and the various bits of evidence gathered, we still seemed to be at a dead end.

'Maybe I need to speak to Rita Sabharwal again,' I said.

'Sir, I meant to tell you, her lawyer has arrived from Delhi,' Thapliyal said.

'When?'

'This afternoon. He called and said he wants to speak with me tomorrow.'

'Did he say what it's about?' I asked.

'No, but I'm sure he thinks we're going to file a case against her,' he said.

'There's really no evidence connecting Rita to the crime, except that she lied to us, and that's not enough,' I said. 'Aside from all of that, I still don't think she's involved, at least not directly. Though she and Ghosh were obviously exploiting Reuben, they had no apparent reason to kill him.'

Thapliyal frowned. 'There's one more thing the lawyer told me that you should know,' he said. 'Rita Sabharwal has been working as a public relations consultant for Dr Pran Vaidya, Kunal's father.'

∽

Ordinarily, I keep my revolver in the lowest drawer of the dressing table. Before going to sleep that evening, I loaded the pistol and put it on the table beside my bed. So far, there didn't seem to be any danger that the killer would strike again but as the case grew more complicated, I couldn't rule that out. Everyone in town knew that I was assisting with the investigation and whoever was responsible for the crime might have reason to threaten my life, though we were nowhere near solving the case.

Since returning to Debrakot, a year and a half ago, I've occasionally thought of getting a dog but haven't had the courage. Two years ago, I put my last dog down and I still haven't recovered. Lili was a stray puppy that adopted me when I was posted in Delhi with the CBI. I'd found her curled up beneath the steps of my flat in Lodhi Colony. She was devoted to me, affectionate, obedient, and a terrific watchdog even if she weighed no more than twelve kilos. Her shrill bark could raise the dead, though she seldom made a sound unless she sensed a genuine threat. One night an intruder climbed on to the balcony and was trying to break in. Lili woke me with her loud, hysterical yelping. As I sat up in bed, I saw the man leap off the balcony in a panic. After I left the CBI, I was posted in Haldwani. Lili came with me and on two more occasions she warned me of danger. Once it was a cobra that entered the house, slipping in through the outside door to the bathroom of the bungalow where I lived. Lili's frantic barking alerted me to the danger and I was able to kill the snake. The second threat was a man I'd put in jail years ago, who arrived drunk in the middle of the night carrying a knife, with revenge on his mind. Though Lili's high-pitched barking didn't scare him off, it was enough to alert the police sentries at the gate, who tackled the man and disarmed him.

Lili lived until the age of fourteen but in the end, her hind legs gave out and she was in so much pain I finally had to call the vet to put her to sleep. It was the hardest thing I've ever done and I wept like a child, swearing that I would never get another dog. Lying in bed at Thornfield sometimes, surrounded by the silence of the mountains, I've often wished that Lili was still with me, for the companionship, of course, but also her street dog instincts and ear-splitting cries of alarm.

Nothing happened that night and the next morning I unloaded

the revolver and put it out of sight in the drawer of my bedside table. Though my fears had been unfounded, there was a lingering premonition of danger.

Around nine o'clock, as I was reading in my study, I heard a conversation in the kitchen and recognized Suraj and Raipal Singh's voices. A few minutes later, Badlu came to the door, coughing softly to alert me.

'Yes, what is it?' I said, my eyes still on the page.

'Your goat has arrived,' he replied.

I got to my feet and followed him back to the kitchen. Tied to the tap stand outside was a young goat that was struggling to get loose from the rope around its neck. Suraj seemed proud of the creature he had procured. With stubby horns, it had drooping ears that dangled on either side of its face, and doleful eyes that conveyed a look of aggrieved innocence.

'What is this you've brought?' Badlu demanded for my benefit. 'It probably has no more than two or three kilos of meat on its bones.'

'There were larger ones,' said Suraj, 'though none of them were black.'

'Is it male or female?' I asked.

'A male,' said Raipal. 'Females are never offered for sacrifice.'

When I went forward and leaned down to pat the goat's head, it butted my hand resentfully. I wondered if the goddess would approve of my offering.

'How much do I have to pay for him?' I inquired.

'Sahib, the owner wants a thousand rupees,' said Suraj.

'Get lost,' Badlu exclaimed, always looking out for my interests. 'It isn't worth five hundred.'

'You can pay whatever you like,' Raipal said.

'Do you think the Devi will be happy with this offering?' I asked.

'Of course, sahib,' Raipal said with a smile. 'You are sacrificing it for a good cause, to find out who committed the murder.'

'How do you know that?' I demanded.

'Charan Das told me what happened at the jagran. It is an auspicious sign when the Devi asks for blood,' the milkman responded.

I was glad to know that the news had spread, though I hoped it wouldn't become too much of a spectacle.

'When are you holding the sacrifice?' Badlu asked.

'Four days from now, on Wednesday,' I said. 'I've been told it's an appropriate date and the stars are properly aligned. The only question is: who's going to chop off the goat's head? I'm certainly not planning to do it myself. Raipal, what about someone from your village?'

'I've done it several times in the past, when I was a young man,' Raipal replied, cautiously. 'And I have a paathal with a good, sharp blade. But these days we don't often perform sacrifices. It's discouraged....'

'Maybe one of the younger men,' I suggested. 'In fact, Suraj, what about you? I'm sure you can perform the sacrifice for me.'

His eyes grew wide with alarm and he drew back.

'What? Are you afraid of blood?' I asked.

Suraj shook his head but remained mute.

'Of course, he'll do it,' said Raipal, putting a hand on his son's shoulder.

'Good,' I said with satisfaction. 'That problem is solved. Let me have your mobile number, so I can contact you, in case there's a question.'

Suraj recited the number and I wrote it down on a scrap of paper.

'Sahib....?' Raipal said, pausing with hesitant curiosity, as if he was afraid to ask a question.

'What?'

'I thought you were a Christian...these customs aren't part of your faith,' he said, with an apologetic smile.

'We Christians celebrate our sacrifices too,' I said. 'But this is not for me. The goat will be slaughtered on behalf of the victims, to identify their killer.'

Raipal nodded in agreement. 'Yes,' he agreed. 'The goddess never lies.'

'Meanwhile, what do we feed this animal?' I said.

'Leaves, grass,' said Raipal. 'It will eat almost anything you give it.'

Taking a thousand rupees from my wallet I handed it to Suraj.

'Why not get a longer rope and let it graze in the yard,' I said. 'That way it will crop the lawn and we won't have to cut the grass for another week or two.'

Everyone, even Badlu, seemed pleased with this suggestion.

Twenty-one

I waited until eleven o'clock that morning, before walking across to Komal and Kaju Rao's house, which lies about fifteen minutes' walk away, on the north side of the ridge. It wasn't a visit that I was looking forward to, and I'd put it off longer than necessary, but eventually I needed to explore all of the possible explanations for the murder. Despite my umbrella, the mist swept in from all sides and my hair and clothes were damp by the time I reached the driveway to Middlemarch.

The gateposts were adorned with the regimental insignia of the Fifth Gurkha Rifles, two khukri knives crossed beneath the lion capital and the numeral 5. Beneath this on one side was the nameplate: Lt Col. K. B. Rao YSM (Retd). Both sides of the driveway were marked out with white lines painted on the concrete and the flower beds were edged with bricks tilted up against each other, in the style of every cantonment garden, as if standing at attention for review. Middlemarch had been a guest cottage for a larger home that now lay in ruins and was entangled in a contentious legal dispute between two brothers who had inherited the property but could not agree on an equitable share of ownership. One of them had torn down the old house and the other refused to let it be rebuilt. Before the dispute erupted, Kaju had been able to buy the cottage and a small parcel of land. He and Komal had moved here after his retirement ten years ago. My mother was fond of Komal for the two of them shared a love of gardening. They could sit for hours chatting about ranunculus, godetia, or dozens of other flowering plants.

Coming down the path, I found Komal kneeling in front of a line of potted begonias that were still in bloom—yellow, red, and pink blossoms that were so bright, they looked artificial. She was wearing a loose salwar kameez with gumboots and gloves. Not wanting to startle her, I called out from a distance and Komal looked up with a distracted expression, using one forearm to brush away the hair from her eyes. Even from twenty metres away, I could see the anxiety behind her smile.

'Good morning,' I said. 'Forgive me, my phone is dead, or I would have called before coming over.'

'Welcome, Lionel,' Komal said, rising clumsily to her feet and holding her gloved hands away from her body because they were covered in dirt. 'It's always nice to see you. Please come in.'

'I have a book to return to Kaju,' I said, gesturing toward the pocket of my jacket.

'Of course,' she replied, with a hesitant look of relief. 'He's inside. Please go on in and give him a shout. I'll join you in a minute.'

When I entered through the front door, knocking loudly as I went inside, I heard a gruff bellow from somewhere at the back. I'd been in the house a couple of times before and guessed the colonel was in the drawing room but it was empty. Just then, Kaju appeared in the far doorway with a large khukri in one hand, its steel blade glinting in the half-light coming through a window curtained with lace.

'Aha!' he cried with his usual bluster. 'Good to see you, Lionel!'

'Komal told me to let myself in,' I said, apologetically.

'Come along, back here,' he said, then realized that I was staring at the knife. 'Sorry. I've been polishing my khukris. If I'm not careful, the blades get rusty this time of year.'

He led me through to a large anteroom that was furnished like an officers' mess, with photographs on the walls and the head of a sambar stag that looked a bit worse for wear, as well as a tiger skin that was losing its fur. On one wall was a display of khukris, at the centre of which was a plaque bearing the regimental insignia of the Fifth Gurkhas. The whole room was a shrine to military valour. On a small side table, I could see where he had spread newspapers and was oiling and polishing his weaponry.

'Are you getting ready for battle?' I asked.

'No, no!' he said. 'Nothing but a bit of housekeeping. My battles are all behind me.'

'Have you ever used any of these khukris?' I said. 'I mean, to defend yourself?'

He shook his head and his moustache seemed to bristle at the question.

'Purely ceremonial. I've collected them over the years. This one was given to me by Field Marshal Manekshaw in 1972.' He showed me an inscription on the blade, then pointed to a framed photograph of himself as a young officer, saluting Sam Manekshaw.

'It looks lethal,' I said.

'Yes, in the hands of the right man a khukri gets the job done!' he said, with intended understatement. 'Some of the johnnies in my regiment could lop off the head of buffalo with one stroke. We used to let them carry out sacrifices during Dussehra, though it's frowned upon now...all of these animal rights activists.'

I nodded and muttered. 'Slaying the demon and slaking the goddess' thirst for blood. In fact, I'm going to have a goat sacrificed day after tomorrow at the Devta's temple.'

He looked up at me with surprise. 'Why would you do that?'

'Superstition,' I said, with a smile, then reached into my jacket pocket and pulled out a book he'd loaned me a couple weeks ago. It was a recently published history of the 1971 Indo-Pak War and the liberation of Bangladesh.

'I just wanted to return this,' I said. 'Thank you.'

'What did you think of it?' Kaju demanded, putting the knife down and wiping his hands on a cloth duster.

'Fascinating,' I lied. The book was as tedious as any military history.

'Did you see where he mentions me?' the colonel asked.

'Of course. How could I miss it? You'd underlined your name in red ink.'

He nodded. 'I remember it as if it was yesterday. The surrender of Sylhet.'

Just then, Komal came into the room, having shed her boots and gloves.

'Tea?' she asked.

'No, we'll have some beer. It's almost noon,' Kaju insisted and his wife obediently withdrew to carry out his orders. Waving me into a chair, he began to recount his exploits during the Bangladesh War. When Komal returned five minutes later with a large bottle of Kingfisher and two glasses, I watched her as she poured, tilting the glasses so there would be less foam at the top.

'If you'll excuse me,' she said. 'I need to finish with my begonias....'

'Actually,' I said, before she could get away. 'I had a question for you, Komal, if you're not in too much of a rush.'

She paused in the doorway and gave me a hesitant smile. 'Yes?'

'I heard you attended some of Reuben Sabharwal's meditation sessions,' I said. 'Is that true?'

'I did,' she replied, nodding.

'Bloody waste of time, if you ask me,' Kaju interjected.

'Was there anything you noticed that might explain what happened to him?'

Komal shook her head and said, 'It was several months ago. I only went three times.'

'Why did you stop?'

'I lost interest,' she said, glancing at Kaju. 'It wasn't what I expected and the house was very depressing and filthy. I'm also allergic to mildew and found myself sneezing the whole time.'

'You never went back?'

There was the slightest hesitation as she shook her head.

'Where did Reuben hold these sessions?' I asked.

'In the prayer room, off the entry hall,' she said.

'Were others there?' I asked.

'Yes, two or three young men and a couple of women,' she said.

'Do you remember any of their names?' I asked.

'No,' said Komal, 'I'm afraid not.'

'Do you think one of them was the second victim?' I asked.

'I couldn't say,' she answered. 'I don't know what the victim looked like. Besides, we didn't really speak or pay much attention to each other. Everyone was focused on Reuben.'

Taking a photograph out of my pocket, I handed it to her. Komal blinked then looked away with revulsion. It was a picture of the young man hanging from the noose, before they cut him down.

'Do you recognize him?' I asked.

She handed the picture back and nodded. 'Yes, it's one of the men. I don't recall his name.'

'Kunal?' I said.

'Could be....' she replied.

'Let me have a look,' Kaju demanded and I handed the picture to him.

'Bloody hell,' he said, with disgust. 'The bugger's wearing lipstick!'

Komal's eyes were fixed on me now, as if she was bracing herself for whatever question I might ask next. But my reason for coming to their house was not to expose her infidelities. I felt sure she was innocent of anything more than a brief affair. Being married to a duffer like Kaju, I couldn't blame her.

'Thank you,' I said. 'Sorry to put you through that.'

She nodded and looked as if she was fighting back tears as she left the room.

'Well, cheers!' said Kaju, holding up his glass.

I raised mine and we both drank our beer as he changed the subject back again to the surrender of Sylhet.

*

My plan of allowing the goat to crop the lawn at Thornfield turned out to be a disaster. Badlu had followed my instructions and tied the animal to a long rope that allowed it to wander about the yard within a ten-metre radius but its reach also extended halfway into the garden. Instead of feeding on the overgrown grass, the goat turned its attention to the flower beds and finished off most of the gladioli and other monsoon flowers. When I returned from Middlemarch, he was standing contentedly amidst a bed of marigolds, most of which had been devoured. Pulling him back into the yard, I had to yank hard and the goat bleated at me with an angry, resentful look, tossing his head, attempting to escape.

Looking at the animal, I tried not to think of it being killed, and its blood flowing on to the flagstones in front of the temple. Something about the crime scene at Shambles had made me think of a ritual sacrifice, as if Reuben had been knifed to death in order to absolve whatever evil may have occurred in the house. Or was he the demon that had to be destroyed? Of course, if I thought about it rationally, I knew this couldn't be true, though it still seemed as if the two murders may have had some symbolic meaning, connected to Reuben's cult.

The picture that I had showed Komal was one of a set of photographs that Thapliyal had given me, all of which were taken on the morning when we first arrived at Shambles and found the two bodies in the kitchen. Vipin Verma, the photographer, had more than a hundred shots on his camera and Thapliyal had chosen fifteen of these. They were glossy, 5' x 7' coloured prints, tucked into an envelope from Rajhans Studios. Once I had hauled the goat out of the flower beds and shortened its lead, I went into my study and dealt out the photographs on to my desk, as if I were playing a gruesome game of solitaire.

Switching on a lamp, I studied the pictures carefully, using a magnifying glass that had belonged to my mother, with which she read the newspapers or consulted her dictionary to do crosswords. As I looked over the photographs again, I tried to clear my head of all the theories and suppositions that had accumulated in my mind, and simply focused on the two bodies, one of which was now buried six feet underground and the other burned to ashes and carried away by the sacred waters of the Ganga.

After fifteen or twenty minutes, I was about to give up, when I caught sight of something that made me stop and look again. In one picture, Kunal's body had been photographed at an angle that showed the right arm hanging loosely by his side. Suddenly, I remembered noticing a small abrasion when I first observed the body. In the confusion that ensued that morning, after we discovered that the dead woman was actually a man, I hadn't examined the victim's wrists, as I should have done. The post-mortem report had also missed this minor injury, focusing primarily on the fatal wound at the back of the head, which revealed that the corpse hadn't died by hanging. In the process of cataloguing the most startling evidence and determining the cause of death, we had overlooked what seemed inconsequential at the time but now hinted at another, more disturbing explanation of the crime.

In the photograph, I could distinctly see a mark on the inside of the right wrist and when I studied the image under the magnifying glass, it was clearer still. Hurriedly, I re-examined the other photographs, hoping to find a picture of the victim's left hand but there were none. Only the right hand was visible, exposing what now looked suspiciously like a rope burn. It hadn't broken the skin but had left what appeared to be the faint shadow of a bruise.

Twenty-two

Rita's lawyer, who had arrived from Delhi, turned out to be a Supreme Court advocate named Mohan Ghorpade, well known for handling high profile cases. While I was with the CBI, he had been able to get an acquittal for a wealthy industrialist we had charged with foreign currency violations and money laundering. Ghorpade was reputed to be one of the most expensive lawyers in the country, representing a number of political clients in corruption cases. At first, it seemed odd that he would come to a small town like Debrakot to take on a murder case in which no charges had been filed. But Thapliyal informed me that Dr Pran Vaidya was also in town. The two of them had arrived by helicopter and were staying at the Aranya Nivas Ashram, along the Jhirnawalla branch road.

All of this was an intriguing and worrying development. Sitting in Thapliyal's office, as we scrolled through the entire collection of digital photographs taken on the morning after the murder, I wondered what sort of pressure the SHO would face. Studying the images of Kunal Vaidya's body on the computer screen, it was clear that more revelations were sure to emerge, but I was determined to solve this piece of the puzzle before other matters distracted us.

'If the victim's hands were tied,' said Thapliyal, 'What does it prove?'

'Nothing, really,' I said, 'Except that he probably wasn't Reuben's killer. From the post-mortem we know that Kunal died from a blow to the back of his head. Whoever caused that injury is probably the same person who tied his hands. It's also very likely that the same rope was used to string him up from the ceiling after he was dead.'

'Ghorpade wanted a copy of the post-mortem report,' said Thapliyal, scrolling through a series of pictures of Reuben's blood-soaked corpse.

'Did you give it to him?'

'No, I told him it hasn't been signed by the medical examiner and until formal charges are filed, I have no authority to show anyone the report,' Thapliyal replied.

'What did he say to that?' I asked, leaning forward as several more pictures of the body appeared on the screen.

'He threatened to get a court order requiring me to share evidence.' Thapliyal smiled. 'Even if he does, it will take several days.'

'Did he say why Dr Vaidya has come to Debrakot?' I asked.

'Because he is distraught over his son's death. Doctor sahib is in mourning.'

'And what did he say about Rita?' I asked.

'He claims she had nothing to do with her brother's murder and the fact that she was seen arguing with him the day before he died doesn't prove anything.'

I nodded, squinting at a photograph that showed the victim's left arm, though the wrist was turned in the wrong direction.

'Yes,' I said. 'But if she's working as a public relations consultant for Dr Vaidya, why wouldn't he distance himself from Rita, under the circumstances? Hiring an expensive, high-profile lawyer and accompanying him to Debrakot only brings more attention to the case. The media will pick up on it sooner or later.'

Thapliyal fell silent for a minute as we examined the photographs on the screen. 'Here's one,' he said, at last.

As he enlarged the image, I could see Kunal's left hand, hanging within the draped folds of the cotton sari. Though the magnification blurred the photograph, a scuffed bruise was visible on the wrist.

'That's it!' I said with satisfaction, though I regretted not having discovered the evidence earlier.

'But, sir,' said Thapliyal. 'This won't prove anything in court. The photographs aren't clear enough to convince a judge. And the post-mortem report doesn't mention these injuries.'

'You're absolutely right,' I said. 'But it's not the judge I'm worried about. I simply wanted to convince myself. Now that I know for sure that Kunal Vaidya was tied up before he died, I can begin to put the rest of the pieces together.'

After Thapliyal made a copy of the digital photograph and saved it for future reference, he sat back in his chair and looked at me with a hesitant expression.

'Sir, there's one more thing that you should see,' he said, cautiously.

At this point, I was about to rise from my seat and take my leave. After an hour of staring at the computer screen in the police station, I had the beginnings of a headache and was looking forward to the walk back home. But Thapliyal clearly had more to show me.

'All right, what is it?' I said, puzzled by his evasive manner.

Unlocking a drawer in his desk, he took out a slim mobile device, which I recognized. It was Kunal Vaidya's iPhone.

Switching it on, Thapliyal looked uncomfortable as the screen came to life, revealing a digital keypad. With his index finger, he tapped in a code, unlocking the phone and revealing an assortment of icons.

'I'm afraid it's offensive, sir,' Thapliyal apologized, as he handed me the phone.

'Okay. Okay,' I said impatiently. 'I'm sure it isn't something I haven't seen before. Which button do I press?'

He reached across and tapped the screen to start the video, before leaning away and averting his eyes.

To begin with, there seemed to be nothing objectionable in the video—a young man seated on an unmade bed with his back to the wall. It was Deepak Kanojia. Someone was speaking to him off camera, a muffled voice that was almost unintelligible though I picked up a few suggestive phrases. After about forty-five seconds, another person appeared in the frame and I recognized Kunal Vaidya. His long hair was pulled back from his face with a plastic headband but he wasn't wearing a sari. In fact, he wasn't wearing anything at all. Soon enough, I understood Thapliyal's discomfiture as the two men embraced and began to have sex. The person who was shooting the video on the phone's camera moved around the foot of the bed to the other side and then leaned in closer so that Kunal's face was clearly visible. The video was clumsily shot but as graphic as any pornography I've seen. Watching it on the small, rectangular screen added to its voyeuristic quality, as did the soundtrack, which left no room for imagination. Altogether, the video was about five minutes long, though it seemed to take forever.

When it finally ended, Thapliyal took the phone from my hands and quickly laid it inside the drawer, face down.

'There are two more videos,' he said. 'Do you want to see them?'

'Perhaps later,' I replied. 'Are they any different?'

'Not really,' he replied. 'All three are of Kunal Vaidya and Deepak Kanojia.'

'Are you able to see who is filming them?' I asked.

He shook his head.

'Do you think it was Reuben?'

Thapliyal shrugged. 'Probably, but it's impossible to tell. They were definitely shot in his bedroom. You can see the bedside lamp and ashtray.'

For a minute or more, I fell silent, glancing across at the computer on which the photograph of the hanging corpse was still frozen on the screen.

'Does the lawyer Ghorpade know about this?' I asked.

'I couldn't tell,' said Thapliyal. 'He said nothing about it.'

'And these are the only copies?' I asked.

'As far as I know,' said Thapliyal. 'I haven't shown them to anyone else, but it would have been easy enough to forward a copy.'

⁂

From the back gate at Thornfield, a narrow footpath winds its way down the slope and joins an old mule track heading back into the hills. Before motor roads were constructed this used to be the main route from Debrakot to pilgrimage sites in the upper Himalaya. A dense oak forest extends along the crest of the ridge which overlooks higher ranges to the north and a broad, cultivated valley to the south. The new bypass road, constructed three years ago, joins the pilgrim route about two kilometres farther on. Just before that point lies the Devta's temple, situated on a grass-covered knoll, amidst an outcropping of large boulders and overshadowed by a massive deodar tree.

I sometimes take this route for my evening walk, though during the monsoon the footpath is overgrown with stinging nettles and wild balsam. The path is infested with leeches too, but I took my chances. It hadn't rained since the previous evening, and I wanted to visit the temple where the sacrifice would be performed. Bushwhacking a path through the weeds with a walking stick, I checked my shoes carefully when I reached the broader mule track. One of the bloodsuckers was inching its way up to my laces but I was able to flick it off before carrying on towards the temple.

Eventually, the trail joined another footpath that led me through patches of barberry bushes and a scrub jungle of stunted oaks. One branch of the ridge angled off to the north before opening on to a grassy meadow that fell away steeply on both sides. For the first time in days, I saw that the sky was beginning to clear, revealing a line of snow peaks to the north, their white summits protruding through the clouds. The Devta's temple faced the high Himalaya and was surrounded by limestone crags that looked as if they had been arranged in a loose circle around the small shrine with its slate roof covered in moss.

I had been here many times before and the view has always made me linger near the temple, peering down into the valley, where a tiny stream threads its way through a mosaic of terraced fields. Raipal and Suraj's village, Ranglana, stands on a ridge about five hundred metres below the temple. Other villages and settlements dot the slopes further down in the valley.

The giant deodar growing next to the Devta's temple cast its spreading shadow on the shrine and surrounding rocks. Embedded in the exposed roots of the huge tree were two iron tridents, probably left there by wandering mendicants, as well as a number of coins wedged into the bark as offerings. Saffron and vermilion threads had been wound around the deodar's trunk. Though I am not a believer, there is something in these surroundings that invokes a sense of reverence and awe. I always ring the brass bell that hangs in front of the locked doors of the temple. It emits a shrill clamour that echoes for a moment or two before the silence of the mountains is restored.

One of the Brahmins from Ranglana attends to the shrine, though it is locked most of the time and no one lives here. The Devta is a folk deity represented by a crude stone image of a man on horseback wielding a sword. His consort, the goddess, is symbolized by another stone idol of a female figure with multiple arms. As I circled around the temple, my mobile phone began to ring. The sound surprised me because the device never works at home, though there was clearly a signal here. My ringtone is an irritating jingle that Chunky Rawat chose when he sold me the phone and I haven't been able to figure out how to change it.

Removing the mobile from my pocket, I saw a number on the screen that I didn't recognize and for a moment I thought it might be a marketing call. With some hesitation, I answered it.

'Mr Carmichael?' A man's voice inquired.

'Yes, who is this?'

'Mohan Ghorpade,' he said. 'I'm representing Dr Pran Vaidya. We were wondering if you might be free to meet us tomorrow morning. I can send a car across to pick you up and bring you to the Aranya Nivas Ashram. Do you know where that is?'

'Yes,' I said. 'But what's this all about?'

'It's regarding a family matter. Dr Vaidya's son, Kunal,' he explained. 'I believe you are involved in the investigation.'

'Informally, yes,' I said.

'If it's not too much trouble, the car will be there at 9 a.m.,' said Ghorpade.

Twenty-three

After entering the ashram gate, we drove through a pine forest that lined the driveway. Two hundred metres on ahead, after rounding a sharp bend, we arrived in front of the main building, which was a modern marble structure with shallow steps ascending to an arched portico that looked like the entrance of a posh hospital. Originally, the property had been a brewery, which was abandoned years ago, and the ashram was built on this site.

Ghorpade met me on the front steps as the car arrived. He was wearing an expensive grey suit with a bright pink tie. Though he shook hands with a brusque, no-nonsense manner there was something comical about him. His legs looked too short for his body and his arms too long, a bit like a caricature of a lawyer whose limbs have become distorted because of his theatrical gestures in court. He had a pinched face, full of nervous self-importance.

The automatic glass doors opened, and we passed through a gleaming lobby, also clad in white marble. Carved panels on the walls depicted images of swans and lotus blossoms. Without explanation, the lawyer gestured towards a staircase as two young women appeared at the top to receive us. Both of them were wearing cream silk saris, their faces glowing with good health. Strings of jasmine blossoms were braided into their dark tresses. Folding their hands in greeting, they ushered us into a large sitting room. Again, the floors and walls were marble while the sofa and chairs were upholstered in spotless white fabric. Two intricately carved ivory tusks were displayed on the wall, framing a circular mirror. A vase of white roses was arranged at the centre of a low coffee table made of clear glass. Through a large window I could see a helipad just below the ashram. The distant snow peaks were wreathed in clouds, as if the view had been chosen to match the colour scheme of the room.

Before we could sit down, a door opened and an elderly gentleman entered. He was wearing an immaculate white dhoti and kurta, crisply starched, though his hair had been dyed jet black, as well as the pencil-thin moustache that creased his upper lip like two hyphens. I recognized him from photographs I'd seen in the newspapers. He did not smile but greeted me with a perfunctory namaskar and pointed to the two chairs facing the sofa, instructing us to take our seats.

'My condolences on the loss of your son,' I said.

Dr Vaidya didn't react, except for a stern blink of his eyes. On the fingers of both hands were several gold rings set with different stones, each of which I imagined had auspicious properties. One was a pearl the size of a mothball.

'Do you speak Hindi?' he asked in a thin, rasping voice.

'Yes, of course,' I answered.

He sighed and nodded. 'I prefer to speak my own language,' he said, glancing across at Ghorpade with momentary disapproval. 'You live in Debrakot?'

'Yes. On the other side of town,' I replied.

He didn't react.

'And why are you involved with this case?' Vaidya asked.

'I'm helping out because the SHO asked for my advice,' I said.

Ghorpade began to explain that I am a retired police officer but Vaidya lifted one hand to silence him.

'I know who he is,' he said, with a note of impatience. 'But I was asking why you've chosen to interfere. This is none of your business.'

'A murder is everyone's concern,' I replied. 'Especially for those of us who live here.'

His eyes met mine for the first time with a suspicious glance.

'Do you think that the local police are incompetent?' he asked.

'No. Not at all,' I responded. 'But they have limited resources to carry out a thorough investigation.'

'What is there to investigate?' Vaidya asked. 'Two men are dead. Beyond that, what more do we need to know?'

'Don't you want to learn who killed your son?' I asked.

Again, Ghorpade tried to intervene. 'Of course, Dr Vaidya wants the police to uncover the truth....'

'My son meant nothing to me,' said Vaidya. 'I do not care who killed him. He was dead to me long before this happened.'

'Why is that?' I asked.

'He was dissolute and defiled his body with drugs and indecent habits. He wasted his life,' said the doctor. 'I tried to discipline him, but he would not listen. After a point, he was no longer a child and I let him go.'

'Did you throw him out of your home?' I asked.

'I didn't need to. He left on his own.'

'You must have supported him,' I said. 'He had no job.'

'His mother spoiled him,' said Vaidya. 'I suppose she must have given him money, now and then, but from me he got nothing.'

'You must feel some sadness, being his father,' I said, seeing Ghorpade twitching in his seat.

Vaidya didn't respond.

'As much as any father would feel, mourning his son,' the lawyer interjected quickly.

'Then why have you come to Debrakot?' I asked.

'Because my ashram is here,' said Vaidya. 'I am an old man. I need to retreat into the forest at this age and leave the material world behind.'

'So, it has nothing to do with Kunal's murder?'

He shook his head. 'That is my lawyer's business, not mine.'

'Why do you need a lawyer if the murder means nothing to you?' I asked without looking in Ghorpade's direction, though he was the one who answered my question in English.

'We want to make sure that the facts in the case aren't twisted or taken out of context,' said Ghorpade. 'You would understand that better than anyone, Mr Carmichael.'

'Actually, I don't understand,' I said. 'But perhaps you can help me.'

Vaidya looked at me with disdain. 'What do you want to know?'

'To begin with, Rita Sabharwal. What does she have to do with all this?' I asked.

'Nothing,' said Vaidya.

'I understand that she works as a public relations consultant for you.'

'Not any more,' said Ghorpade. 'We've severed all ties with her.'

'But she *was* working for you,' I said, keeping my eyes on Vaidya. 'Her brother was the other victim. Kunal was living with him. It's not as if you can erase all of that, just by firing her.'

'She is nobody,' said Vaidya. 'Her brother was a corrupt, wicked man.'

'What makes you say that?' I asked.

Out of the corner of my eye, I could see that Ghorpade was growing increasingly nervous, worried that his client might say too much. But Dr Vaidya didn't hesitate.

'He tried to blackmail me,' he said.

'How?' I asked.

Ghorpade now coughed and spoke to his client directly. 'Doctor sahib, it would be better if we discussed this later....'

'Sabharwal sent me a video of my son,' the old man continued. 'He wanted thirty lakhs, or else he would release it to the press.'

'If your son meant nothing to you, why would it matter?' I responded.

'Have you seen the video?' Vaidya asked, his jaw clenched.

'Yes,' I replied. 'One of them.'

I could now see the anxiety behind his gaze.

'It would have been used against me,' he said, 'to discredit my work. Personally, I could care less if my son humiliated himself, but my company represents traditional values. This would have given people a reason to criticize our message of well-being and good health.'

'Then why didn't you pay Reuben? Thirty lakhs is not a lot of money for someone like you,' I said.

'I didn't trust him,' said Vaidya. 'He would have given me copies of the video but kept the originals for himself.'

'Is that why you sent Rita here to negotiate with him?' I asked.

Vaidya gazed at one of the stones on his left hand.

'Who showed you the video?' he asked. 'Was it the police?'

I didn't answer for a few seconds and then shrugged.

'It was on your son's phone,' I said.

'And where is the phone?' he demanded, a hint of anger breaking through the cold, ruthless demeanour.

'All of the evidence has been sealed,' I replied. 'It will only be made public once the case goes to court.'

'Nonsense,' Ghorpade said. 'The police must share the evidence with us. Did Inspector Thapliyal forward a copy of the video to you?'

I smiled at him without answering to let them draw their own conclusions.

'Carmichael,' Vaidya said after a minute of silence had passed. 'You haven't answered my first question. Why are you interfering in this case?'

'Curiosity, perhaps,' I said and then added, 'as well as a sense of duty.'

'Duty?' said Vaidya, sarcastically.

'Once a policeman, always a policeman,' I answered.

'But you are retired. Nobody is paying you to investigate this murder,' he persisted.

I shook my head, wondering briefly if I really had an answer to his question.

'Not everyone needs to be paid to do what is right and just,' I said, though my words sounded hollow and meaningless.

'I will pay you thirty lakhs to bring me that phone,' said Vaidya, after another pause. Every syllable he uttered was tinged with venom.

'Why would you trust me?' I said.

'Because I've been told you are an honest man,' he answered.

'Then why would you try to bribe me?' I said.

'Everyone has a price,' Vaidya murmured, looking away towards the mountains beyond the window.

∞

When I eventually got home to Thornfield, I found I had an unexpected visitor. Badlu had grudgingly allowed her into the house and Rita was seated in the sun room. She rose from her chair as I entered.

'This is a surprise,' I said. 'Have you been waiting long?'

'Half an hour,' she said, glancing at the slim gold watchband on her wrist.

Today she was dressed in a sari again, pale green chiffon.

'What can I do for you?' I asked.

'I'm sorry I got upset the other night,' she said. 'I shouldn't have walked out on you.'

'Perhaps I should have been more sensitive,' I said. 'I'm sure this has been a difficult time for you.'

She turned and looked at me with an earnest expression on her face.

'No, you have every reason to be suspicious of me,' she said. 'I'd like to explain.'

I gestured for her to sit down and she dropped into the chair with relief, as if the tension between us had suddenly eased.

'Before you say anything,' I warned her. 'You should know that I'm coming from the Aranya Nivas Ashram, where I met Dr Vaidya and his advocate.'

She gave a disinterested smile.

'Did they tell you I've been sacked?' Rita asked.

I nodded. 'Were you surprised by that?'

'No,' she replied. 'Dr Vaidya is a ruthless man. All he cares about are his traditional values and the bottom line.'

'I got that sense. He is a cold fish,' I said.

'Exactly,' she replied, with a laugh. 'I've always thought of him as a frozen prawn.' Then, seeing the puzzled look on my face, Rita added, '*Pran* Vaidya.'

'Ah,' I said, surprised at the joke. 'I hope they gave you a generous severance package.'

'No,' she said. 'That isn't his style. I was paid what I was due but not a paisa more and they threatened me with a libel case if I spoke to anyone about the work I did for him and his company.'

'So, that's why you came to see me,' I said.

'I'm not afraid of him,' she said. 'Public relations is a bit like a laundry service. You try to bleach out the stains but it doesn't always work.'

At this point Badlu appeared carrying the tea tray and he glanced at me with disapproval for entertaining Rita.

'So, why exactly did he hire you?' I asked, after the cook had gone.

'To deal with my brother, mostly,' she said. 'His son, Kunal, had fallen under Reuben's spell. Vaidya wanted me to get him out of there and cover up whatever scandal might emerge.'

'He told me that he had nothing to do with his son,' I said.

'That isn't true. Kunal was the only person Vaidya cared about. Everyone else, he treated like dirt—his wife, his other children....'

'How many others are there?'

'A daughter and the youngest son. Kunal was the eldest. His first-born favourite,' she said.

'That's not what he told me,' I said.

'He's lying,' Rita insisted. 'Vaidya spoiled him silly and like all spoiled brats, Kunal rebelled against his father and did everything he could to embarrass and humiliate him.'

'What did Reuben have to say about him?' I asked.

'He was cynical as usual,' she said. 'He encouraged Kunal to get money from his father to pay for whatever drugs they used.'

'And what did you say to Reuben?' I asked.

Rita watched me pour a cup of tea for her.

'I told him that Vaidya would pay him whatever he asked for, as long as he agreed not to have anything more to do with the old man's son,' she said. 'There was also a video that Reuben took of Kunal fooling around.'

'You mean having oral sex with another man,' I said.

She raised her plucked eyebrows. 'You've seen it?'

'Yes, I have,' I said.

'Reuben was trying to extort thirty lakhs. He'd sent a copy to Dr Vaidya,' said Rita. 'Threatening to give it to the press.'

'So, what happened?' I said.

'My brother wasn't a reasonable man. He needed the money, desperately,' said Rita, 'But at the same time, he calculated that he could get much more. I tried to talk him out of it but he wanted a crore.'

'Would Vaidya have agreed to pay him that much?' I asked.

'Not all at once. I was told to negotiate staggered payments over a period of five years, as long as Reuben threw Kunal out of his house and had nothing more to do with him,' Rita explained. 'He also had to give us the phone.'

'Did he agree?' I asked.

'Yes. We argued about it but in the end, he accepted Vaidya's offer.'

I waited a moment, stirring a spoon of sugar into my tea before adding milk.

'And what did B. K. Ghosh have to do with all of this?' I asked.

'B. K. was working on promotional videos for the Ayurvedic Wellness Centre. You know, those glossy biopics celebrating the vision and leadership of the CEO.' said Rita. 'B. K. is very good at making everything look nice.'

'Ghosh told me that he was going to pay Reuben fifty thousand rupees the day before he was killed,' I said. 'He gave me some cock and bull story about your brother suddenly discovering that he had two hundred thousand followers on the internet and wanting a share of the profits.'

Rita hesitated for a fraction of a second, then nodded. 'Yes, Reuben was insisting on getting some cash. Vaidya wouldn't give him anything until he got the phone, so I persuaded B. K. to pay him something. Earnest money, I suppose. But then, he died that night.'

'What about Reuben's podcasts? Were you serious about those?'

'That was all B. K.'s idea,' she said. 'I couldn't imagine why anyone would want to listen to Reuben ranting on about spirituality.'

'But it seems he said things that some people wanted to hear,' I said.

'Yes, I suppose,' Rita agreed. 'But I'm not sure it would have succeeded in the long term. Reuben himself thought it was a joke.'

Twenty-four

At night, the goat was kept locked up inside the wood godown at the back of the house. I had put down some straw for bedding and made sure there was a bowl of fresh water. We kept the animal tied, even with the door closed, because he was still intent on escape. Aside from the grass in the lawn, which the goat had grudgingly cropped, Badlu fed him vegetable peels and other kitchen scraps. I too offered him some of the cuttings from the garden as a treat. In his own belligerent way, the goat had grown used to my presence and even nuzzled my hand when I reached out to pet him.

After Rita departed, I settled down to read for a while, simply to take my mind off the case. There is always a point when you begin to overthink a problem and it's necessary to clear your mind. Reading for me is a form of meditation and I am always happy to escape into a good book. Having finished *Burmese Days*, I chose another old favourite, Jean Rhys's *Wide Sargasso Sea*. It's a slender volume in which the author retells the story of Mrs Rochester, the mad wife in *Jane Eyre*, reconstructing her past, growing up in the West Indies, where Rhys herself was raised. The associations with Thornfield have always added significance for me.

The novel was short enough to finish by 10 p.m. As I set the book aside and began to switch off lights in preparation for bed, I suddenly heard a commotion outside, coming from the direction of the wood godown. It sounded as if the door was being rattled and I heard the goat bleating anxiously.

My first thought was of a leopard that had been prowling the hillside in recent weeks. It had carried off a couple of dogs and killed a cow near the dhobi ghat. Hurrying to my bedroom, I picked up a torch and my revolver. The quickest route outside was through the kitchen. From there I set off in the direction of the godown. By this time, all sounds had stopped, and I flashed the torch across the yard, seeing nothing beyond the pale blue blossoms on a hydrangea bush. Turning the corner of the house, I expected to see the leopard's gleaming eyes staring at me in the torchlight. The pistol was fully loaded, and my thumb was on the safety catch.

But there was no sign of the predator and as I shone the light on the godown door, I could see that it was still locked. Just then, I heard a sound to my left and turning, I spotted a figure running up the path. The mist diffused the torch beam and all I could see was the back of a man disappearing into the moist shadows. Instinctively, I called out for the intruder to stop but by then he was already fifty metres up the path. There was no point in giving chase.

After waiting a minute or more, I went across to inspect the door and found that whoever it was had wrenched off part of the hasp, though he hadn't been able to free it completely and the lock was intact. When I shone the torch through a crack in the door, the goat bleated at me with a plaintive but healthy cry.

At that point, it began to rain lightly and I retreated indoors, wondering who might have tried to steal the goat. Badlu obviously hadn't heard me call out and I figured there wasn't much chance that the thief would return. For an hour or so I lay in bed listening, but the only sound was the soft spattering of rain on the roof. The revolver and torch remained by my bedside but, eventually, I drifted off to sleep and my dreams were a strange combination of images from the book, banana trees, and coconut palms combined with panthers prowling through a burning house.

※

Six hours later, I woke up to a pounding on the kitchen door as faint streaks of dawn filtered through a gap in the curtains. For a moment, I was disoriented as I emerged from sleep, realizing that I had gone to bed fully dressed. Picking up the revolver, I thought better of it and replaced it in the bedside drawer before going out to see who was at the door.

Badlu was there, along with Pintu, the Darcys's driver. On opening the door, I was informed that Gerry had died of a heart attack sometime in the night. Vinny had sent the driver across to ask for my help. The shock of this news woke me up completely and I told Pintu that I would be ready to leave in a few minutes. Returning to my room, I remembered my last conversation with Gerry and tried to reconcile myself to his death, though as I put on a fresh shirt and combed my hair, I felt a combination of sadness and disbelief.

Pintu had brought the Darcys's car to the turnaround point and drove me across to Xanadu. On the way, I asked him a few questions to which he had no answers, saying that the memsahib had woken him up less than half an hour ago.

The front door of the house was ajar and I hurried inside, calling out Vinny's name. She replied from the bedroom. 'In here.'

When I stepped through the door, I could see that Gerry was in bed with the covers pulled up to his shoulders. His face was turned towards me, and his mouth was open, as if he were about to speak. Vinny was sitting in a chair to one side, wearing a dressing gown and looking at me with a lost expression. Going across to her, I put my hand on her shoulder and could feel her shaking.

'Oh, Lionel....' she said, reaching up to grab my arm.

'What happened?' I said.

'He must have gone early this morning,' she said. 'I woke up about five, feeling something was wrong. When I switched on the light, I found him like that.'

I went across to the bed and looked down at his face. There was obviously no need to check for a pulse and in the light from the bedside lamp, his skin was as white as his hair and beard. Gerry's blue eyes were staring straight ahead. Reaching down, I closed the lids and then brushed my hand over his shoulder beneath the blanket in a helpless, futile gesture.

Unlike the scene of the murder at Shambles there was a peaceful quality to this death, as if it had happened so naturally there was nothing anyone could do but accept the stillness and inevitable silence that awaits us all at the end of our lives.

Turning back to Vinny, I saw she had risen from her chair and instinctively I put my arms around her and we held each other for several long minutes. She was weeping softly and I could feel her body shuddering with emotion until, at last, she pulled away and wiped her eyes.

'Gerry always said he wanted to die in his sleep,' she said.

'If you've got to go, it's the best way, I suppose,' I said. 'Last time we spoke, he said he was suffering from angina.'

Vinny nodded and looked away out the window, where sunlight was spilling through the wisteria vines.

'Is your telephone working?' I asked. 'We'll need to make arrangements for a funeral. Did he ever tell you what he wanted, a cremation or a burial?'

'Burial, I think. He never went to church but he used to say that he'd been baptized as a boy,' she said, with a wan smile.

'I'll call Reverend Isaac, as well as Dr Manchanda,' I said. 'We'll need to arrange for the paperwork.'

'Thank you, Lionel,' she said. 'I didn't know who else to call.'

―

There is a lot of wisdom in the tradition of getting a body into the ground before sunset. Debrakot has no facilities for embalming and in Gerry's case, he had obviously died of natural causes, so there was no need for a police inquiry. He had two children from a previous marriage, one of whom was in Australia and the other in America. Vinny found phone numbers for each them and asked me to call, which I did. Both children were understandably upset by the news but agreed that there was no need to delay the funeral on their account.

Reverend Isaac arranged to hold a service in St. John's at 4 p.m., immediately followed by the burial. Unlike Reuben, there seemed to be no question that Gerry could claim his two metres of sanctified ground, even if he wasn't a member of the congregation. More than once, he had confided in me that he was a non-believer. Word spread quickly around the hillside and almost all of the neighbours came by the house, offering to help in whatever way they could. Vinny put on a brave face and greeted everyone with affection, accepting the condolences and words of sympathy with a composed expression of grief.

The church service was short and formal, with a prescribed litany of Bible readings and hymns. Reverend Isaac was wearing a long white cassock with a red stole. The coffin maker had produced a box, covered this time in black satin with a large white cross nailed on top. I knew that if Gerry had been sitting beside me, he would have made a remark about the 'dubba' as he liked to call it. Komal Rao and Mrs Chopra had taken on the task of attending to Vinny, never leaving her side, and I was happy to retreat three rows back to the pew that my mother always sat in. Listening to the prayers and the words of reassurance and salvation, I couldn't help thinking of the prayer room at Shambles and the occult rituals that Reuben performed. In a sense, it was all the same thing—an attempt to understand the ultimate mysteries of mortality and act out a forlorn hope that death was not the final full stop on the page but only a semicolon that permitted us to believe in the possibility of an afterlife.

The same team of Nepali labourers had dug the grave and after the service we all trooped down behind the coffin. There was some delay at the last minute, as Reverend Isaac had forgotten his prayer book in the church and one of the young men from the congregation was sent back up the hill to fetch it.

To my surprise, I found Geeta Arjunsingh standing beside me. She has always treated me with a certain amount of reproachful disdain, perhaps because my mother was unsuccessful in persuading me to show any interest in her, though I may be flattering myself with that explanation. In any case, she has a severe, judgemental manner and I sensed that she wanted to give me a piece of her mind.

'Lionel,' she hissed, under her breath.

'Yes,' I whispered back.

'Is it true that you're planning to sacrifice a goat?' Geeta asked.

Given the circumstances, with a hushed gathering waiting by the graveside for the prayer book to arrive, I didn't have much choice but to nod silently, without trying to provide any justification.

'How could you be so cruel and heartless?' Geeta continued with anger in her eyes. 'Haven't you ever heard of animal rights?'

'Of course,' I whispered. 'I'll explain...a little later.'

'Shameless. Disgusting,' she said. 'Your mother would have been horrified!'

Of course, my mother was resting peacefully on the terrace above us, and I felt that Geeta had taken a cheap shot, invoking her presence.

'It's not what you think,' I said, conscious that others were now looking in our direction, curious to know what was being said.

Just then, I was saved by the young man who came bounding down the slope with the Book of Common Prayer in one hand. Geeta retreated a couple of steps, as if consciously distancing herself from me. I've always known that she is an ardent proponent of animal rights and has taken up the cause of stray dogs, cats, ponies, mules, monkeys, etc. All of these are noble, compassionate causes, but I had a murder to solve, and the thought crossed my mind that perhaps Geeta had something to do with the man who had tried to steal my goat.

Meanwhile, Reverend Isaac started the graveside service and within a few minutes I heard the familiar refrain '...we therefore commit this body to the ground, earth to earth, ashes to ashes, dust to dust....'

Throughout the day, I'd held my grief in check, but Gerry was now being lowered into the pit. Each of us tossed a fistful of earth on to the coffin as a gesture of farewell. As I did this, I was surprised to find there were tears in my eyes and I tried to take a deep breath that caught in my throat. Retreating from the grave, I quickly escaped, not wanting anyone to see me weeping. Hurrying back up the hill, I left the other mourners to follow at their own pace.

Twenty-five

The drumbeats sounded like a stampede of hooves galloping across the mountains. Charan Das led our procession with his dhol, the two-sided drum, suspended from a shoulder strap. In his right hand he held a stick with which he beat a rapid tempo. The open palm of his left hand produced a slower, pulsing rhythm. The drumming echoed across the valley and set the pace as we headed down the path from Thornfield, leading to the Devta's temple.

I had the goat on a rope, which was doubled up and looped through a collar around his neck. Happy to be free from the confinement of the yard and godown, the animal frisked back and forth in front of me, stopping occasionally to snatch a mouthful of leaves from the side of the path. It was eight o'clock in the morning when we left the house and there were nine of us altogether. Charan Das's daughter accompanied him, walking quietly behind her father. Badlu had reluctantly agreed to come along. His wife, son, and daughter-in-law decided to join us too, as much out of curiosity as any sense of devotion. Two other men who'd been at the jagran arrived with Charan Das and one of them had tied a red scarf trimmed with gold tinsel around the goat's neck.

Half a kilometre beyond Thornfield, at the point where we joined the old mule track, several others were waiting to accompany us to the temple, mostly hillmen, as well B. K. Ghosh, who had a cameraman and audio technician with him to film the sacrifice. Earlier in the morning, Raipal had come by the house to deliver milk before we left and he had promised to circle back as quickly as possible, after making his rounds of the hillside. He said that Suraj would meet us at the temple, where one of the pundits from their village had agreed to perform a puja.

It was a bright morning, with only a few traces of clouds in the sky, and I was now convinced that the monsoon was actually in retreat. The air was clear, with a nip to the breeze, and the young goat seemed to be kicking up his heels as we went along. A little further on, when we started uphill, the drumbeats changed, slowing the pace slightly. Where the trail narrowed, we walked single file along the gravel track. Overhead, a griffon vulture was wheeling on the thermals and I wondered if the bird had sensed that our little procession would end in death.

B. K. had caught up with me and asked, out of breath, 'How much farther?'

'Haven't you been to the temple before?' I replied.

'No,' he said. 'I hadn't heard about it, until you told me.'

'Another kilometre or so,' I said. 'Has Rita left?'

'She drove down to Delhi yesterday,' he said. 'Have you crossed her off your list of suspects?'

I looked at him with a questioning glance, as the goat pulled at the rope, tossing its head in an attempt to get free.

'Let's see,' I responded, with a vague gesture. 'This sacrifice is supposed to reveal something.'

'Do you actually believe it will work?' said B. K. 'I thought you were a sceptic when it came to these sorts of things.'

'I am a sceptic,' I said. 'But I also believe in the power of suggestion. You can never rule out how a person's actions will be influenced by faith or superstition.'

The path had grown steeper and B. K. fell silent, though I could hear him panting for breath. A few minutes later, where the path levelled out, he spoke again.

'It was sad about Gerry,' he said. 'I saw you at the funeral yesterday.'

'Yes, very sudden,' I replied.

'What do you think Vinny will do?'

'It's hard to say,' I answered. 'Most of her family are back in England.'

'She has her friends here,' he continued. 'But living on her own....'

'It's not easy,' I said, 'especially, after twenty-five years of marriage.'

'At least he died peacefully,' said B. K.

I didn't bother to answer as we carried on to a fork in the path, where we headed up on to the shoulder of the ridge at the end of which lay the temple. From here we got our first view of the snow peaks. The high Himalayas were swaddled in clouds, but the white summits poked through, jutting up against the blue sky.

A few minutes later, when we arrived at the temple, I could see a cluster of villagers gathered near the shrine. Suraj was among them though he sat by himself, to one side. Charan Das paused when we came in sight of the temple and he beat the drum even louder, as if to rouse the deities from their celestial slumber. B. K. had gone ahead to supervise the camera crew. I didn't know exactly what to expect as we crossed the open field and arrived at the flagstone courtyard that skirted the temple. One of the men blew a conch and the priest rang the brass bell suspended above the portal of the shrine.

The goat was not impressed and looked about with a petulant gaze as the drumming finally ceased and several of the men stepped forward to touch the threshold of the temple and then fold their hands in obeisance. The priest had begun the puja, with a tray of offerings including a coconut, puffed rice, sweets, and a smouldering cone of incense. On a low stone platform, to one side of the temple, I noticed a large paathal, its broad steel blade freshly sharpened.

At that moment, my phone buzzed. It was in my shirt pocket, and I had switched off the annoying ringtone. Taking the phone out, I saw a message from Thapliyal, asking where I was. Typing with one finger, while trying to restrain the goat on its lead, I kept my reply short: 'At temple. All well.'

By now there were about twenty-five people altogether. My eyes were soon fixed on Suraj, who had risen to his feet and was standing with his arms folded across his chest. He did not look in my direction but seemed to be watching the priest with a troubled expression. Though he had agreed to behead the goat, I could tell that he was having second thoughts about performing the sacrifice.

Meanwhile, I could see that Charan Das's daughter, who'd sat down at the edge of the courtyard when we arrived, was back on her feet again, circling the temple with a shambling gait. At that moment, I saw Suraj reach into his pocket and take out his mobile.

He had obviously received a message and, as I watched, he studied the device in his hands with an intent and anxious look. I was about fifteen metres away and started to move in his direction. The goat came with me, tugging at the rope.

I could see the look of panic on Suraj's face, as he put the phone back in his pocket and our eyes met for a moment. Retreating a step backwards, he turned and took off running across the open field towards the forest on the north side of the ridge. He looked as if he was being chased by a swarm of bees.

At the same moment, I let one end of the rope slip free and the goat was released. The startled animal looked back at me for a second and then bolted. Three men in the crowd set off after it with shouts of dismay, which only made the goat run faster. Dashing across the open field, in the opposite direction from where Suraj had gone, it soon reached a rocky outcropping and darted up the crags, pausing briefly at the top and then disappearing out of sight. Seeing that any further pursuit was pointless, the men who were following the goat gave up and turned back. Meanwhile, the rest of the crowd looked at me with surprise and confusion as I gathered the loose rope into a coil and tried to look as perplexed and disappointed as everyone else.

Though the sacrificial offering and its executioner had both fled, the priest completed the puja and the ceremonies ended in an anticlimax. I left a generous offering at the shrine, mostly to placate the pundit who daubed my forehead with a vermilion tika.

'What happened?' B. K. demanded in a baffled voice, as we headed back home. 'Why did that boy run away?'

'Who knows?' I said, 'Maybe he has a guilty conscience.'

'And how did the goat get free?'

'My clumsiness,' I said with a smile. 'I should have held it more tightly.'

Seeing the look on my face he said, 'You let it go on purpose!'

'Of course, I did,' I said.

'But why?' he asked.

'Because it had served its purpose,' I said. 'Haven't you ever heard of a scapegoat?'

From his expression it was obvious that he didn't know what I was talking about, so I explained. 'In the Old Testament in the book of Leviticus, the Jews were admonished by god to set aside one day of every year to atone for their sins. On that day, two goats were brought to the altar and lots were drawn. One of the animals was sacrificed while the other was released into the wilderness, carrying away with it all of the sins and transgressions of the tribe.'

B. K. shook his head. 'I still don't understand.'

'Never mind,' I said.

A short while later, when we rejoined the mule track, I saw Raipal Singh hurrying up the trail towards us carrying his empty milk cans.

'Is it over already?' he asked

I nodded and then explained how the goat had got loose and escaped. He shook his head in dismay. 'It's a bad sign,' he said.

'Perhaps,' I responded. 'But your son also ran away.'

'What for?' he said, further confused.

'I don't know,' I said, 'When you see him, tell him that if he doesn't come to my house by eight o'clock tomorrow morning, I'll send the police to get him.'

⁂

Three days earlier, I had gone to see Savitri. This time, I'd made sure that Charan Das was there as well. By then, the goat had been delivered to my house and the date for the sacrifice was set. When I had asked him, Charan Das happily agreed to lead the procession with his drum and Savitri said she would come as well, though she had no memory of the jagran, and the goddess' demand for a sacrifice.

'Do you know Raipal Singh's son, Suraj?' I had asked.

'Yes, he sometimes delivers milk,' said Charan Das.

'Was he friendly with Reuben?' Holding up a hand, I indicated that I wanted Savitri to answer.

After a pause, she confirmed that he had come to Shambles two or three times on different occasions, along with some of the other young men.

'Was he a devotee of Reuben's?'

'I don't know,' she'd said.

'Did he come to the house on the night of the murder?'

She'd then looked at her father, as if unwilling to speak.

'Go ahead,' Charan Das had said. 'Tell the DIG sahib what you know.'

'Usually, I work only in the mornings, but sometimes Bhagwan would call me down in the afternoon, if there was extra work,' she explained. 'That day I went to wash some clothes for him and when I entered the kitchen, Kunal and Suraj were sitting, having tea and smoking. Suraj seemed embarrassed to see me and after a few minutes they went inside. That's all I know.'

'And this was the day before the murder?' I confirmed.

'Yes,' she'd said. 'I don't know what happened after that. The next morning, when I came to clean up, that's when I found the bodies....'

She shuddered at the memory of what she'd seen.

'Do you think Suraj had anything to do with their deaths?' I'd asked.

'I don't know.'

'Was Reuben with him and Kunal?'

'Bhagwan wasn't in the kitchen,' she answered, 'He was probably inside.'

'Was anyone else there?'

Savitri shook her head.

'What about a woman? She was arguing with Reuben outside,' I said.

'That was earlier in the day. I didn't see her but I heard them shouting,' Savitri replied.

I asked her a few more questions though it was obvious that she had no further knowledge of what had taken place.

'Suraj is an innocent boy,' said Charan Das. 'He isn't capable of murder.'

'Are you sure?' I said. 'He agreed to sacrifice the goat....'

'But that is different,' the old chowkidar said, shaking his head. 'Killing a goat as a sacrifice is a ritual act, but stabbing a person to death.... I've known Suraj since he was a young boy and I can't believe he did it.'

'He disappeared for three days after the murder and claimed he had gone to Landsdowne to try and join the army,' I said.

I watched Charan Singh's reaction when I told him this and it was obvious that he knew nothing about it.

'But why would he have killed them?' the chowkidar said in disbelief.

'That's what I'm trying to find out,' I said. 'Did you know that the woman who was arguing with Reuben was his sister?'

Charan Das nodded.

'Yes, but I didn't know this at the time, only later,' he said. 'That day I thought she was one of his followers.'

'Did you hear what they were arguing about?' I asked.

'No,' he said. 'They were speaking in English.'

'Nobody else came to the house that day?'

Charan Das thought for a moment.

'I don't remember,' he said, 'with everything that's been happening.... People were always coming and going from the house, but that day.... I don't think anyone came by, except Suraj.'

Through all of this, Savitri had remained silent, staring at the ground with a dazed, bewildered look.

'Do you think the Devi will tell us the truth?' I asked.

'Of course. Whoever committed the murders, we will find out,' Charan Das replied with complete confidence.

Twenty-six

In the afternoon, following the events at the temple, I went across to Xanadu, and called on Vinny. I hadn't spoken to her at Gerry's funeral and felt I needed to ask her if there was anything more that I could do to help. When I arrived, she was sitting on the veranda with Geeta Arjunsingh. I could see that Vinny had been crying but she gave me a cheerful smile despite her teary eyes. Without her make-up she looked younger and more vulnerable. Geeta, on the other hand, met me with a stern scowl of disdain.

'Lionel, what is this I hear about you conducting an animal sacrifice?' said Vinny, after I had kissed her on the cheek.

I shrugged. 'It was part of my investigation.'

Vinny exchanged a glance with Geeta, as I sat down on one of the cane chairs.

'What are you talking about?' she asked.

Looking at Geeta, I replied, 'There was no sacrifice. I let the goat go free.'

'Thank God,' said Vinny. 'I thought you'd lost your mind.'

'The poor animal must have been traumatized,' said Geeta.

'Not really,' I said. 'The goat had no idea what was going on and it was well fed. By now it's probably found its way home to the village.'

'I still don't understand what all of this had to do with Reuben's murder,' said Vinny. 'Have you solved the crime?'

'Not yet,' I said. 'But I'm getting closer.'

'And, of course, you won't tell us anything,' said Vinny. 'Why do you have to be so mysterious?'

'I don't mean to be,' I said, then changed the subject. 'Anyway, I just came by to see how you're doing and ask if I can help in any way.'

Vinny closed her eyes for a moment, and I saw the grief return to her face. Geeta reached out and put a comforting hand on her arm.

'I'll be fine,' said Vinny, after taking a deep breath. 'It's just so hard to accept the fact that Gerry's gone. You live with someone for twenty-five years and it becomes a routine, then all at once, you're on your own.... Honestly, I don't know what I'm going to do. There's a part of me that just wants to run away from here. I spoke to my sister in London and she wants me to come stay with her for a bit. At the same time, I don't want to leave.'

'Well, you shouldn't let it overwhelm you,' I said. 'Take your time....'

'And all of us are here to help you,' Geeta added.

'Of course,' said Vinny, a tear trickling down her cheek. 'Thank you. I'm so grateful to Lionel. Yesterday morning, I didn't know what to do. Then he arrived and took charge and handled all the arrangements, such a practical, sensible man.'

'I suppose that comes from being a policeman,' said Geeta, without looking at me. 'They know all of the correct procedures.'

'I haven't done anything,' I said. 'But I did want to ask if, perhaps, we should inform the High Commission in Delhi. Both of you are British subjects and I'm sure they can help sort out whatever formalities are required. I can also deal with the Foreigner's Registration Office.'

'Of course,' said Vinny. 'Bureaucracy! It never ends.'

'I'll just need to get a copy of Gerry's passport,' I said.

She nodded.

'He kept it in the upper right-hand drawer of his desk, in his study,' said Vinny. 'Would you mind getting it? Mine's there too, if you need it.'

I rose from my chair and went to the front door, which was open. Stepping into the drawing room I remembered arriving the day before and seeing Gerry in bed, his mouth open and the lifeless blue eyes staring into space.

His study was at the back of the house and up a flight of stairs. I knew the way. Gerry and I would often sit there, talking about whatever seemed interesting or important at the time—politics, books, religion. The room was exactly as I remembered it, afternoon sunlight slanting through a large window that overlooked the garden. Two of the walls were lined with bookshelves and there was a laptop open on the desk, as well as a copy of Monier–Williams's *Sanskrit–English Dictionary* and a sheaf of papers that looked like the printout of a manuscript.

Never having been in the study when Gerry wasn't there, I felt like an intruder. His absence was palpable in the hollow stillness of the room, an empty coffee mug sitting on a side table near the window, the framed paintings on the walls, including a Kangra miniature of Krishna playing his flute. A number of objects had been carefully placed on the shelves, a round copper jar, engraved with Devanagri script, a pine cone picked up on a walk, and a collection of blue and green jars. There were a few photographs too, including one of Vinny at their wedding, wearing a sari. The odour of paper and ink filled the room. Gerry had carefully curated the space, surrounding himself with everything that mattered to him.

'The Orientalist in his lair!' He used to proclaim, with a mixture of irony and pride. I could almost hear his voice.

'Do you know what an Indologist is?' Gerry had asked me once, when we were sitting in this room. From his expression I knew what was coming.

'No, tell me, what's an Indologist, Gerry?' I asked, playing along with the joke.

'Somebody who's an expert on indolence!' he'd replied with a laugh.

I hesitated before pulling open the desk drawer and finding the passports neatly tucked into one corner, with the royal crest stamped on the covers. Checking, I opened one and saw Gerry's photograph staring back at me with an amused look in his eyes. Vinny's passport was there too. In her photograph she had longer hair and wasn't wearing glasses. I put both passports in my pocket and closed the drawer.

Taking a last look around the room, I wondered what would become of his library, most of which were arcane tomes on classical Indian literature and spirituality, a lifetime of intellectual inquiry that now seemed bereft of any meaning beyond the rank and file of books on a shelf. And then, as I was about to leave, something else caught my eye and made me freeze. On an upper bookshelf, in a gap between the leatherbound spines of encyclopaedias and a stack of notebooks, stood the alabaster statue of Anubis.

It was exactly as Rita had described it. The stone had a creamy lustre and streaky patterns like pale toffee. She'd told me that she remembered it from when she was a child and the statue had always fascinated her. I had to lean over one corner of the desk and stretch out my arm to reach it. The smooth, polished shape felt cold in my grasp, as I took the statue down and studied the workmanship. The jackal's features were delicately carved, with intricate detail, but the rest of the image was stylized, an elongated body that seemed to conform to the natural shape of the rock. The forepaws too were expertly fashioned and Anubis was seated with his tail tucked to one side, atop a small, square pedestal.

Carrying the statue out on to the veranda, I asked Vinny how they'd got it.

'Oh, that! Gerry bought it from Reuben,' she said. 'Not too long ago.'

'Do you know what he paid for it?' I asked.

'No idea,' she replied. 'You can have it, Lionel, if you'd like. When Gerry told me what it was...something to do with Egyptian tombs and mummies, it gave me the creeps. You're welcome to take it.'

'Are you sure?' I said, 'It's not for myself. Reuben's sister was looking for this and if it's all right with you, I'll send it to her.'

'Please do,' said Vinny. 'She's welcome to have it.'

∞

Suraj didn't show up the following morning but when Raipal Singh delivered milk to the house, he swore that his son would come to see me soon and begged me not to send the police to their village.

'Is he at home?' I asked.

'Yes, but what has he done?' the milkman asked, a worried look on his face.

'He could be in a lot of trouble,' I warned him, 'unless he comes to me and explains himself. I need to talk to him.'

'Is it about the murders?' Raipal asked.

'Yes,' I said. 'Did you know that your son was spending time at Shambala Villa with Reuben and his devotees?'

He shook his head and looked down at his feet.

'All he told me was that Reuben had promised to get him a job in Delhi,' said Raipal. 'Suraj believed him, though it was all a lie.'

'What kind of job?' I asked.

'I don't know. In some company,' said Raipal. 'He built up his hopes but in the end there was nothing....'

'I'll wait another day,' I said. 'But if he isn't here by tomorrow, the police will come to your house and arrest him.'

Our conversation took place in the garden, out of earshot of Badlu, who was watching from the kitchen window. When I came inside, the cook gave me a questioning glance.

'What is it?' I demanded, knowing that he had something on his mind.

'You are wasting your time with these people,' he said. 'They will never tell you the truth.'

'Why do you say that?' I asked.

'Because they are simple, uneducated fools,' he said. 'They don't trust anybody and nobody can trust them. That's how it is in the hills. This whole business about the jagran and the sacrifice, it's nonsense. You spent a thousand rupees on that goat and it's gone... just like that....'

He made a gesture, as if snapping his fingers to show that I was left empty-handed.

'Perhaps,' I said. 'Do you think I should have chopped off its head?'

'It wouldn't have proved anything,' said Badlu.

'So, what's the difference?' I said. 'I learned more by letting the goat go, than I would have done if it had been killed.'

He gave me a puzzled look. 'What did you learn?'

'We'll see....' I said.

Just then, Thapliyal showed up, with two constables in tow. Signalling for his men to wait outside, he followed me into the drawing room.

'You'll have some tea this time?' I said.

He tried to refuse but I insisted and went to tell Badlu to make it in a degchi with milk and sugar, enough for the two constables as well as us. When I returned to the room, Thapliyal was studying his mobile phone.

'There is no signal here,' he said.

'I know,' I replied. 'Not only is my landline dead but if I want to make a call on my mobile, I have to walk halfway up the path. That's why I never use it.'

'What would you do in an emergency?' he asked, with a worried look.

'I suppose, I'd just wait for the police to show up,' I said.

He shook his head with disapproval and disbelief.

'So, what brings you here today?' I asked.

'Unfortunate news,' said Thapliyal. 'This morning I got word that Deepak Kanojia died of a drug overdose.'

'You're sure of that?' I asked.

'Yes, his body was found yesterday. It seems he'd been dead for several days. Someone alerted the police because of the smell.'

'Were you able to trace any of the calls he made before he died?' I asked. 'Was he in touch with anyone about the murders?'

'No, the only calls he made were to a local drug dealer,' said Thapliyal. 'The Najibabad Police identified the number.'

'Do you think it was an accidental overdose? Or intentional...a suicide?'

'It's impossible to know. There will be a post-mortem report but I doubt if it will tell us much,' said Thapliyal, 'Either way, I suppose he killed himself.'

Twenty-seven

I had been reading by the fireplace in the drawing room, and was about to go to bed, when I heard a hesitant knock at the kitchen door. It was half-past ten. Badlu had gone home, after clearing the dining table and washing the dishes. Earlier in the day, when Thapliyal had come to see me with the news about Deepak Kanojia, we'd agreed that I would accompany the police party to Ranglana the next morning. Despite messages I'd sent through his father, Suraj hadn't shown up to turn himself in. It would be a long walk to the village, but I felt a responsibility to be there when the boy was arrested, partly to gauge his reaction but also to make sure the constables didn't beat him up in the process.

The kitchen lay in darkness but a bulb on the veranda outside was burning and dozens of moths were flitting about, attracted to the light. Peering out the side window, I couldn't see anyone at the door and I wondered if the sound I'd heard might have been a bird foraging in the rain gutters or wind blowing a magnolia branch that tapped against the windowpane. But the night was still and there was no sign of any movement outdoors. Beyond the circle of light that extended to the edge of the flower beds, I could see nothing at all.

Unbolting the door, I pushed it open, along with the outer screen. It was a cool, clear night. A pygmy owlet was calling somewhere in the forest below, a pulsing sound, as if someone were blowing the same four notes on a flute, again and again. Through the branches of oaks at the edge of the yard, I could see the glittering lights of the town in the distance. Moths fluttered about my head.

Suddenly, I sensed that I was in danger but before I could turn around, an arm encircled my neck in a choke hold, as someone tackled me from behind. Caught off balance, my knees buckled under me, and I fell heavily on to the concrete floor. Though I tried to call for help, the wind had been knocked out of my lungs and all I could utter was a breathless curse. Of course, I should have had my revolver with me, but it wouldn't have been much help for my assailant pinned me to the floor and pulled my arms behind my back. I tried to struggle, though it was too late. He quickly tied my wrists together while one of his knees pressed painfully into the small of my back. Whoever it was, he'd obviously done this before. With the loose end of the rope, he tied my ankles together as well, then stuffed a rag in my mouth, so I couldn't make a sound.

Finally, when I was completely immobilized, he turned me over on to my back, so that I was staring straight up into the glare of the veranda bulb. My attacker was silhouetted against the light, his face covered by a dark blue ski mask, with three holes for his eyes and mouth. He seemed to be alone, and I tried to make a mental note of the clothes he was wearing, as well as his size and build, anything that might reveal who he was. His lightweight jacket was pale grey with a Nike logo. His jeans were faded and torn at one knee. From his strength and agility, I guessed he was in his twenties, weighing five or six kilos less than me and a few centimetres shorter, but easily capable of overpowering a sixty-four-year-old man.

He didn't seem to be carrying a weapon. Other than knocking me to the ground, the attacker didn't strike or injure me, though I knew he probably would have used more force if I had fought back. As I slowly recovered from the shock and tried to think if there was any way I might escape, he studied me for a minute with his anonymous gaze. Was he trying to decide if he should finish me off? A selection of kitchen knives lay on the counter inside, next to the stove, and if he opened the top drawer of my dressing table, he would find the revolver, fully loaded. I blamed myself for having stepped outside without taking precautions and, for a moment, felt more foolish than afraid, as the man stepped over me and entered the house.

After the initial surprise of being knocked down and hog-tied, as Americans like to say, everything seemed to slow down. Lying on the cold veranda floor, staring up at moths circling the light, I tried to imagine the man moving about inside my house, as if in slow motion, his shadow creeping across the floor and his silhouette passing through the walls like a ghost. There was no sound of footsteps and I could only guess where he might be—in my study, perhaps, or in the drawing room. The book I'd been reading lay on the coffee table, where I'd placed it face down, the pages splayed open to mark my place. I wondered if those would be the last words I'd ever read and whether he would stab me eighteen times or slit my throat. There was no reason to hang me from the ceiling, but I was already imagining the next morning, when Thapliyal would be standing in the kitchen looking down at my corpse, blood seeping from my wounds like liquid shadows.

In a perverse, irrational moment, I thought that maybe Reuben himself had returned from the dead to re-enact his murder in my home with me as the victim instead of himself. I tested the rope that bound my hands and feet, finding that the knots were secure. There was no chance of twisting my wrists free. For a moment, I remembered the goat running loose, wishing that I could do the same, yet knowing that even if I rolled over and stood up, my ankles were hobbled. Perhaps the man who had tied me up would bring a cleaver from the kitchen and chop off my head with a single, sacrificial stroke.

The owlet was still calling in the darkness, as if counting down the final seconds before my death, a syncopated, steady sound like time leaking from a dripping tap. I wondered if the intruder had entered my bedroom now and whether he would find my wallet on the dressing table. Perhaps he'd take whatever cash I had to make it look like a robbery, though I knew that wasn't his motive. He was here because of the murders at Shambles, and I felt sure he must be Reuben's killer, the same person who struck Kunal Vaidya on the back of his head, then strung him up to make it look as if he'd hanged himself. But why? What violent reasoning had brought him here? Was he afraid that I might discover his identity? Would he torture me to find out what I knew? Or would I simply die without understanding anything more, bleeding out on the floor before the case was solved.

Above me the moths orbited the bulb. Some had settled on the screen door like petals falling from withered flowers. Their shadows spun around me and the night seemed to be disintegrating on their wings, neither darkness nor light, but fragments of both, swirling around the overhead bulb, as I waited for the masked assailant to return. Would he show his face before he killed me? Or taunt me with a familiar voice? I wanted to shout, as if speaking to Gladys. I imagined her playing cards with my mother and the Tandon sisters, dealing out a hand at bridge...an ace of clubs, a jack of hearts. The moths looked like spades and diamonds.

It was like being trapped in one of those nightmares when you try to call out, either in fear or in anger, but no sound emerges from your mouth. Even if I had been able to shout, there was nobody to hear me. Badlu's quarters are a hundred metres away, beyond a stand of chestnut trees. At night, he locks himself and his family indoors with all the windows closed and shuttered. My closest neighbour is ten minutes' walk away and Thornfield lies at the end of the path, so that nobody passes this way after dark.

With my hands tied behind my back, there was no way of looking at my wristwatch and I couldn't tell how many minutes had gone by. My mind continued to prepare for death, running through everything I would leave unfinished, like the book I'd been reading this evening—a Western by Louis L'Amour, *The Man from the Broken Hills*, part of a collection of paperbacks I've kept since I was a boy. From time to time, I still read them, when I get tired of serious literature. Also, on the list that I was making in my head were repairs in the guest bathroom. For months I'd been meaning to replace the cracked sink. The last visitor I had was an old friend from Lucknow who came up for a couple of days in April. I thought of the garden going to seed. All of the mundane chores that I'd put off until now filled my thoughts as I lay there waiting for the intruder to return with a knife in his hand. They say that just before you die, your life passes in front of you, but in my case, it was only those things left unresolved, including the murders at Shambles.

A moment later, the screen door opened and the man's shadow fell across my face, blotting out the blinding light above. He looked down at me through the expressionless eyeholes of his mask. The moths seemed to have abandoned the light and the owlet had fallen silent. The door clapped shut and I tried to turn towards him, looking for the knife in his hand as he stepped over me again. All I could see was the zipper on his jacket glinting for a second and the scissor-like movement of his legs as he carried on down the two steps off the veranda before disappearing into the night.

It was all over and I had survived. The garden gate creaked, as the intruder departed, followed by silence. He was gone. I wasn't dead. The rag in my mouth tasted like mud and I tried to push it out with my tongue, though it had been wadded into my gums and cheeks. Fortunately, I could breathe through my nose.

Though I had lost track of time, my assailant couldn't have spent more than a quarter of an hour in the house. What had he been searching for? I hadn't seen anything in his hands before he left. Though I finally rolled over and got up on to my knees, it was a pointless effort because there was no way for me to stand or walk with my ankles tied. After struggling for half an hour, I gave up and lay down again. It was going to be a long night. Badlu would only show up at 8 a.m. Until now, I hadn't felt cold, except when my face or hands touched the concrete floor. But the temperature was sure to drop as the night wore on, and I wished I hadn't taken off my cardigan in preparation for going to bed. Nevertheless, the chill in the air was strangely reassuring. It proved that I was alive.

Earlier, when I was anticipating death, all sorts of crazed anxieties had gone through my head, but now I felt my reasoning return, trying to figure out who the masked man might have been and whether he was acting on his own or if he'd been sent by someone else. After a while, I gave up trying to unravel the questions that kept spinning through my mind. The rope pinched my wrists and ankles whenever I tried to move, though it wasn't tight enough to cut off my circulation. Remaining still and calm was the only option I had, and I began to think about myself in ways I hadn't done before. Living alone, as I was, I'd been too complacent but in a situation like this, I realized how vulnerable I was. The first decision I made was that I needed to get another dog. Had Lili been here with me, she would have warned me that someone was outside.

In a strange way, being tied up like this made me reflect upon and resolve other aspects of my life. I had often thought of Farleigh, the crazy old recluse I'd met when I first came to Debrakot, so many years ago. As I grew older and less sociable, there was no doubt that I could easily turn into a hermit like him, locking myself away in Thornfield and shutting out the rest of the world. I felt a depressing sense of inevitability, growing old and senile, losing my mind in this quiet, secluded place. After deciding to get a dog, I also told myself that Thapliyal's suggestion about widening the path from the turnaround point to the house and making it motorable was a sensible idea. First thing, next week, I would call a contractor and get an estimate for the work. Perhaps I might even get an internet connection and a booster for my mobile phone.

The hours went by slowly and the owlet began to call again, as if someone had set a pendulum in motion, the sound as relentless as a metronome. I thought of the first time I'd heard the bird's call years ago, when I came to stay with the Augdens. The four notes—whoo who-who whoo—had puzzled me and I'd asked the brigadier what it was. He told me it was a pygmy owlet, and showed me a picture in a bird book. Later on, after Sylvia and I got married, I remember lying in bed with her, having just made love. She heard the owlet's call and wanted to know the source of the sound. When I told her what it was, she didn't believe me and said it must be a cricket or a frog. Finally, I made her get up and we put on our clothes and went out with a torch to look for the bird in the trees. There it was perched on a branch, bobbing its head up and down as it called. Sylvia had kissed me and apologized for doubting my word, after which we went indoors and made love again with the eager exuberance of youth.

Just over a year ago, I got a letter from Australia. For a brief moment, I imagined that Sylvia had finally written to me, though the handwriting on the address was different from hers. When I tore the envelope open, I found it was from a mutual friend who had also emigrated and now lived in Melbourne. He was writing to tell me that Sylvia had recently died of cancer. After reading the letter twice, I set it aside with a feeling of desperate sadness, knowing that she was gone. Though I hadn't heard from Sylvia since our divorce, and I often felt resentful and angry about her betrayal, receiving word that she had died left me hollow and bereft. Until then I had almost erased her from my mind but imagining Sylvia's last moments in a hospital bed—my friend didn't say what kind of cancer it was—I wished that I could have seen her one more time. A few days later, I burned the letter in the fireplace, hoping that it might bring closure, though I still felt a helpless sense of being entirely alone.

By now I could see the sky brightening through the deodar trees on the eastern side of the house. I hadn't slept at all, though I wasn't tired, only numb from the cold. My hips and shoulder hurt from lying on the hard concrete and I desperately needed to empty my bladder. A number of birds had started calling, a dawn chorus of chirps and whistles greeting the new day. I recognized a barbet wailing and the shriek of woodpecker, the shrill arpeggio of a whistling thrush and half a dozen other cries that I couldn't identify.

In the middle of these songs, I heard a harsh, squealing sound. At first, I thought it was some unknown species welcoming the dawn until I realized it was the garden gate. Sunrise is about 6.30 in September and I could see the yellow light touching the tops of the trees. A figure was coming up the path and I panicked for a moment, thinking my assailant had returned, until I recognized who it was.

Seeing me lying on the veranda, trussed up as if for slaughter, Suraj stopped dead in his tracks. The electric bulb was still burning overhead. He must have recognized me but there was a moment of hesitation before he ran towards me, thinking perhaps I was dead. Kneeling beside me, he pulled the rag out of my mouth. I took several deep breaths before I could speak.

'What took you so long?'

Fumbling with the knots in the rope, Suraj stammered, asking me what had happened. Instead of trying to answer, I cried: 'Damnit, get a bloody knife and cut me loose!'

Twenty-eight

'Why didn't you come earlier?'
'I was afraid.'
'Of what?'
'The police would arrest me and put me in jail.'
'If you behave as if you are guilty, there's every reason for us to suspect that you are the murderer.'
'I'm not. I didn't kill anyone!'

Suraj shook his head, anxious and distraught. After he had cut the rope and freed me, I went to the bathroom and cleaned up, then made a cup of tea for each of us. It would be another hour before Badlu arrived and I wanted to speak with Suraj alone. A cursory inspection of the house revealed that the intruder had spent most of his time going through my study, leaving the desk drawers open, with books and papers scattered on the floor. He had searched the bedroom too but hadn't taken my wallet or my revolver. Nothing else seemed to be missing, though I would examine the house more carefully later on. But first, I needed to question Suraj.

'Why did you run away before the sacrifice?'
'I got a message on my phone,' he said.
'From whom?'
'From Kunal,' he replied.
'But he's dead.'
'That's why I was frightened,' said Suraj. 'The SMS came from his phone.'
'What was the message about?' I asked.
'It was a photograph....'
'Of what?'

He took several seconds to reply. 'Some clothes of mine, covered in blood.'

'How did that happen?' I asked.

We were seated on the glassed-in porch. He looked away, holding his teacup with both hands and then placing it on the coffee table without taking a sip. I could tell he hadn't slept much over the past few days. He looked dishevelled and unshaven, his eyes bloodshot. The torment and fear must have been enough to drive him mad. When he didn't answer my question, I tried again.

'Whose blood was on your clothes?'

'Bhagwan's,' he whispered, with a terrified look in his eyes.

'If you didn't murder him, then how did you get covered in blood?'

'I tried to stop him,' he said.

'Who?'

Suraj looked up at me with an earnest, anxious expression.

'Deepak.'

'Deepak Kanojia?' I said, trying not to sound surprised.

'Yes. He was stabbing Bhagwan with the knife and I tried to come between them, but he pushed me aside and threatened to kill me too. There was blood everywhere, all over the floors and wall. Then after Deepak ran away, I tried to lift Bhagwan, but he was dead, and I realized that my clothes were stained. Everyone would think that I had done it....'

His words spilled out in a flood of emotion as tears flowed down his cheeks.

'Are you sure that Deepak Kanojia killed Reuben?' I demanded, leaning forward. 'You recognized him?'

'Yes. I'd met him twice before,' Suraj said. 'Deepak was Kunal's friend and he had gone away for a few days. That night, he arrived at the house unexpectedly and entered the kitchen, where Kunal's body was hanging from the rope. Deepak screamed at Bhagwan, accusing him of killing his friend. I was inside but came out to see what was happening. Bhagwan was trying to explain that Kunal had hanged himself but Deepak didn't believe him. He picked up a knife from the counter and stabbed Bhagwan in the stomach. Then he raised the knife again, two, three times, stabbing Bhagwan in the arms and chest. When I tried to grab Deepak's arm, he swung around and threatened me. After that, he slashed Bhagwan's throat and kept on stabbing him. Finally, he threw the knife aside and ran out the kitchen door. I stayed behind. I didn't know what to do.'

He stopped and covered his face with both hands, sobbing.

'Who would believe a story like that?' I said, without any sympathy in my voice.

'Nobody,' he answered, after a moment. 'That's why I hid myself.'

'Upstairs, in the attic room?'

He nodded. 'It was a secret place.'

'What was it used for?'

'Kunal slept there.'

'Why did he sleep in that room? There were plenty of other beds in the house?'

'He told me that his family were hunting for him,' Suraj answered. 'He didn't want to go back home and he had to stay hidden most of the time, so nobody knew where he was. He told me that's why he disguised himself as a woman.'

'And called himself Meena?'

'Bhagwan gave him that name,' he said.

'How well did you know Kunal?'

'I only met him a few weeks back. He was friendly but seemed lonely and troubled. After we exchanged numbers, we used to talk sometimes on the phone.'

'How did he die?'

Suraj looked at me with a puzzled expression, as if the answer was obvious.

'He hanged himself.'

'No, he didn't,' I said, sharply. 'Don't lie to me!'

I could see the indecision on his face, a trapped look of anguish. For a moment, I thought he might run away again.

'Go on. Tell me what happened,' I said. 'If you lie to me, the police will lock you up and beat you. I'm expecting them to be here in another hour. This morning I was planning to accompany them to your village and take you into custody.'

He looked at me with tearful, worried eyes.

'I'm not guilty,' he said. 'Please believe me.'

'Then, who murdered Kunal?'

His whole body seemed to shudder, as he inhaled.

'Bhagwan,' he whispered.

'Speak up!' I said, 'I can't year you.'

'Bhagwan hit him,' said Suraj, raising his voice slightly. 'They were arguing in the bedroom. I was in the kitchen, cutting onions for dinner. There was a loud thumping sound, like something falling on the ground. Nobody else was in the house. I went inside to see what was wrong. When I entered the bedroom, Bhagwan was standing in the doorway with his back to me. He had an iron pipe in one hand. It was kept near the fireplace for blowing on the flames. Suddenly, he turned and saw me, anger in his eyes. That was when I noticed Kunal lying on the ground, face down with his hands tied.'

He took a deep breath and wiped his nose on the sleeve of his shirt before he continued.

'At first, I thought that Bhagwan would attack me with the pipe but then he told me to help him. I was so frightened I couldn't speak and did whatever I was told. He got me to help him untie Kunal's wrists, though my hands were shaking so much I couldn't loosen the knots, just as I couldn't untie yours, sahibji, this morning....'

'Did you know that Kunal was dead?'

'I wasn't sure. At first, I thought he was unconscious but when Bhagwan and I picked him up, his head rolled to one side. We took him into the kitchen and Bhagwan made me bring the stepladder from the storeroom....'

'Why didn't you run away?' I said.

Suraj gave me a blank stare. 'I was so shocked. It was like a nightmare. Bhagwan was giving me orders and I obeyed.'

'Did he tie the rope to the ceiling?' I asked.

Suraj nodded. 'First, he made a noose and then he tied a knot to the hook. After that we lifted Kunal up and put the noose around his neck. It was difficult and we struggled. The sari came loose and Bhagwan had to retie it. After we finished and I'd put the ladder away, Bhagwan spoke to me in a stern but quiet voice. He told me that if anyone came, we would tell them that Kunal had hanged himself. He made me promise not to say anything else.'

'What happened then?' I prompted.

'I went inside and sat on a bed, thinking what should I do? My mind was so confused. After a while, I decided that I would leave and go back to my village as soon as it was light. But then, as I told you, Deepak arrived....'

'What about the chowkidar, Charan Das, and his daughter? Where were they all this time?' I asked.

'In their quarters, up above. I only saw them earlier in the day,' Suraj answered.

Studying him in silence for several minutes, I replayed the story in my mind to see if there were any inconsistencies.

'Why were you at Shambala Villa that night?'

'Bhagwan had asked me to help him with some repairs. One of the rain gutters had fallen down in a storm and some of the metal sheets on the roof had come loose,' said Suraj. 'We had to replace the bolts because it was leaking in the sitting room.'

'Was anyone else at the house that afternoon?' I asked.

'Yes, a woman arrived about three o'clock. She didn't come inside but Bhagwan met her outdoors. They were arguing for a while,' Suraj recalled.

'Do you know who she was?'

'No, I didn't see her and Bhagwan didn't say anything about her.'

'Did you often come to the house?' I asked.

'Only during the past few weeks,' said Suraj. 'Earlier, I used to deliver milk occasionally but it was only recently that Bhagwan even spoke to me.'

'What did he say?'

'One morning, he started asking me questions. How old was I? Had I finished school? Then he offered to help find me a job, in Delhi,' said Suraj.

'What kind of job?'

'He didn't say,' Suraj answered. 'I was ready to do anything.'

'Did he offer you drugs?' I asked.

Suraj looked puzzled, shaking his head. 'No.'

'Was Kunal taking drugs?'

'I don't know if he was. He said nothing about it to me.'

'But he showed you his room,' I said.

'He needed some help moving boxes in the attic, that was all.'

I watched him carefully but there was nothing to suggest he was lying.

'Why didn't you go home to your village after finishing the repairs?' I said.

'It was growing dark. Bhagwan told me to spend the night. He was in a cheerful mood and said we would cook something special for dinner. I had brought fresh mustard greens from the village. Kunal also encouraged me to stay. I felt happy being with them. But then, a little while later, Bhagwan began to argue with Kunal,' said Suraj. 'His mood changed so quickly and I could hear him shouting.'

'What was the argument about?'

'I don't know for sure,' said Suraj. 'All I could hear was something about a mobile. Kunal kept saying he'd lost it. But Bhagwan accused him of giving it away. I tried not to listen. They were in the other room.'

By now the sun had risen and the garden, outside the glazed porch, was bathed in yellow light. It was a bright day, and I found it hard to imagine all of the violence and terror that Suraj had described.

'So, after Reuben was killed, you went and hid in the attic?' I asked.

'Yes, I was confused. I couldn't go home covered in blood. I was afraid Deepak might come back and kill me. Seeing Kunal hanging from the rope and Bhagwan stabbed to death, it made me crazy. I just wanted to hide.'

'How long did you stay up there?'

'Two nights. Once the police came the next morning, I wasn't able to leave.'

'You could have come downstairs and told them the truth,' I said. 'I was there too. You could have told me.'

He looked down at his feet. 'I know. I heard your voice. But I was sure that nobody would believe me.'

'So, you just stayed upstairs, waiting?'

'Yes,' he said. 'I changed into some of Kunal's clothes. Then, after the second night, I was hungry and knew I had to escape. There was nothing to eat except a packet of biscuits which I finished. Finally, in the early morning, on the second day, before the sun rose, I slipped quietly downstairs and went out through the back door. Nobody saw me leave.'

'A constable was on duty,' I said.

Suraj shrugged. 'He must have been asleep. There was only a little light. When I returned home to my village, I made up the story about going to Landsdowne. A friend of mine had tried to join the army a few months before, so I knew that I would be rejected because of my height.' For the first time, he smiled cautiously. 'I'm sorry, sahibji, I lied to you.'

'But now you're sure you're telling me the truth?' I demanded.

'I swear!'

'What about the man who attacked me last night?' I said. 'Who was he?'

Suraj waved one hand in a helpless gesture. 'I have no idea.'

'I thought it might be you,' I said.

'How?' he responded, fear returning to his eyes. 'I would never....'

'The man had on a mask. I couldn't see his face,' I said. 'He was about your size.'

'No. No,' Suraj protested. 'It wasn't me.'

'Then why did you decide to come and see me this morning?' I asked. 'After waiting three days? I sent word with your father that I needed to speak to you urgently.'

'I didn't know what I would say to you,' he stammered. 'When you asked me to get the goat and perform the sacrifice, I didn't want to do it, but I knew that if I refused you would think I was hiding something.'

'You *were* hiding something,' I said.

'Yes, but I knew I wasn't guilty of killing Bhagwan or Kunal. I thought that if the sacrifice took place, the Devi would reveal it was someone else. I was afraid, but I also thought it might be a way of proving my innocence,' he said.

'Were you the one who tried to steal the goat from the godown, three days before the sacrifice?' I asked.

He nodded. 'After I brought the goat from the village and you asked me to perform the sacrifice, I was afraid. I didn't want to do it.'

'But, in the end, you came to the temple and were ready to kill the goat,' I said. 'What happened then, to make you run away?'

'I could tell that you suspected me, and I wanted to show you that I wasn't guilty. I was even willing to kill the goat though I kept thinking of Bhagwan's blood all over the floor...all over me...on my hands. Then just as the puja started at the temple, I got a message on my phone from Kunal's number and there was a picture of my bloodstained clothes. It seemed as if he was accusing me, though he was dead. Who wouldn't have been afraid?'

'But you haven't answered my first question,' I said. 'Why did you finally decide to come here this morning?'

Suraj put his hands over his face for a moment and wiped away his tears, then looked me in the eye.

'I couldn't keep hiding forever and I knew that if I tried to run away, the police would catch me. Finally, I decided that I would come and touch your feet and beg you to forgive me,' he said.

'Forgive you for what?' I said.

'For lying to you. For not having told you what I witnessed—Kunal and Bhagwan's murders,' he said.

'You keep calling him Bhagwan?' I said. 'Do you still believe he was a god?'

'Maybe,' Suraj replied. 'Kunal used to say that if we did what Bhagwan told us to do, he would treat us with love and kindness but if we disobeyed him, he had a terrible temper. He would never forgive those who betrayed him.'

'A cruel and jealous god,' I said in English, under my breath.

'Sahibji, do you believe me, that I didn't kill him?' Suraj's voice was pleading.

'I don't know what to believe,' I said. 'But the only way we're going to prove your innocence is if you make an honest statement to the police and explain everything to them, just as you've done with me.'

Twenty-nine

Inspector Thapliyal was, naturally, alarmed and disturbed to hear what had happened to me, though I assured him that I was perfectly fine, and the only injury I'd suffered was a badly bruised ego. After inspecting the veranda, where I'd been tied up, as well as the mess in my study and the bedroom, the SHO shook his head with disapproval.

'Sir, you must take more precautions,' he said, 'living here on your own. I will post two of my men to guard the house.'

'I'm sure that's not necessary....' I protested.

'But who do you think the intruder was?' he asked in an anxious voice.

'I have no idea. As far as I can tell nothing was stolen from the house.'

Taking charge of the situation, Thapliyal ordered his men to search the yard and the paths leading away from the property, to see if they could discover any evidence of my assailant.

'I doubt if they'll find much. Whoever it was, he seemed to know what he was doing,' I said, 'a professional thug or goonda working for someone else. Maybe it was just a warning, an attempt to intimidate me.'

'Obviously, it's connected to the murder,' Thapliyal insisted.

'No doubt,' I agreed.

'You're sure it wasn't this boy, Suraj?' he suggested.

'No, not him,' I said. 'I'm convinced he's innocent.'

Thapliyal remained suspicious. As I told him what I'd learned about the murders at Shambles, he listened carefully with a sceptical frown. Being a good police officer, he still had his doubts, but after I'd outlined the sequence of events that Suraj had recounted, he grudgingly admitted that the story was plausible. At most, Suraj was guilty of withholding information and being coerced into helping Reuben cover up Kunal's murder.

'I'll have to take him to the station and record his statement,' said Thapliyal.

'Yes, of course,' I agreed. 'Correct procedures should be followed. But the boy has been through a lot already. He's badly traumatized. Please ask your men to treat him gently and I don't think there's any need to keep him in custody. I can assure you that he will make himself available for further questioning, as necessary.'

Thapliyal nodded. 'It would have been much better if Deepak Kanojia was alive, so we could have got a confession out of him. But, if you believe this boy is innocent, sir....'

'I do,' I said. 'And it's not just instinct. His account of the two murders makes much more sense than our original theory that Kunal Vaidya killed Reuben and then hanged himself. I never believed that version of events.'

'Maybe not,' said Thapliyal. 'But Suraj behaved as if he was guilty.'

'Because he was afraid,' I argued. 'I added to that fear by organizing a bogus sacrifice to scare the truth out of him. Anyone who believed that Reuben was a god, would surely believe a sign from the goddess.'

'Yes, sir,' said Thapliyal with a smile. 'But, remember, I warned you that we wouldn't be able to call the Devi as a witness, even if she revealed who the killer might be.'

'It was a desperate ploy,' I admitted. 'By the way, I haven't told Suraj that you were the one who sent him the photograph of his bloodstained clothes, using Kunal Vaidya's phone.'

Thapliyal smiled. 'I was only following your instructions, sir.'

'Perhaps technology can be useful sometimes....' I started to say, then stopped myself, as I suddenly realized something I'd missed. Getting up from my chair, abruptly, I went straight to my bedroom. Thapliyal followed on my heels.

The charger chord was plugged into the wall, but my phone was gone.

'It was there yesterday,' I said. 'That's what he took! I use the damn thing so seldom, I completely forgot.'

'What kind of phone was it?' Thapliyal asked.

'A cheap Chinese model I got from Chunky Rawat's store. It seldom worked because there's no signal here at the house,' I said.

'Why would he have taken it?' Thapliyal wondered aloud. 'We should be able to trace it using your number.'

Just then, through the bedroom window, I saw one of the constables hurrying up the path from the garden gate. He was carrying something in his hands. When we went outside, he showed us what he'd found on the path below Thornfield.

My phone had been smashed with a rock and totally destroyed. Picking out a piece of shattered circuitry from the constable's palm, I examined the glittering fragment closely.

'It's hard to imagine that all of these bits and pieces allow us to communicate with each other,' I said. 'I always wondered what was inside.'

'Sir, can you think of a reason why it was stolen?' Thapliyal persisted.

'Yes, I know exactly why it was taken and destroyed,' I said. 'Of course, we won't be able to prove a thing, but Pran Vaidya must have sent the man who tied me up and broke into my house.'

'Dr Vaidya?' said Thapliyal, with surprise. 'What would he want with your phone?'

'He knew I'd seen the video that Reuben was using to blackmail him and probably thought I had a copy. When I met him last week, he offered me thirty lakhs to get him Kunal's phone.'

Thapliyal was silent for a moment.

'I was offered ten lakhs,' he replied, with a smile.

'Reuben had sent the video to Vaidya,' I said. 'And he was desperate to destroy any copies that existed.'

'Kunal's phone is still at the station,' said Thapliyal. 'I've kept it locked in the safe. We will need it as evidence.'

'Perhaps,' I said. 'But I doubt it. Now that both murderers are dead, along with their victims. The case can be closed.'

'Sir....' Thapliyal said, reluctantly. 'Will you be filing an FIR?'

'For what? The incident last night?' I said. 'No. It will be a waste of time....'

'But, sir. It would be the correct procedure,' Thapliyal suggested.

'To hell with procedure. Life's too short!' I said. 'We'll never be able to connect the intruder to Vaidya, even if you catch him, which is highly unlikely. And I certainly don't want to file a report that will tie me up for the rest of my life. I've already spent too many years showing up in court, just to have judges and lawyers delay the proceedings month after month. No.... Let it go.'

He looked at me with an uncertain expression.

'Are you sure?'

'Absolutely,' I insisted. 'The important thing is that the murders at Shambala Villa have been solved. Congratulations!'

After another moment's hesitation, Thapliyal stiffened and surprised me with a brisk salute, which I returned with as much dignity as I could muster.

⁂

By the time the police party left, taking Suraj with them, it was already eleven o'clock. I hadn't had breakfast though the adrenaline from last night's events kept me going. Asking Badlu to make me a cup of coffee, I went into my study to survey the damage. Picking up a couple of books off the floor, I replaced them on the shelf and began to sort through the contents of a drawer which had been dumped on my desk. The statue of Anubis watched me from the top of a bookcase, where I'd put it for safekeeping until I could pack it up and send it to Rita. A short while later, when my coffee was delivered, Badlu gave me an accusing look.

'What is it?' I asked.

'You could have been killed,' he said, as if the whole thing had been my fault.

'I don't think so,' I said. 'The man wasn't armed.'

'Why didn't you shout for help?' he said. 'I would have come right away.'

'I had a rag stuffed in my mouth,' I said. 'Besides, what could you have done? He would have tied you up as well.'

'What if he comes back?'

'He won't,' I said. 'In any case, the SHO is insisting on posting two constables here on night duty, for the next couple of weeks.'

'That's good,' said Badlu, nodding with approval. 'But you need to be more careful and not get involved with these cases, now that you've retired.'

'Yes. Yes,' I said, trying to dismiss him, though he wasn't ready to leave.

The old cook shuffled his feet. 'If you had died, what would happen to me?'

'Is that what you're worried about?' I said. 'Badlu, you're much older than I am. Chances are....'

I stopped myself because I could see that he was genuinely upset.

'More than thirty years, I worked for your mother,' he said. 'If she was alive, she would never have let this happen.'

'What do you mean?' I said.

'Going to Charan Das's house for the jagran. Getting a goat for a sacrifice. It's not right,' he said, with a note of indignation. 'And entertaining strange women from Delhi, whom you hardly know. Your mother wanted you to get properly married.'

'Yes, I know,' I said. 'But that's not likely to happen.'

'You need someone at this age, to share the last years of your life, instead of sitting alone reading books all night,' he scolded.

'Okay, that's enough,' I said, in a gentler tone. 'Thank you for your advice.'

He shook his head with frustration and turned to leave.

'I'm making eggplant and dal for lunch. Do you want roti or rice?'

'Roti,' I replied. 'And I'll eat as soon as the food's ready.'

My afternoon nap was longer than usual since I hadn't slept the night before. When I woke up, it was already half-past four and I lay there in a brief but blissful state of amnesia. Gradually, however, the events of the last twenty-four hours came back to me, and I was relieved to find that my hands and feet weren't tied. My bed was certainly softer than the veranda floor. For a while, lying there,

I thought about Shambles and the lives that had been lost within those crumbling walls.

Reuben had lived a lie, which he inflicted on others and used to exploit and abuse his vulnerable and desperate followers. The pathetic, tawdry cult that he constructed around himself was as degraded and corrupt as the building in which he lived. He lured his devotees to Shambala Villa, using drugs and promises of employment, as well as spiritual perversions, all for his own narcissistic self-gratification. In the end, he murdered Kunal Vaidya, in a fit of rage but, in a sense, he also killed himself. Though Deepak Kanojia had picked up the knife and stabbed him, out of tortured anguish, the simple truth of it was that Reuben Sabharwal was entirely responsible for his own death.

⁂

By the time I'd had my tea, I was feeling restless, now that the case was solved. The two constables assigned for my security arrived at 5 p.m. and I recognized one of them as the young man who had been posted at Shambles.

'Are you still afraid of ghosts?' I asked.

He gave me a sheepish grin.

I needed a walk to clear my head and decided to go across to see Vinny. Gerry's death certificate had been signed and stamped. Thapliyal had helped expedite the paperwork. Though it would be dark before I came back, I made sure I was carrying a torch. When Badlu insisted on knowing where I was going, I assured him that there was no danger of being waylaid on the path.

The sun was heading for the horizon by the time I arrived at Xanadu. When I knocked on the front door, a maid unbolted it and led me into the drawing room. Several minutes later, Vinny emerged looking worried.

'What's all this about you being attacked?' she said.

'Nothing, really,' I said.

'I heard you were knocked unconscious and tied up all night,' she looked at me with a worried expression.

'No, I was conscious the whole time,' I said. 'News travels quickly.'

As we sat down, Vinny quizzed me for several minutes, insisting that I tell her everything including the latest news about the murders at Shambles. It took a while before her curiosity was satisfied.

'And how are *you*?' I finally asked.

'Okay...mostly,' she said with a sigh. 'I'm busy packing. Day after tomorrow, I fly to London.'

'So soon?' I said, reaching into my pocket. 'It's good I brought your passports back.'

She took them from me and flipped one open. I could see it was Gerry's and a look of sadness crossed her face as she studied his picture.

'My sister persuaded me that I need to get away from here,' she said.

'Of course.'

'Would you like some tea?' she asked.

'No, thanks! I've had my quota for the day,' I replied.

'Then we'll have a drink,' she insisted. 'The sun's going down.'

'Why not?' I said. 'I think we both need a drink. I'll do the honours.'

The bar was in one corner of the drawing room and I took out two glasses.

'What will you have?' I asked.

'There's an open bottle of Laphroaig. Gerry's favourite.'

I found it and poured us each a generous peg of whisky.

'To Gerry!' Raising my glass, I took a sip and sat in silence for a minute as the peaty warmth spread from my throat and into my chest.

'I'm not sure when I'll be back,' said Vinny. 'Maybe in a couple of months, or after the winter is over. More than likely, though, I'll pack up and sell this house. It's funny, Gerry is the one who loved it here in India. I'm much happier in England. Now that he's gone there's not much reason for me to stay.'

'Most of your family is there,' I said.

She spoke for a while about her sister and nephews, as well as the son from her first marriage. He was a doctor in Edinburgh. When

I told her that I had an aunt who lived in Scotland, she looked at me with a curious expression.

'Didn't you ever think of emigrating?' she asked.

I finished what was left in my glass and shook my head.

'No, I'm happy enough here,' I said. 'I wouldn't know how to behave in Britain.'

'So, you'll stay on in Debrakot forever?'

'Probably,' I said, getting up to pour us each another drink.

I was glad to have someone to talk to this evening and I could tell Vinny felt the same way, just listening to the sound of someone else's voice. We reminisced for a while and gossiped about our neighbours.

'I remember, you told Gerry and me once how you came up to Debrakot the first time, as a young man, running away from Lucknow because of a love affair that went wrong,' said Vinny.

'Yes, it was a long time ago,' I said.

'You got the girl pregnant, didn't you?' said Vinny.

'That's right,' I said, looking into my glass.

'What was her name?'

'Sujeeta,' I said.

'What happened to her?' said Vinny.

I was about to brush the question aside, feigning ignorance, but then I glanced up at Vinny, who was watching me with a curious look in her eyes.

'It's strange you ask,' I said. 'For a number of years, I had no idea where she was or what had happened to her. But then I was posted in Lucknow, briefly, back in the nineties, after Sylvia and I got divorced. On an impulse, I made some inquires...discreetly, of course. It's one of the advantages of being a policeman. I learned that Sujeeta had got married, soon after I'd moved up here. She must have had an abortion or lost our child but there was no record of that. Her husband was a wholesale grain merchant from Kanpur and she'd moved there. They had three children, two boys and a girl.'

'You never tried to get in touch with her again?'

'No,' I said, 'Of course not.'

'Do you think she's happy?' Vinny asked.

'I suppose....' I said, leaving the rest unsaid.

It was getting late, and I needed to head home before Badlu decided that I'd been abducted and raised an alarm. Putting down my empty glass, I stood up.

'I should be going,' I said. 'Take care of yourself.'

Vinny got to her feet and smiled

'While I'm away, if there are any of Gerry's books that you'd like to borrow, come over any time,' said Vinny. 'I'll tell the maid that you're welcome to help yourself.'

I thanked her and we hugged each other goodbye.

Thirty

A week after Suraj came to my rescue, he showed up at the house again, soon after sunrise, delivering milk and bearing a gift. It was a puppy, about two months old, and he handed it over to me with a grin.

'What's this?' I said, surprised.

'A bhotia sheepdog,' he explained. 'I got it from some shepherds that were camped near our village.'

The scruffy creature was mostly hair, with two small black eyes like peppercorns and an inquisitive nose that sniffed at my hand.

'But what am I supposed to do with it?' I protested, trying to hand the puppy back to him, though he refused to take it.

'I brought it for you. It will make a good watchdog,' Suraj insisted. 'Bhotias are fierce and protective. It will grow this tall.' With one hand he indicated about waist high.

'Thank you very much, but I really can't....' I said.

'They live outdoors mostly and protect the flocks from leopards and bears.'

'But I'm not a shepherd,' I said.

'Then it will chase off monkeys from your garden,' said Suraj.

The puppy's fur was mostly black with tan patches on its chest and the inside of its legs. After nuzzling my hand, it began chewing on the cuff of my shirtsleeve, gnawing at the button.

'I can't look after a dog,' I said. 'It takes a lot of time and effort.'

'Don't worry,' said Suraj. 'These dogs take care of themselves, and they have a loud bark that will scare everyone away.'

At that moment, Badlu arrived from his quarters and gave me a questioning look.

'First you asked him to bring you a goat,' he said. 'And now this?'

'I didn't ask for it,' I complained.

'Is it a male or female?' Badlu wanted to know, as he went inside to get a pan for boiling the milk.

Lifting the puppy up, I checked.

'A male,' Suraj confirmed.

The puppy stank of goats, and he probably had fleas. When I pointed this out to Suraj, he laughed.

'That's because he was raised with the shepherd's flock. After a bath, he won't smell at all,' he reassured me.

'Here, give him some milk,' said Badlu, placing a saucer on the veranda.

Suraj poured out an inch and I put the puppy down. At that point, I saw Badlu and Suraj exchanging a glance, realizing that they had conspired behind my back. The puppy dunked his face in the milk and began lapping it up.

'See how his tail curls up,' said Suraj. 'And he already has a lot of strength in his legs and shoulders.'

Badlu was smiling now, and they both seemed pleased with themselves.

'Do I have a choice?' I asked.

They shook their heads in unison. By now the pup had finished the milk and was licking the inside of the bowl. Reaching over, I picked him up again and brushed the hair away from his face, which was entirely black, except for two pale spots on his forehead, one above each eye.

'That's a sign of good luck,' said Suraj. 'He has four eyes, to keep a sharp lookout for danger and to see from this world into the next.'

By now the constables had come around from the front of the house to see what was going on. They nodded with approval when they saw the pup.

'Nobody will dare enter your house when he grows up,' one of them said.

'And our night duty here will be over, sir!' said the other, laughing.

'I'm still not sure it's a good idea,' I said, reluctantly. 'Owning a dog is a big responsibility.'

'I'll look after him,' said Badlu. 'Don't worry.'

Realizing that there wasn't anything I could do, I patted the pup and put him down again. He immediately began to chew at my shoelaces.

'We'll have to call the vet to give him his shots and deworming pills,' I said. 'I'll also think of a suitable name.'

⁂

Leaving the puppy in Badlu's care, I walked across to Glenwood that afternoon. Gladys was seated in her usual chair, next to the window, playing solitaire on a small, folding table.

'Lionel, where have you been?' she cried, putting down her cards as I entered. 'I've been wanting to see you! What happened?'

'I'm sorry, I've been preoccupied,' I apologized.

'No. No. I'm just playing patience. Of course, I wish it was bridge! If only your dear mother was still here!'

'How have you been?' I asked. 'All well?'

'Yes, my dear. But *you* tell me. I hear you solved the murders!' she exclaimed.

Sitting down in a chair to her left, I began to explain how Reuben had killed Kunal, when she interrupted me.

'Wait a minute! That's my bad ear!' she said. 'Come to the other side.'

I knew it would make no difference, but I did as I was told.

When I started again, she tilted her head and listened intently, though after a minute or two, she waved a hand at me impatiently.

'I know all that!' she said. 'But why did this young man kill Reuben?'

'Because he had murdered his friend. He also abused them both....'

'Jealousy? Were they lovers?'

'I don't know. It doesn't matter, does it?' I said.

'Shocking, really shocking!' she said.

'Reuben pretended to be god but turned out to be a demon instead,' I said.

'How much money?' she cried.

'No, Gladys. It wasn't because of any money...at least not directly.'

She gave me a puzzled look.

'I hear that Lala Satish Aggarwal has taken possession of the house, now that the police have left,' Gladys said, pointing out the window at Shambles. 'I'm sure he'll tear it down and put up some hideous eyesore on the site. Hopefully, I'll be long gone before it gets built. You can be sure that our side of the hill is going to be destroyed just like the rest of Debrakot.'

'Well, change is inevitable, I suppose,' I responded.

'Of course not,' she said. 'Charan Das won't vacate his quarters unless he's paid a packet. He's nobody's fool!'

'That isn't what....' I started to say, but Gladys took off on her own tangent.

'Believe you me, I'm not one of those people who gets nostalgic about the past,' she said. 'It's a good thing we got rid of the British when we did. I'm proud to be an Indian, even if I have some English blood in my veins. My husband died for this country and nobody can question my allegiances.... But it does get depressing when you see everything being managed in such a corrupt and ugly way!'

I nodded, realizing that whatever I might say, it would, literally, fall on deaf ears, so I told Gladys exactly what was on my mind.

'Sometimes I wonder whether I'll die peacefully in my sleep or if I'll suffer a violent death,' I confessed.

'Absolutely!' Gladys replied. 'We used to always think of Debrakot as a sleepy little town tucked away in the hills, until the motor road arrived....'

'When I was younger, I felt invincible,' I continued. 'I wasn't afraid of dying and put my life on the line more than once. It didn't bother me back then but now that I'm retired and no longer need to take any risks, suddenly it worries me sometimes.'

'Thornfield is such a lovely house, one of the oldest on this hillside. The Augdens always invited me to have Christmas dinner with them and a few other friends. Natalie would get drunk and Teddy would roll his eyes. We all laughed and played Christmas carols on the phonograph. But that was all before your time. Back then, the properties were well maintained and full of life. Even

Rosemary McKenzie kept Cairngorm in reasonable shape, not like the shambles it is now.'

We were speaking at cross purposes, both of us carrying on our own separate conversations, but somehow it didn't seem to matter.

'I wonder if Sylvia and I had stayed married, whether she would have ever come back to Debrakot,' I said, looking Gladys in the eye. 'Who knows?'

'Yes, who knows?' she answered, having caught my last phrase. 'Rosemary actually believed all that rot. Nobody can speak to the dead, at least not in this life. People say that Debrakot is full of ghosts. I think it's all made up. Each of these houses has its stories but that's all it is...stories...somebody's imagination!'

I confessed: 'There are times I feel completely alone, especially when I finish reading a book. Novelists write about love and loss, but they never seem to get it right, because they have to bring their stories to an end, while some things can never be resolved completely. The words may run out and a full stop might punctuate the last sentence on the final page, but the story keeps on going...even after you close the book.'

Gladys looked at me with a suspicious glance.

'I say, what are you talking about? Such rot!' she burst out, with a laugh, and for a moment I thought she'd heard what I'd said, but then she carried on, 'Debrakot will outlast us all. It's the kind of town that defies bloody history.'

'Yes, Gladys, we can agree on that!'

Acknowledgements

Sincere thanks to former DGP Aloke B. Lal for kindly agreeing to read the manuscript of this book and commenting on it. His corrections and suggestions were invaluable but he should not be held responsible for any errors or exaggerations that may have crept into this story, which is fiction, after all.